SEE JANE DANCE!

A West River Mystery

Jolene Stratton Philo

Midwestern Books

ISBN-13: 979-8-9880628-2-0

Library of Congress Control Number: ?

Cover design by: eBook Cover Designs

Published by Midwestern Books
801 W Washington Ave, Polk City, IA 50226

Contact: info@midwesternbooks.com

Chapter 1

My knees knocked as I stood outside my apartment. I jabbed the key into the lock and heard the phone begin to ring.

"Coming!" I yelled as I worked the key with both hands. It refused to budge, so I pulled out the key and examined the bolt lock. It was hoary with frost and looked icy cold. Man, oh man, a frozen lock was no way to welcome a weary traveler who'd driven five hundred fifty miles from Sioux City, Iowa to Little Missouri, South Dakota on the day after New Year's.

The phone rang again. "Be there in a minute." The wind cut through my blue jeans. My knees knocked harder. I pulled off my gloves with my teeth and tightened my grip on the key. The cold metal numbed my hands, and I couldn't feel my fingers. Time for another tactic.

I put on the gloves and bent over until my lips were nearly touching the lock. The phone kept ringing as I blew huge lungfuls of hot air into the keyhole. Condensation formed around the metal, and I tried the key again. Wahoo! Once inside, I ran straight for the phone and picked up the receiver.

"Happy New Year!" My unabated shivering made the greeting come out thin and reedy. I sounded more like a retired country schoolteacher than a first year rookie.

"What took you so wong to answer?" Betty Yarborough asked. "I seen you drive into town and waited to caww untiw Merwe said your car was parked beside the schoow and you was headed to your apartment."

"The lock was frozen. How cold is it?"

Little Missouri's official switchboard operator was sure to know. She kept diligent watch over our tiny town's citizenry and its weather. If the temperature shifted so much as a degree, she not only knew it but also broadcast the information far and wide. With gusto.

"Fifteen bewow."

"Fifteen below?" I gritted my teeth to stop chattering.

"The Farmer's Awmanac says we'ww be in the deep freeze most of January."

I groaned. "Please Betty, say it isn't so!"

"You better get used to it. But here's something guaranteed to warm you up," Betty warbled.

My body tensed involuntarily. During the almost five months I'd been teaching in Little Missouri, I'd grown wary of Betty's warble. It meant that she and my mother, to whom I'd bid farewell about thirteen hours ago, were up to something again. They had bonded during phone call after phone call while I spent an unfortunate night stuck in a snowbank a few days after Thanksgiving. Since then, they had spent considerable time and effort trying to set me up with every unmarried rancher or cowboy in the area. Mom hadn't so much as hinted of their latest scheme during the two weeks of Christmas vacation I'd spent with her and Dad. Betty and Mom must have cooked it up while I'd been on the road.

"We signed you up for square dance wessons!" Betty paused for dramatic effect. She relished dramatic effect.

I did not. "Who is we?"

Her clipped reply suggested my response had not been what she expected. "Me and your mother."

I closed my eyes and bit my tongue. Part of me wanted to tell Betty to mind her own business. But the part of me that needed something to distract from below zero temperatures, as well as mid-winter's short days and long, dark nights, wanted to hear more. "Go on."

She perked right up. "The first wesson is tomorrow night. Seven o'cwock at the dance haww."

"How much do they cost?"

"Don't you worry about that," she sang. "Me and Vewma spwit the fee."

Velma? The school janitor? She and I had what is best described as a love-hate relationship. I loved it when my students used glitter in art class, and she hated vacuuming it up. Somehow, we'd become friends despite our differences. And now she and Betty had gone halvsies on my square dance lessons. This was not the girlfriend group I'd envisioned in August when I had arrived in Little Missouri. Then again, in a town of ninety-two people, I couldn't afford to be choosy.

"Your mother said to put some of the chocowate chip oatmeaw cookies she sent home with you at the snack tabwe."

I closed my eyes and prayed. "Lord, give me strength." In case he couldn't handle the job, I began counting to ten. I made it all the way to four before Betty cut me short.

"Another caww is coming through. Got to go."

The line went dead. I put the phone receiver in its cradle, relieved our conversation was over. Fifteen below could do a number on my new 35 millimeter camera and several other items in my car. I hurried outside and brought in the first of three boxes full of equipment and supplies. I'd purchased them on the sly during Christmas vacation. A few, like the camera, had been purchased on my own dime. The majority would be paid for by the Tipperary County Sheriff's Department once Sheriff Sternquist received the receipts. I set the box on the kitchen counter and noticed the envelope propped up against the salt and pepper shakers on the table. Where had that come from?

I reached for the envelope. My name was scribbled on the front in nearly illegible writing. The note inside was equally illegible. Had I not spent the last semester deciphering my third grade students' cursive, the message would have remained a mystery forever. After a few minutes decoding the note, I identified Dick Phillips as its author. He was inviting me to supper at Round the Bend Café on Friday night.

We hadn't seen one another since he'd given me an unexpected gift early on Christmas Eve as I left for Iowa. That morning he'd shown a side of himself that was new to me. I wanted to see more of it. And him.

Two questions came to mind as I picked up the phone receiver. First off, how had Dick's envelope gotten into my apartment? Equally important, if I accepted Dick's invitation over the phone, how long until Betty leaked the news to the entire town? The answer to the first question required some investigating. The answer to the second was simple. About ten minutes.

I put the receiver back in its cradle. Getting in touch with Dick would have to wait. My first order of business was to unpack the Beetle before night fell. My track record for courting trouble in broad daylight was impressive, yet it paled when compared to my ability to cozy up to it after dark. I tucked Dick's note into its envelope and stuck it in the drawer beside the stove. Then I stepped outside as the sun slipped below the western horizon.

Frigid air stung my cheeks. I pulled my stocking cap further down over my ears, tucked my chin into my coat collar, and hurried to my car. Ten steps later, I crashed full force into an object that blocked the sidewalk. Gasping, I stumbled backward and lost my footing. At the last instant, I shifted my weight to land in a snowbank instead of on the cement sidewalk. An arm, deep black against the night sky, shot out. Strong, calloused fingers closed around my wrist.

Oh no, you don't! I twisted my arm and fought to break free. *This time, I'm not going down without a fight.*

Chapter 2

A wet, schleppy whistle of air pierced the darkness. "We-ull," Merle Laird said. My crusty old neighbor tightened his grip on my wrist and heaved me to my feet. "Welcome home."

"What are you doing running around out here in the dark?" I sputtered, knowing that my reply was out of line since Merle's top speed was a slow, painful limp.

"You know, I come close to dropping the eggs and milk I'm givin' you by way of saying Happy New Year. You ain't gonna survive 1978 in one piece if you don't watch where you're goin'."

That sucked the huff right out of me. "Want to come in for some coffee?"

"Nah." He lifted one flap of his Elmer Fudd hat and rubbed at the bristles on his ear. "You best get unpacked and ready for that new batch of kind-ee-gartners coming in the morning. Talk around town is that they is so excited to start school, they is scheming to show up early and break the door down if you don't let 'em in."

The kindergarteners! Between the square dance news and Dick's note, I'd forgotten all about them. Having just spent much of the drive across South Dakota wondering how to keep a bunch of non-readers in their seats while I taught the first, second, and third graders their lessons, the diversion had been a welcome reprieve.

"They may be ready for me, but I don't think I'm ready for them." I dusted snow off the seat of my pants. "Thanks for pulling me out of the snowbank. And for the eggs and milk. Would you put them in my refrigerator while I unpack the car?"

"Nope." Merle paused. "But I will unpack your car while you put what I brung you"—he handed the eggs and milk to me—"where they belong."

It was a prudent division of labor. I put away the food and then hurried into my classroom in the north half of a double wide, double long trailer that also housed my apartment. Since the beginning of the school year, I'd gotten the hang of teaching my seven primary school students, but who knew what would happen when four kindergarteners entered the mix. My stomach knotted as I checked over my lesson plans. Was there enough to keep the littlest kids busy all day? Was that even possible?

The apartment door banged shut. Merle had finished and was leaving. I flipped on the porch light and poked my head outside. "Thank you!" I watched him gimp along the sidewalk. "Can you come tomorrow morning and entertain the kindergarteners?"

He raised an arm in farewell and spoke as he hitched along, favoring his bad hip. "You'll have them wrapped around your little finger before I got the eggs gathered. Now git back inside before you let in any more cold air."

***

Merle's faith in me led to absolutely zero inspiration regarding the kindergarteners before they and their parents showed up the next morning. Thanks to a terrible night's sleep, I was up and in my classroom bright and early. Liv McDonald and her daughter Keeva were the first to arrive. No surprise there, since Liv taught the upper grade students. Her classroom was in a modular building identical to mine. The only difference was their placements. Her trailer bordered the northern edge of the playground. Mine ran along its west side. Her classroom was in the east half of the building. The other half was empty and ready for duty if it was needed.

Keeva and I had become buddies in the fall during a series of suppers followed by board games at her parents' ranch. She was small for her age, with mousy brown hair braided into two stiff pigtails behind her ears. Only her bright blue eyes belied her astonishing spunk, which was most visible when she was atop a horse so big I wouldn't think of riding it. Not that I was inclined to ride a horse of any size. Not even a pony.

Keeva bounded into the cloakroom. "Where's my cubby?" she demanded.

"Keeva, say hello to your teacher." Liv's brown eyes danced in her tan, windburned face.

"Hello, Miss Newell." She scanned the compartments mounted on the cloakroom walls and pointed at one. "That's my name!"

"You found it! Put your lunchbox here." I patted the shelf right above her name. "Then hang your coat on the hook below it and put your snow boots on the newspaper on the floor underneath. After that, find your desk and put your school supplies inside."

Keeva got right to it. Liv gave her an amused glance. "I don't think she needs me anymore. Is it okay if I leave?"

I glanced out the window. Three more children and their mothers were clustered at the base of the landing. "Go ahead. It's about to get crowded in here."

"I'll go out the other way." Liv crossed my classroom and went through the exit at its far end.

I opened the door. "Come in and get out of the cold."

The three children, who chattered like squirrels until I greeted them, grew quiet and shy. Their mothers coaxed them to climb the landing stairs. Grace Berthold was the first to gather her courage, perhaps reassured by the presence of her brother Renny, a third grader.

Strangers were surprised when told they were related. Grace's dark hair, dark eyes, and olive skin were a stark contrast to Renny's strawberry-blond hair, hazel eyes, and freckles. Average in height and weight, she moved with athletic grace while the baby fat clinging to Renny's small frame made him appear clumsy.

I was marveling at their physical differences when inspiration hit. "Renny, will you go in with Grace and show her what to do?"

"Your brother will take good care of you, Gracie." Trudy Berthold gave her daughter a pat and a wave. "You two walk to Round the Bend after school."

Next to make the upward trek was grey-eyed Jeremy Gibson, the only boy in the bunch. A tuft of white-blond hair escaped his hood onto his forehead. All I knew about him was that his older sisters were in Liv's room, and he was the baby of the family. His mother Linda, whom I'd never formally met, looked far more worried than her son and held his hand tightly.

Jeremy pulled away from his mother. "I can go in by myself." He raced up the steps.

That left a tiny, green-eyed girl wearing a pink stocking hat. "You must be Winter Swensen," I said.

"Winter Skye," she corrected me. "My sisters are Spring Day, Summer Rose, and Autumn Breeze. They are in Mrs. McDonald's room, and our middle names are as important as our first names. Right, Mom?"

"Right," said the petite woman beside her. She smiled at me. "I'm Galva Swensen." Her attention returned to her daughter. "You go in with Miss Newell before she turns into an ice cube. I'll see you after school, sweetie."

Winter—make that Winter Skye—marched up the stairs and joined Jeremy in the cloakroom. They found their cubbies and put their coats and boots where they belonged. They were loading school supplies in their desks when Liv rang the bell. I went to bring in the first through third graders. When Elva entered the classroom and saw her third grade classmate Renny assisting Grace, she volunteered to be Keeva's buddy for the day. No sooner had I given her the go-ahead than second grader Cora Barkley asked if she could do the same for Winter Skye.

Saying yes to Cora spurred the other second grader Tiege Sternquist into action. He bounced across the room and skidded to a stop, the toes of his cowboy boots touching the toes of my sensible pumps. "That makes me Jeremy's buddy, right Miss Newell?"

I hesitated. Tiege was one-third rootin' tootin' cowboy and one-third Tigger from Winnie the Pooh. The remaining one-third was Murphy's Law personified. I wasn't sure Jeremy would survive six hours under Tiege's enthusiastic tutelage.

"Well—"

"Please, Teacher, please. Cross my heart and hope to die." He made an X over his heart, pitched forward, and nearly took me down with him.

He righted himself, and against my better judgment, I approved Tiege's request. By day's end, I was pleasantly surprised by his thoughtfulness. He, Renny, Elva, and Cora made the kindergarteners' first day of school a success. Even so, I was hoarse from fielding their oddball comments.

"My dog barfs when I feed him chocolate chip cookies."

"Mom picked out my favorite pink underpants for today. Do you want to see them?"

"Does your mom choose your underpants, Miss Newell?"

"Which way to the bathroom?"

Once the classroom emptied at three thirty, I laid my aching head on my desk and closed my eyes. My mind emptied, and I was drifting toward delicious sleep when the phone jangled. My head shot up with a snap.

I went to the phone and croaked, "Little Missouri School, Miss Newell speaking."

"You sick?" the voice on the line croaked in return.

There was no mistaking the school janitor's voice. "No, Velma, I'm not sick. Just a little hoarse from explaining everything to the kindergarteners today. I should probably bow out of tonight's square dance lesson." I held the receiver a few inches from my ear.

"Sometimes," she hissed, "you can be as big a la-dee-da sissy as you was when you first come out here. Me and Betty plunked down good money for your lessons, and we mentioned you was gonna be there to several eligible bachelors—"

"What?" It was my turn to be outraged. "You have no business doing that!"

"I don't know why you are all hot and bothered when me and Betty is just looking out for you. Besides, that Dick Phillips who cracks a smile every other year grinned big as you please when I told him you'd be there. He said he's gonna come."

Hold on! Here was the way to accept Dick's dinner invitation and take care of Velma's habitual overreach.

I breathed deep to rein in my excitement. "My social life doesn't need a manager, and I can find my own dance partners. If you want me there tonight, you have to promise something."

"Go on," she growled.

"You stop throwing hissy fits when my students use glitter."

"How long?"

"The rest of the year."

Long pause. "You drive a hard bargain, young lady."

"Deal?"

Longer pause. "Deal."

Without a word I high-fived the phone and hung up.

Velma Albright, you've been had!

Chapter 3

The dance hall was a dumpy, stucco building in need of paint. Even though it was only a couple blocks south and east of the school, it was too cold out to walk. Several pickup trucks were parked on either side of the main entrance when I arrived, so I nosed my car into a spot on the other side of the street between Velma's trailer and the back door of The Bend.

I grabbed my plate of chocolate chip oatmeal cookies and scurried toward the dimly lit entrance to the dance hall. The squat building's rounded roof put me in mind of a repurposed Quonset hut and made me inadvertently duck and hunch my shoulders when I went inside. Someone had said that the town's ambulance and fire trucks were stored in the garage on the opposite side of the building. I wondered if the ladders had to come off the fire engines to get them through the garage doors.

I entered the dance hall half of the building. It was also used for community basketball games, family celebrations, holiday parties, and more. I tossed my parka on one of the wooden movie theater chairs that lined the walls. My underwhelming wardrobe of worn blue jeans, scuffed loafers, and a moth-eaten brown sweater as dumpy as the dance hall had been chosen to send an unequivocal message. Contrary to anything Betty or Velma had said or implied to anyone, I was not hunting for a husband. In case my clothes weren't enough to get the message across, I twisted my stocking cap while pulling it off to ensure that my honey-blond hair was at peek frizziness.

Based on the horrified reactions of my students' parents scattered around the dance hall—the Barkleys, the Bertholds, the Gibsons, the Swensens, the Borgesons, and Liv McDonald and her husband Axel—my methods may have been too effective. As for the single men in attendance, their reactions were priceless. Dick Phillips blushed with his mouth hanging open. Not a good look for him. State trapper Rique DuPeuss, a dead ringer for Daniel Boone who had once offered to prepare me a deworming tincture made from boiled tree bark, wrinkled his nose. I didn't know the name of the handsome guy in a red flannel shirt with a hundred-watt smile, but it went dark as he took in my toilette.

Sheriff Rick Sternquist, older brother of Tiege, laughed. Instead of his sheriff's uniform, he wore jeans and a blue western shirt that matched his eyes. His dark-blond hair was neatly clipped around the sides and wavy on top. He hadn't impressed me when we first met. That had changed ever so slowly as I'd uncovered evidence in two different murders he'd been investigating. Fine with me.

When I took my plate of cookies to the snack table, Rick whispered, "You auditioning for a horror movie?"

An ear-piercing screech kept me from answering. We both covered our ears and looked toward the stage. A thin man with a jet-black pompadour was bent over an amplifier adjusting knobs. The screeching stopped. The man stood upright. He wore cowboy boots, jeans, and a western shirt. Not the standard plaid and pearl-snap type worn by the ranchers in the room. This guy's shirt, along with his jeans and boots, were studded with rhinestones and as black as his hair. Every inch of his tall, thin frame sparkled when he held a microphone to his lips.

"Good evening, everyone. I'm Oscar Rumble." His voice was schmoozy, oozy, and wholly repugnant. "I've been calling dances since I was ten and teaching lessons since I was seventeen. How many of you are new to square dancing or feel rusty?"

All but a few hands went up.

Oscar chuckled. "Well then, I guess I'm gonna earn my keep with this bunch. Arrange yourselves gent-lady-gent and so on in a big circle. The extra ladies can take a seat for now. I'll switch you pretty little fillies in and out."

I swallowed a whinny and found a spot between Dan Barkley and the stranger. His hundred-watt smile was back. Oscar Rumble met my eye, wiggled his eyebrows, and licked his lips like a hungry dog.

The stranger's smile dimmed again. "You know that guy?"

I scowled at Oscar. "Not yet. And I hope not ever."

Rumble licked his lips once more. He turned his gaze upon the surplus dancers—Dick, Rique, and Rick sitting in the chairs along the wall. "I can't hardly believe my eyes," Oscar said. "That's the first surplus of stallions I've seen in forty years."

Next, he addressed the dancers in the circle. "We'll work on several basic calls tonight. Start by introducing yourself to the person on either side of you."

I already knew Dan Barkley and his wife Pam, who stood on his far side. Their children, Cora and Bennan, were two of my students. I turned to the stranger.

He spoke first. "I'm Rocko Vander Meer. I work at the Forest Service."

I took in his black hair and blue eyes, his red flannel shirt, blue jeans, and tennis shoes. He didn't dress like he was from here. His last name sounded familiar, and I tried to place it. "Jane Newell. I teach school here."

"So you're the teacher from Iowa."

"Who told you that?"

"It'd be easier to mention who didn't. You know we're the only two Iowans in town, don't you?"

My eyes widened. "Are you related to the Vander Meers who own the bakery in Le Mars?"

Oscar spoke into his microphone. "Now everyone join hands and circle right."

Rocko's answer would have to wait.

"Now circle left." Following Oscar's singsong instructions, we switched back and forth. After a few minutes he stopped us and explained two new calls. "Here's how to do allemande right and allemande left. For allemande right, gents join your right hand with the right hand of the lady on your right and turn her in a circle."

Once we could do that move without stepping on one another's feet, he explained and had us practice allemande left. Then we all joined hands again, and Oscar alternated circling and allemanding right and left. When he was satisfied with our progress, he brought in Dick, Rique, and Rick so they could learn the steps. Dick took Rocko's place and proved to be a quick learner.

Oscar announced a short break. A few people put on coats, presumably for a smoke break or to visit the bathrooms, which had their entrances outside and around the corner. Most people went straight for the snacks and the coffee urn. When Oscar called us back to the circle, Dick downed the chocolate chip oatmeal cookie he was holding in two bites. From the crumbs on his chin and the smear of chocolate on his cheek, I guessed the cookie in his mouth hadn't been his first.

"Now, ladies and gents," Oscar announced, "let's try tonight's steps to a dandy new tune called *There's Somethin' 'bout You Baby, I Like*."

While Oscar started the record player and lowered the needle, I stood on tiptoe and whispered in Dick's ear. "Supper on Friday night sounds wonderful. I'll meet you there. Say six o'clock?"

His expression didn't change, but there was an extra spring in his step as Oscar called the dance. I wasn't familiar with the song. I don't think Dick was either because when Oscar sang the last line of the chorus, which repeated the song's title, my Friday night supper date blushed bright red.

During the next half hour, Oscar taught us how to do-si-do and elbow swing. After each new move, he added it to what we'd already learned. First we practiced without music, and then with it, rotating the extra men in and out at regular intervals.

"And that, ladies and gents, is enough for one night," Oscar finally said.

I went to find my coat and saw Dick leave so fast there was no chance to talk to him again. Darn!

"The bakery's run by my uncle and aunt."

I turned around and there was Rocko. I smiled. "My dad loves that bakery."

"Are you from Le Mars?"

"No. Sioux City, but Dad's always up for a road trip if food's involved. How about you? Did you grow up in Le Mars?"

"Orange City."

"Then we were practically neighbors."

"Nice to meet you, neighbor." He extended a hand, and we shook. "Would you like to get coffee and pie at the café with a fellow Iowa transplant?"

"I would love to. Though you should know that if we are seen in the café together, the entire town will assume we're getting married soon."

His flashed his hundred-watt smile. "It's worth the risk."

"Jane!" Pam Barkley beckoned from where she and Dan stood visiting with Rick Sternquist, Axel and Liv McDonald, Bram and Mary Borgeson, and Linda Gibson. "Can you come here for a minute?"

"I'll catch up with you at the café in a few minutes," I told Rocko and moved into the empty space next to Linda. "Am I taking Scott's spot?"

"Don't worry about it," she whispered. "He's in the bathroom. Too much coffee during the break."

We turned our attention to Mary Borgeson. I caught the end of her sentence.

"—a few more couples to take lessons. And three more women or girls so the extra men don't have to sit out."

We tossed names around and came up with a decent list. Rick would ask his parents. The Borgesons would bring their daughter Elva and invite the Kellys, who ran the store. The McDonalds would bring their daughter Rosalie as well as Axel's parents, Frost and Fannie McDonald. Pam Barkley would approach Gus and Betty Yarborough.

"What about the switchboard?" I asked, though what I really wanted to know was why they thought Betty's blind husband Gus would want to take square dance lessons.

"There's a list of people who've asked Betty to show them how to operate the thing," Dan said. "It's about time Betty let somebody else near it."

"Maybe Garth and Galva Swensen's older girls?" I ventured before turning to Linda. "Or yours?"

The conversation took longer than I'd anticipated. When the group broke up, I ran across the street toward the back door of the café. It's owners, Glen and Trudy Berthold, didn't like people to use the rear entrance, but Rocko had been patient long enough. Plus it was too cold to go around to the front. The light over the door was off, so I grasped the metal railing and gingerly climbed the wooden steps to the landing.

A large black garbage bag blocked the entrance. Intending to drag the bag out of the way, I reached down and searched for the drawstrings. They proved elusive, so I pulled off one glove and felt around for them again. When my fingers touched cloth rather than plastic, I moved my hand in increasingly large circles. I felt skin and then hair and snatched my hand away as though burned. I hadn't touched a garbage bag. I'd touched a person.

Chapter 4

I took a small flashlight from my pocket and pointed its beam at the body on the small porch. The person lay prone, and I tilted the light to illuminate the partially hidden face. At first my mind refused register what I was seeing. A triangle of a red plaid flannel peeking above a coat collar. A nasty gash near the left temple. A head of black hair. A mouth I feared would never again shine its hundred-watt smile. And blood. So much blood.

I pounded on the door. "Help! Please, help! Rocko Vander Meer's been hurt! I think it's bad!"

Glen Berthold pulled the door open and took in the scene. "I think the sheriff's still at the dance hall. I'll get him and tell Dick Phillips and Mary Borgeson to bring the ambulance." He leaped over Rocko and ran across the street.

I yelled at his retreating back. "Dick left when you did." I knelt beside Rocko and applied pressure to the gash in his temple.

"Betty'll find him." Glen burst into the dance hall and the door banged shut.

With my free hand I searched for Rocko's carotid artery. His skin was still warm, and he had a faint pulse. "Oh God," I prayed, "keep him alive." I applied pressure until Mary and Rick arrived.

"Is he alive?" she asked.

"Barely. He's lost a lot of blood."

Mary put a hand on my shoulder. "Dick's bringing an ambulance. I'll take over."

My brain knew that Mary, a trained EMT, could do far more for Rocko than I. I tried to get out of her way, but my legs refused to obey. I whimpered and began to rock forward and back. Forward and back.

Rick gently pulled me to my feet and walked me to the Beetle. "Keys?"

"In my coat pocket."

He propped me against the car until he found them. Then he folded me into the driver's seat, started the engine, and turned up the heat. "Stay here and warm up until I get back. Okay?"

I nodded and sat on my freezing hands. He shut the door. The ambulance pulled up beside me, obstructing my view of Round the Bend's rear entrance. I stared out the window, then pulled my hands out of my pockets and stared at them. They were covered with dried, brown blood. I rubbed at the stains. Much more blood had covered Rocko's face and pooled under his head. How could he survive after losing so much blood?

A knock sounded on my window. I looked up. Rick motioned for me to roll down the window. His expression confirmed my fear. Rocko was dead.

"Mary and Dick did everything they could," Rick said. "They're waiting in the ambulance until I give them permission to remove the body."

"He must have bled out."

"That could be, though head wounds usually look bloodier than they are. It could be that the force of the blow and lying outside in thirty-degree-below weather killed him."

I rubbed at the blood on my hands again.

Rick misread my action. "Roll up the window so the heat stays inside. Wait here while I call the Rapid City crime investigation team." He jogged off.

My mind cleared as I closed the window again. Rick wouldn't be calling the crime team unless he suspected foul play. When he returned and slid into the passenger seat, I questioned him. "Are you saying someone attacked him?"

"That will be determined once the team from Rapid City completes their analysis. Due to the cold and the fact that it's night, they've decided to come in the morning. That leaves me to conduct tonight's preliminary investigation so the body can be moved before it freezes solid." He leaned his head against the seat back and exhaled. Then he looked at me, his expression grave and his voice gentle. "Stumbling onto Rocko had to be a big shock, but if you're up to it, I could use your help."

Rick had resisted my involvement in his investigations after I'd moved to Little Missouri in August. That had changed before Christmas vacation when Rick learned that I'd been a criminal justice major until my mother blew a gasket and insisted that I go into elementary education. He asked me to set up a forensic lab and assist in investigations. I said yes before he finished his question.

Now as we sat snug and warm in my car, with Rocko's body alone and exposed to the elements, I said yes. Soberly, sadly, but once again without hesitation. "What do you need me to do?"

"Am I right to assume you bought a new camera in Iowa?"

"I did. Plus a flash attachment, film, and darkroom supplies."

"Excellent. I'll stay here with Rocko. You get the camera, plenty of film, and whatever else you need." He got out and shut the door. I put the car in reverse and zoomed off.

Less than fifteen minutes later, I was photographing the scene. Poor lighting hampered our efforts. Glen Berthold offered to replace the bulb above the back door. Rick said no. He didn't want to compromise the area more than necessary. After much discussion, he positioned his sheriff's vehicle and Dick Phillips moved the ambulance so their headlights illuminated the porch and the body. The arrangement was a great improvement, though it created shadows and distortions. I took photos from every possible angle, first with the headlights on and then off so we could compare them. I shot two rolls of film before Rick called it quits.

"That's enough for now, Jane. It's time for Mary and Dick to transport the body." Rick motioned me toward his truck. "You warm up while I update Glen. I'll join you as quick as I can." He returned soon with steaming mugs of coffee and handed one to me before climbing into the cab. "Compliments of Glen and Trudy."

I wrapped my hands around the mug. The warmth pricked my freezing fingers. I tried to wiggle my toes. The extra socks and warm boots I'd donned during my quick stop home were no match for thirty below zero. I moved my feet closer to the heater. "What happens next?"

"I secure the area and cozy up here in my cab until the team from Rapid arrives in the morning."

"So you do think there's foul play involved?"

"I have no idea. But it's always best to play it safe."

I stifled a yawn and checked my watch. Ten o'clock. "What's my assignment?"

"You've done plenty for one night." He sipped his coffee. "Glen'll bring me some sandwiches and coffee after he closes. You head on home."

"You talked me into it." I got out and paused before shutting the door. "Would you do me a favor tomorrow?"

"You name it."

"Update me tomorrow about what the team from Rapid found."

"Consider it done."

Ten minutes later, I was piling extra blankets on my bed and getting into in my warmest pajamas. I took the hot water bottle into the kitchen and filled the teakettle. While it heated, I ran warm water into the sink and scrubbed my hands. I washed every speck of dried blood down the drain and then scrubbed some more. If only I could scrub away the memory of Rocko lying on The Bend's porch, his beautiful face pressed into the rough wood. I was still scrubbing when the tea kettle began its angry, insistent keening. The keening continued even after I lifted the kettle from the burner. Only then did I realize the kettle wasn't the source of the keening. The source was me.

CHAPTER 5

My students, all clomping boots and noisy chatter, came inside Wednesday morning. The lively curiosity they brought into our classroom was the opposite of the death I'd witnessed last night. For the next seven hours, they would require all my energy and attention. I welcomed the reprieve.

I was unwinding the plaid scarf from Bennan Barkley's mummified head when his sister Cora tugged at my sleeve. Her dark eyes appeared worried and barrettes in her fine hair were threatening to fall out. "I don't see Winter Skye. Is she sick?"

I undid the barrettes and clipped them back into place. "The kindergarteners come on Tuesdays, Thursdays, and every other Friday. I promise she'll be back tomorrow."

"Okay." Cora skipped to her desk and passed the news on to Tiege.

"What?" He sprang from his desk, scattering pencils and paper in every direction. "Jeremy's crazy for comic books, so I come up with a Batman counting game to teach him."

He was mid bounce when I applied gentle pressure to his shoulders and steered him into his seat again. "Now that's called initiative, Tiege."

"No." Tiege looked puzzled. "It's called Kapow!"

"Kapow?"

"Miss Newell, you're saying it wrong. It's not 'kapow' with a question mark. It's 'kapow' with an *exculma-tion* mark." He struck a Batman pose and *exculmed*, "Kapow!"

That's all the motivation needed for Bennan Barkley, Stig Borgeson, and Beau Kelly—the three first graders who were the charter members of the Tiege Sternquist fan club—to let loose a flurry of kapows complete with super-hero-worthy *exculmation* marks.

As a practitioner of the art of exculmating, I took a deep breath and projected from my diaphragm, "Return to your seats!"

They froze, dumbfounded.

I tapped each boy on the shoulder. "Kapow!"

They thawed and sat down.

I walked briskly to my desk and sank into my chair. "Does anyone have something for show-and-tell?"

One by one the children served up tidbits that fasci-nated their friends. No one mentioned Rocko, not even Renny. That struck me as strange. As a rule, Renny used show-and-tell to report what had happened at Round the Bend the night before. Perhaps his parents had decided to keep Rocko's death to themselves. There was a first time for everything. Lack of sleep took its toll on me as the day progressed. My eyelids grew heavier and my patience thinner. By three thirty, the kapows, which had continued throughout the day, had wormed their way into my skull and were digging an escape tunnel in the middle of my forehead.

When I dismissed the children at the end of the day, my farewell was void of *exculmation*. A wall of cold air chased me into my apartment, where I made hot tea and used it to wash down a couple aspirin. I laid a couple chocolate chip oatmeal cookies on a napkin. I carried the tea and cookies to my desk where I corrected papers, nibbled, and sipped for the next hour. As I set out the next day's seatwork and arranged activities I prayed would take the kindergarteners more than five minutes to complete, a knock sounded at the door.

Not a visitor. Please, no! I was ready for my fuzzy pajamas and some of Mom's leftover bean soup in front of the television, not for conversation. The knock sounded again.

"Coming!" I flipped on the porch light and peered through the window.

Rick stood there looking decidedly unofficial. The flaps of his sheepskin hat hid his ears. Frost coated his eyelashes. The collar of his fleece-lined leather jacket was turned up. His hands were deep in his pockets, and the tip of his bright red nose was dripping.

A wave of pity washed away my peevishness. I let the sheriff in and led him through the children's cloakroom into the entryway of the apartment. "You look like you could use some hot soup and something warm to drink."

"I won't say no to that." He hung up his coat and pulled off his snow-caked boots.

In the kitchen he took a seat at the table. I dumped a

container of frozen bean soup into one saucepan, poured milk into another, and set them on the stove. I whisked cocoa, sugar, and vanilla into the milk and turned on the burners. While everything heated, I fetched the granny square afghan made by my very own granny and draped it around his shoulders. He pulled it over his head and gathered it tight under his chin like a Siberian babushka. The frost on his eyelashes began to melt and his eyelids drifted shut.

I crept into the guest bedroom for my camera, retraced my steps, and snapped his picture.

His lids flew open. "What'd you do that for?"

"The picture could come in handy if you even think about shutting me out of this investigation."

"It's already hit a snag." Every syllable radiated despair.

I poured hot chocolate into a mug and set it before him. "What kind of snag?"

"The area behind The Bend has been contaminated."

"But you were guarding it all night."

He wormed a hand out from under the afghan and picked up his mug. He blew on the surface and took a sip. "Ah, that hits the spot."

I set napkins and spoons on the table and ladled soup into bowls. I slid one to him and waited while he blew his nose into a napkin. I waited some more while he tasted his soup and dipped in for another bite.

I had waited long enough. It was time to move things along. "Either you tell me what happened, or I'll nail eight-by-tens of you in that afghan on every light pole in the county."

"You are the most impatient woman I have ever met."

I threw my spoon at him. "And you are the most stubborn man I know. Who contaminated the area?"

"I believe it's more like *what* rather than *who*."

I took a second spoon from the silverware drawer and let it fly. "Okay, have it your way. *What* did the damage?"

"Hold your fire, and I'll tell you."

"You'd better. I'm moving on to knives soon."

"I'm too cold and hungry to care." He lifted his soup bowl to his lips, drained it, and burped. He wiped his mouth, blew his nose again, and finally spoke.

"I'd been behind The Bend for a couple hours when Dick and Mary returned from delivering Rocko's body to a funeral home in Belle Fourche. Dick said he had today off and offered to stand guard so I could get some sleep. I took him up on the offer, being partial to having my wits about me in time for the investigators to arrive. I went out to Dad and Mom's ranch and slept until dawn. Then I drove to The Bend and found Dick sound asleep in his truck."

"You've got to be kidding."

"Wish I was. I knocked on his window and he was out of the cab like a shot. We went to the scene, and it was a mess. The crime scene tape was torn and trampled in the snow. Garbage cans were knocked over. Bones and food scraps littered the ground. Grease all over the porch and door. Paw prints coming and going from every direction."

Ah yes. *What*, not *who*.

"Our first thought was coyotes. Dick went to Rique DuPeuss's place and asked him to take a look. Right away Rique said they were dog prints, probably from a pack that travels up and down the river. They stay out of town for the most part. Rique thought they were lured into town by the smell of fresh blood."

"Did they ruin everything?"

"That's what the team out of The Hills said. The pictures you took are our best hope now."

I started to stand. "Let me get the film, and you can send it with them."

"No. I asked you to take pictures for my"—he raised a finger—"make that *our* investigation. To be developed in the darkroom of *your* forensic lab."

I settled into my chair and folded my arms on the table. "So I'm involved in the investigation all the time as opposed to when it's to your advantage?"

"All the time. No matter what. Starting yesterday. I'm relying on your lab to analyze the photos and the material evidence we find."

"In that case, we need to get busy." I jumped up. Rick threw off the granny afghan—bye bye, babushka—and followed me into the guest room. I pointed to the cardboard boxes on the floor. "The supplies you asked me to purchase in Sioux City are in there. Once you build the darkroom—"

"Hold on. When was I conscripted for carpenter duty?"

"Would you like me to ask Betty to recommend a handyman and explain why I need one? How long do you think she'll keep that news under wraps?"

He looked around. "You got a yardstick?"

"What? Do you want me to knock some sense into you?"

"No. I want to take measurements for the materials I need to pick up at the hardware store in Tipperary. This weekend, we're building a darkroom."

Kapow!

CHAPTER 6

Rick tucked the slip of paper with the darkroom measurements in his coat pocket. "I'll be here Saturday morning in time for breakfast."

"Would you like oatmeal or Cream of Wheat?" I asked.

He cracked his first smile since arriving. "Oatmeal with Snippy cream if you have it. Enjoy your evening, Jane."

"Same to you."

He shut the door quickly, but not before a stream of frigid air entered and wrapped my ankles in its icy grip. My exhaustion, which Rick's visit had chased away, returned doubled in strength. Before I could cuddle up on the couch with the granny afghan, the phone rang.

I dragged the afghan along and wrapped it around my ankles before picking up the receiver. "Hello?" A whistly schlep sounded in my ear. "How are you doing, Merle?"

"Ain't nothing gets past you, now does it, Teacher?"

Another whistle. Another schlep. "I hear you was up late taking pictures for the sheriff with that fancy new Kodak you brought from Ioway. Now that he's wherever he went to, you got time for some non-skid pancakes?"

"Thanks for the offer, but I ate already."

"With the sheriff?" He sounded jealous. "I thought he looked a good sight more cheerful when he left your apartment than when he first got there."

I was too tired to stroke the ego of a man old enough to be my grandpa. On the other hand, I knew better than to get on his bad side. He was a good neighbor, and I wanted him to stay that way.

"I thawed him out with leftover hot soup and cocoa. Can I come tomorrow night instead?"

"Five o'clock?"

"I'll be there." I hung up and put on flannel pajamas, along with two pairs of socks. Then I turned on *Eight Is Enough* and snuggled under the afghan and two blankets on the couch. When I woke up, my neck was stiff, Dick Van Patten was long gone, and only an hour remained until school would begin. Time to get a move on!

I raced into the classroom seconds before my students entered with their frosty eyelashes and rosy cheeks. The smell of cold rose from them as they peeled off coats, snow pants, boots, hats, mittens, and scarves and hung up their things.

Renny's hand shot up after the Pledge of Allegiance. The gleam in his eye said that he'd heard about Rocko's death and intended to spill the beans. Renny considered such reports to be a public service. I considered them a public nuisance. Beau Kelly was still recovering from his mother's death in August. The hit-and-run driver who killed Beau's mother had been arrested in October and reports about violent acts were off limits in our classroom.

Renny knew that, but he wasn't about to stop trying. His hand waved faster than the flag on the pole in front of the school building. I ignored him and went to the front of the room. "Today is the kindergarteners' day for show-and-tell."

Renny scowled as his hand flopped onto his desk with a thump.

"Raise your hand if you're in kindergarten and brought something." All four raised theirs, shy smiles playing on their lips.

Of the four, Winter Skye Swensen appeared to be the most eager to begin. I nodded at her. "Would you like to go first?"

She sprang from her seat and skipped to the front of the room, white-blond hair flouncing and green eyes shining. I sat behind my desk and encouraged her to begin.

"My dad made me this for Christmas." She held up a cute and cleverly assembled stuffed mouse.

Hands went up faster than snow forts on the playground. Winter Skye pointed at Beau Kelly.

"Your dad makes stuffed animals? Like teddy bears?" he asked.

"No." She recoiled as if the thought horrified her. "Like deer heads and rattlesnakes and foxes. He's a tagsadermist."

I gestured weakly at the no-longer-cute or clever mouse. "Are you saying that's a—"

"A real mouse. Yup. Who wants to pet it?"

Everyone under the age of nine in our classroom stroked the mouse's fur. They commented on how soft and smooth it was. Everyone in the room who was over the age of nine took their word for it. Finally, Winter Skye took the creepy critter into the entryway and put it in her backpack. I stood close enough to watch her zip it securely in a pocket, while remaining far enough away to run like the wind if the mouse came to life. Once my resurrection worries had been quelled, show-and-tell resumed. Keeva explained how she had braided a lanyard using tail hairs from Baby, her horse. Jeremy belted out the Batman theme song while modeling his new superhero cape and mask. Grace Berthold demonstrated how to change her new doll's diaper. Their offerings couldn't top a tagsadermied mouse, but they gave me an idea of what made these kindergarteners tick.

The day felt like a marathon. I struggled to teach four grades' worth of lessons instead of three, to engage eleven students instead of seven. It felt like nonstop motion through subject after subject. Grade after grade. Indoor recess after indoor recess. At dismissal time, the children burst onto the playground as energetic as when they had arrived and oblivious to the sub-zero temperature.

I, on the other hand, had barely enough energy to pull the door shut against the cold. The moment of quiet I had longed for all day had arrived. When I sat down at my desk, the emotions I'd not had time to process since the discovery of Rocko's body rushed in.

We had exchanged only a handful of words, but our conversation and his easy manner had intrigued me. We were both from Iowa, from the same part of the state, yet he had seemed comfortable with Tipperary County's cowboys, ranchers, and Forest Service workers in a way I doubted I would ever be. Even if I learned to ride a horse. Even if I broke my vow to never, ever wear cowboy boots.

Rocko was dead. We would never sit across from each other in a booth at Round the Bend and eat pie while we reminisced about growing up in Iowa. We would never compare notes about our favorite goodies from the bakery his aunt and uncle owned in Le Mars. He would never tell me how someone raised amidst tidy corn and bean fields could adapt to the rugged, untamed short-grass prairie.

Rocko was dead. I laid my unbearably heavy head in my arms. If this was the weight of loss after knowing him for less than a day, how much more devastating must it be for his parents, his family, and his co-workers? Could their lungs still breathe? Could their hearts still pump? Could their eyes do anything but weep? See anything but darkness?

No, I thought as my own tears fell and wet the strands of hair that had escaped from my banana clip. Tears soaked the cuffs of my sweater, but I didn't care.

Rocko was dead, along with the thousands of possibilities his life had contained. I couldn't restore his life. All I could do was help Rick solve the puzzle of his death. If it was an accident, so be it. If it was murder, well that was another matter. If someone had killed him, that person should pay dearly. An eye for an eye. A tooth for a tooth. I raised my head, wiped my nose, and whispered, "A life for a life."

CHAPTER 7

When I entered Merle's kitchen an hour later, bacon was sizzling and spitting in the frying pan on the stove. He pointed a spoon dripping with waffle batter at the offending pan. "You scoot over there and turn down the burner 'fore that hot grease takes our eyes out."

Having no desire to sport an eye patch while on a date with Dick Phillips, I greeted Merle with a hand shielding my face. "Hello to you too."

"Don't get sassy with me, Teacher."

Once the bacon settled down, I dropped my hand. Merle studied my face, and his expression said that walking to his house in the cold hadn't obliterated the evidence of my tears. He dropped the spoon in the bowl of batter and rubbed the hairs on his ear with one hand. "I hear you was the one who found that young man outside The Bend. I'm beginning to believe you is a magnet for dead bodies."

"Not funny, Merle." I sank into one of the chairs at his kitchen table. "Do you know what it's like going to meet a new friend for pie and conversation and stumble over his dead body instead?"

"I am sorry I joked about the sit-ee-ation." He rubbed his ears with both hands. "So the shock ain't wore off yet?"

"I wonder if it ever will."

He didn't speak until after he lifted four gold-en-brown waffles from the waffle iron and refilled it with the last of the batter. "We-ull," he said as he forked bacon onto a plate lined with paper towels, "it's gonna take a goodly amount of time. Less if he died acc-ee-den-tal. More if he was done in and the guilty bastard ain't found. Partway between if the sheriff sniffs out whoever done it."

"The sheriff isn't in this alone, you know—"

Shut up, Jane!

"—Uh, he called in a support team from the Black Hills."

"That so? Then he's got some susp-ee-tions about what he seen." Merle set the plate of bacon on the table, shuffled to the waffle iron to remove the final batch, and added them to the ones already piled on a platter.

I rearranged the clutter on the kitchen table to make room for Merle to wedge the platter between a grease-spotted pile of mail and a chipped sugar bowl. "Little Missouri felt so safe when I moved here. Every-body knows everybody. People work hard. They go to church. They watch out for one another. At least that's what I thought then. Now I'm not so sure."

"Fill yer plate." Merle picked up his fork and waved it at the food. "This talk'll go down better on a full stomach."

When we'd eaten our fill, I cleared the table and began washing dishes. Merle did a little toothpick work before he spoke again. "Little Missouri ain't as safe as it seems. A town this small don't have any place to hide. You learnt that since you moved here. What you ain't learnt yet is that not everbody works as hard as they let on. Not near enough people go to church, and half a those who do don't pay attention to what the preacher says."

On that count, I was as guilty as the next person.

"And they don't so much watch out for everbody to keep 'em safe as to uncover gossip they can pass along. You know a little about that last one, too, if I ain't mistaken."

Did I ever.

Merle threw his toothpick into a battered tin wastebasket. "Just this week I got an earful about them parents that belong to that bunch a girls with them god-awful names. You know who I'm talking about?"

He had me flummoxed. "Can you give me a little more to work with?"

"You know. All them flowers and weather and seasons and the like."

Now I was tracking. "Do you mean Winter Skye Swensen's parents?"

Merle snapped his fingers. "Them's the ones."

"Why would anyone spread gossip about them? They're a nice family."

"People got their reasons."

"What reasons?"

"Oh, dotin' on them girls like they was queens of Sheba and saddlin' them with four of the most impractee-cal names in a three-state area. That's all some folks with an envious disposition and less sense than a chicken with its head cut off need to jump to conclusions." He took a jackknife from the bib pocket of his overalls and began cleaning his fingernails.

"What conclusions?"

"We-ull, what I heard was that Galva ain't happy Garth put up a pole barn for his tax-ee-dermy stuff instead a building them a house like he promised when they got engaged."

My jaw tightened. "I wish I hadn't asked you. That's their business and nobody else's."

"You got a point there, Teacher." He snapped the jackknife shut and returned it to its pocket. "But Galva's got herself a couple bad habits. She says more than she should in front of them girls of hers. They is bright enough to pick up what she's saying, but not old enough to shut their mouths around their friends. And from what I understand, Galva trusts the women she beaut-ee-fies in that little hairdo shop Garth put in the corner of his barn to pac-ee-fy her. There's a few who spec-ee-lize in taking what's said in conf-ee-dence in broad daylight and twistin' it into lies to spread after dark. There's a few of 'em I wouldn't trust with a wooden nickel."

I wrung out the dishcloth and draped it over the faucet before picking up a dishtowel. "I wish I hadn't asked you. I don't want what you said about my students' parents to make me suspicious of them."

Merle dismissed my fears out of hand. "You ain't that kind of person."

He gave me too much credit.

"But I shoulda thought through what I was saying."

He drew in a wet, schleppy breath. "But since you're the one who found that Rocko fellow the other night, there is something about one a your kind-ee-garten families you got a right to know. I been hearing pretty regular that Scott Gibson and Rocko was at loggerheads. I met 'em both and thought they was good men. Figured what I was hearing was damn popp-ee-cock. Still do. But Rocko's dead and Scott's not. With you being thick as thieves with the sheriff, you oughta pass that on to him next time he visits your apartment and stays long enough to raise eyebrows."

That last comment made him sound like one of the folks with an envious disposition and less sense than a chicken with its head cut off. On the other hand, what he said about Scott and Rocko sounded like it contained a grain of truth, so I would pass it along to Rick.

I dried the last plate, set it on the counter, and gazed out the window above the sink. Frost covered the glass, obscuring both moon and starlight. Wind rattled the panes, and cold night air seeped in. I shivered and plunged my hands into the soapy water remaining in the sink. It warmed my hands, but it couldn't touch the chill gripping the center of my being.

Rocko was dead. Perhaps murdered. Scott Gibson had been absent from the dance hall when Rocko had gotten hurt. If Merle's rumor did contain a grain of truth, the father of Jeremy, the kapow king of kindergarten, would become our prime suspect.

For the first time since Rick and I had become a team, I wished we hadn't.

Chapter 8

When I woke in the morning, my misgivings about the investigation were still there. They hung on through breakfast and my preparations for the school day. I was in a bad mood when my students arrived. They came through the door full of little kid magic and pulled me into their world. My dark mood fled and stayed away until Velma came to clean after school.

She looked me up and down with a critical eye. "You gonna do anything about how you look before you go to supper with Dick Phillips tonight?"

I hadn't told a soul about our date. Neither had Dick. At least not in so many words. It was more likely that Velma, the nosiest school janitor in the history of school janitors, had fired questions at him until he blushed and gave himself away without a word.

I thought about using my correcting pen as a dart with Velma as the dart board. But that would never do. An injured Velma would mean no janitor. No janitor would mean I would have to clean the school tonight.

Me cleaning the school would force me to cancel my date. I closed my grade book, laid the pen beside it, and cancelled target practice.

I stood and gestured at my dark-red wool pantsuit and white turtleneck. "What's wrong with what I'm wearing? You don't expect me to wear a dress and heels in twenty-below weather, do you?"

"I got nothing against your duds, but your hair looks like you been combing it with an eggbeater. When's the last time you got it cut? Halloween?"

She wasn't far off. My plan had been to make an appointment at a salon while at my parents during winter break. But Dick Philips had unintentionally given me a shiner a few days before Christmas. Though we'd prevented the drug dealer who had killed a kid from a nearby boys' ranch from flying off into the sunset, the fight had earned Dick and me some dandy battle scars. My black eye had required massive amounts of concealer and foundation, as well as cleverly draped bangs to hide it from Dad and Mom. Keeping it from a hairstylist would have been impossible. Thus the eggbeater look.

I ran a hand over the rebellious frizz that had escaped the barrette at the nape of my neck. "I'll see what I can do while you vacuum."

She shook a finger under my nose. "And don't you even think about sneakin' outta here once you're all dolled up. Me and Betty told your mom we'd make sure you look respectable. She made us promise once she got wind of your getup when you come to the first square dance lesson."

Velma fired up the beast. I left her to it, marveling at Mom's ability to keep tabs on me. We lived five hundred miles apart, but now that she was in cahoots with Betty and Velma, she might as well live next door.

My hair and I duked it out in the bathroom. It took twenty minutes, a battalion of bobby pins, and a can of hairspray, but I emerged victorious and half asphyxiated. When I returned to the classroom, Velma was growling at a bookcase and swatting its contents with a feather duster. I tiptoed over to my desk and wrote a note in my planner to schedule an appointment with Lacey Jo at Dyed and Gone to Heaven in Tipperary asap. Then I tiptoed up behind Velma, brought my lips close to her ear, and spoke in my teacher voice, "Do I look respectable?"

The feather duster flew from her hand, ricocheted off the ceiling, and hit the chalkboard. It slid down its surface neat as you please and cozied up to the chalk in the chalk tray.

"The judge from the United States gives you a perfect ten!" I declared and held up an imaginary score card.

"There you go again, bein' all East River smart aleck." She stomped over to the chalkboard and snatched up the feather duster. She twirled it in a circle. "Turn around."

I did.

She crossed her arms. "Do it again. Slow this time."

I complied while she alternated between exasperated harrumphs and exasperated sighs. Finally she mumbled an exasperated, "It'll have to do."

"Thank you for that vote of confidence." I went to the entryway where I bundled into my winter things and got my purse. On the way out the door, I shouted over my shoulder. "The judge from the United States withdraws your perfect ten!"

***

I stepped outside and slammed into the cold and dark. It accompanied me to my car and permeated the Beetle's engine, which turned over with a painful groan. Once I parked outside Round the Bend, the cold escorted me inside where the warmth generated by the deep fryers and the kitchen grill finally chased it away.

Dick sat at a small table for two. It was wedged into the back corner where the wall between the café and the bar met the plywood partition that partially blocked the kitchen from view. Its proximity to the cash register made it an unpopular spot for most of the year. In the winter, however, its distance from the gusts of cold air that entered with every customer made it very attractive.

The other diners, and there were plenty of them, watched my progress to where Dick waited. More than likely, Betty and Velma had already spread the word, which explained why the café was crowded this frigid night. I lifted my chin and smiled at the customers with their curious stares. Dick's back was toward me, so he couldn't see my approach. That meant he wouldn't stand and pull out my chair for me, an action that would have had the phone lines buzzing all night long.

"Hi," I said and sank into the empty chair at a right angle to his. "Have you been waiting long?"

"No," he mumbled and stared at the table. "Wanna order?"

The rapport we'd enjoyed early on Christmas Eve on a snowy stretch of road shortly after I began to drive to my parents' home in Iowa was gone. Had I imagined the spark between us?

No, Jane. It was unmistakable. Maybe he's just nervous.

I waited for him to blush.

Nothing.

I took off my coat and waited for him to add to the three words he'd said.

Nada.

Chilled silence filled the space between us. I waved Trudy over. "We're ready to order."

She whipped out her pad and cocked an eyebrow at me. "You want the usual?"

"I do."

"Got it. Diet Coke, cheeseburger, and fries." She scribbled on the pad and turned to Dick. "And for you?"

"Hot water."

He was up to five words.

Trudy waited for him to go on.

Nothing.

"Want a tea bag with that?" she asked.

He shook his head.

"You still gotta pay for the tea bag. Something to eat?"

Another shake.

"Okay." She turned around and went straight to the phone. Considering Dick's imitation of a sphinx, I guessed she was about to tell Betty to scrap any wedding plans she'd made for us.

Icy fingers clutched at my heart. I pulled my coat over my shoulders. "Not hungry?"

"No."

Six.

He lifted his head and leveled a frosty gaze at me. Then he stared at the table again as if he couldn't bear the sight of me. I shivered and slipped my arms into my coat sleeves. Trudy came over and surveyed the top of Dick's head. She gave me a weak smile and placed mug of hot water on the table.

"There you go." Her voice shattered the icy silence. "Your food will be out real quick, Miss Newell."

Dick curled his fingers around the mug. When the water didn't freeze over, I asked. "Is something wrong?"

"No."

Seven.

"Is your water hot enough?"

"No."

Eight.

Our conversation remained frozen until Trudy brought my food. I thanked her and reached for the ketchup bottle. She patted my shoulder and tiptoed away.

Dick pushed out his chair. "I'm going home."

To his credit, he uttered words nine, ten, and eleven with a clarity and volume the previous eight had lacked. His declaration reached every corner of the café. Conversation ceased. Diners watched him disappear into his winter gear and tromp off. As he slammed the door on his way out, a framed photograph of the Long Pines baking under a bright summer sun fell off the wall and crashed to the floor.

The attention shifted to me. Pity shone from every eye. I wanted to hide under my chair and melt into a little puddle. Instead, I sat frozen in place. Not even the warmth rising from my food or the aroma of melted cheese, grilled meat, and sizzling french fries roused me to action.

Trudy brought my bill and put my food in a carry

out box. She poured my Diet Coke into a Styrofoam cup while I studied the bill. The cost of Dick's tea bag had been charged to me.

White hot humiliation brought me to my feet. Dick. I slammed my money on the table and told Trudy to keep the change.

She loaded the food and the tea bag into a paper sack. "Might as well send it home with you. You paid for it." As she handed me the sack and my cup of diet Coke, she leaned in and whispered, "I told Betty you're too good for him."

Well then, I told myself on the interminable walk to the exit, Betty will tell Mom and Velma. Though not necessarily in that order. Between the three of them, the combined citizenry of Tipperary County and Sioux City, Iowa will hear about my disastrous date before morning.

I stepped outside, happy to hide in the darkness and cold. The twenty-below temperature that had made me and my Beetle shudder earlier in the evening felt balmy now. Compared to the chill of my date with Dick Phillips, how could it not?

CHAPTER 9

The phone rang and jolted me into wakefulness. I glanced at the clock on my nightstand. Five thirty. My first instinct was to burrow deeper under the blankets and ignore the call. However, if my hunch was correct, the woman on the other end of the line would just keep calling. The only thing to do was to get it over with. I threw back the covers, threw on a bathrobe, and tramped to the phone.

"Hi, Mom."

"How did you know it was me?"

I yawned. "You're the only person who calls this early on a weekend."

"You were still in bed? But it's six thirty." She'd used the same astonished tone every Saturday morning of my teenage years when I begged her to wait to vacuum outside my bedroom until a decent hour.

"In Iowa maybe. It's five thirty here."

"I forgot about the time difference." She sounded contrite. "Would you like me to call later?"

My stomach growled. So much for going back to bed. "Now's fine. What's up?"

"I told the teachers in my building about kindergarten starting this week. They are dying to hear how it went."

I described the adopt-a-kindergartener movement instigated by the second and third graders.

"What an ingenious idea. Good for you, Jane."

"More like good for my students. They thought of it."

"And you capitalized upon it. Don't sell yourself short, young lady."

I accepted Mom's rare compliment with gratitude and told her about Jeremy's Batman costume, Winter Skye's taxidermized mouse, and Tiege's kapow theory of education.

"Hang on a minute, Jane. Your father has got to hear this. I'll hand him the phone."

When he came on the line, I launched into the story again. Dad began laughing when the Batman cape entered the scene. It intensified when the real stuffed mouse made its entrance. With the kapow, his glee crescendoed in an explosion of snorts and hiccups.

Mom's voice came on the line again. "He's laughing so hard he's crying and his nose is running. I need to sign off and get him tissues before he drowns in his own phlegm." She clunked the receiver into its cradle, and that was that.

Grinning, I hung up and checked the clock. Sunrise was still hours away. There was plenty of time to shower and dress before Rick arrived with materials for building the darkroom. Our plan was to haul everything inside while it was too dark for Merle or Velma to see what we were doing.

Thanks to Mom and Dad's call, I was ready for Rick long before he showed up. To kill time, I laid out everything for breakfast and worked in my classroom. When a soft knock sounded at the door, I let Rick in. We unloaded his truck, which he'd parked beside my Beetle, without the aid of flashlight or porch light. Once everything was inside, he drove to Frost McDonald's garage and left it there for an oil change. He walked back to my apartment and was hanging his coat in the entryway as the first pink streaks of dawn appeared on the eastern horizon.

I stuck my head around the corner. "Breakfast is ready. Want some?"

He rubbed his palms together. "Yes, please."

He joined me in the kitchen, and we reviewed the day's agenda while we ate. We filled our stomachs, set our dirty dishes in the sink, and got busy. The first order of business was to install a bolt lock on the door of the guest room we were converting into the forensic lab. The lock was the only way to keep evidence in and Velma out. Next, we turned the room into a hidden workshop, complete with sawhorses, a skill saw, and all manner of hand tools. It was unlikely that any of my neighbors were nosey enough to visit me on a day as cold as this one. Then again, if my neighbors whose first initials were M and V did stop by because they were that nosey, Rick could pull the door shut, and they'd be none the wiser.

Once the necessary precautions were in place, Rick started measuring twice and cutting once. I dumped stew ingredients in my slow cooker and turned it on high in hopes that it would be ready for a late lunch. My part in our subterfuge was to stick to my Saturday routine of working in my classroom. Since that routine included bopping between my apartment and the other half of the building throughout the day, it was easy to check in with Rick now and then.

Around twelve thirty, I admired the framework of studs he'd erected. "Wow! You've gotten a lot done. Will you be able to take a lunch break in about a half hour?"

"Sooner if you want. Whatever's been cooking all morning is making me hungry."

"As soon as the drop biscuits come out of the oven, I'll let you know."

Twenty minutes later, we sat down to eat. I was about to dip a spoon into my stew when Rick offered to say grace. I set down my spoon and bowed my head.

"Thank you for this day, good company, and good food. Give us wisdom and provision to discover what led to Rocko's death. Amen."

I blew on a spoonful of stew while Rick buttered a biscuit and drizzled it with honey We ate in silence until the edge was off our hunger.

"Has the team from the Hills sent a preliminary report yet?"

"They have, but it doesn't say anything we didn't know already. Their final report may tell us if Rocko's death was accidental or deliberate." He split open another biscuit and buttered it. "If it's the latter, your photos could be the evidence needed to build our case."

"Will the darkroom be finished today?"

"It's not a one-day project. I hope to run the wiring and maybe put up some of the paneling and hang the door by dusk. I wish I could stay later, but I told Frost I'd pick up my truck before supper."

"Is there anything I can do to help?"

"You should stick to your normal Saturday routine just like we planned." He ladled more stew into his bowl. "While you're at it, come up with a reason for me to visit you whenever we need to discuss the case."

I laughed. Sometimes men, even a bright young sheriff who could usually put two and two—though in this case, perhaps one and one was more apropos—were clueless creatures.

He looked put out. "What's so funny?"

"Even though you and I know that we are colleagues and nothing more, the rest of the residents of Tipperary County do not. All we need to do is be seen together more than usual, and the rumor mill will rev up. It's a perfect cover for what we're really doing. No one will suspect anything else."

"Give me a minute to think it over." He sipped his coffee and finished his stew before pronouncing his verdict. "We need to do a couple things for this to work."

"Okay." I couldn't imagine what he meant.

"First, my parents have to be in on the secret. They think the world of you, and I don't want them hoping there's something between us. They know how to keep their mouths shut and won't tell a soul."

"Not even Tiege?"

He barked a laugh. "Most certainly not Tiege."

"Then tell your parents. With my blessing. What's the other thing?"

"You have to tell your principal what's going on."

"Mrs. Dremstein? Why?"

"Because your apartment is school property. If I'm here more than some believe to be proper, they'll complain to her. She's a strong woman who backs up her teachers. Still, she deserves fair warning before the storm of protest hits."

"I'll call her Monday and set up a time to meet with her." I rose and took my dishes to the sink. "Do you want more stew?"

"No more room." He patted his stomach and stacked his dishes.

"I'll take care of those. You get back to work."

Shortly after dusk, he found me in the kitchen taking a pan of sugar cookies out of the oven and setting it on a hot pad.

"Mmm. Smells good in here."

"We're going to decorate them in art class this week. I made extra, so help yourself. The ones on the counter won't burn your tongue."

"That's an offer I can't refuse." He bit into a cookie. "These are good, but I like your chocolate chip oatmeal ones better. Do you have any of them?"

"Not until tomorrow." I slid another pan in the oven. "How's construction coming along?"

"The walls are up, but that's it. I'd like to come early tomorrow morning and get right at it again. Is that okay with you?"

I straightened. "You're going to skip church?"

"What choice is there? We need to finish so you can develop film and make prints." He nabbed a couple more cookies and carried them into the entryway.

I followed him and leaned against the doorjamb while he put on his coat. "Tomorrow it is then. Get here well before sunrise. If anyone sees you sneak in on Sunday morning, and we both skip church, Mrs. Dremstein will have to fire me. Then what will become of me and my orphaned cookies?"

Rick grinned as he pulled his hat snug around his ears and wound a muffler around his neck. "Don't give the cookies another thought. I'll give them a good home."

"And what about my job?"

"You're on your own there." He put a gloved hand on the doorknob. "But I'll bring breakfast tomorrow so you can save your pennies for when you're unemployed."

I grabbed my stocking cap and threw it at him.

He ducked, cracked the door open, and looked outside. "The coast is clear. Gotta go."

As he slipped out into the cold, I snatched a mitten from a shelf, lobbed it at his butt, and hit the bull's eye. *Score!* The years I'd spent picking on my younger brother Jeff were paying off.

I allemanded into the kitchen and opened the oven door. I took out the pan of cookies and set it on a wire rack to cool. They were crisp and lightly browned around the edges and a light yellow in the middle, just the way my little brother liked them. Rick too, from what he'd let on. I'd never had an older brother before. From what I could tell, I was going to like it.

CHAPTER 10

Rick trooped in an hour before dawn. In a plummy British accent laced with West River twang, he announced, "Breakfast is served." He held a square something swathed in towels in one hand and a cardboard carton in the other. The carton was bigger than a breadbox, but not by much, and the aroma of yeast mixed with cinnamon emanated from it.

I snatched it from Rick's hands and tore off the lid. A dozen caramel rolls sat in a nest of wax paper. These weren't just any old rolls. These had been made by Cookie Sternquist, and they were legendary in a county that boasted scads of fabulous bakers. They brightened my Sunday morning like sunrise on a clear day.

"When you're done drooling over those, could you take this pan so I don't track snow into the kitchen?" He held up the square bundle. "I parked behind a snowbank near the fair building and hit some deep drifts on the way here."

There was a pan in there? I carried the bundle to the

table. While Rick removed his snow boots and parka, I unwrapped towel after towel in search of what was hidden within. When I reached the center and opened the pan, sausage patties and sunny-side-up eggs, steam still rising from their glistening yellow centers, winked at me. In a flash I set the table and poured coffee. We sat down, and I said grace, mainly thanking God for Cookie Sternquist, before the food went cold.

"Your mother is a marvel." I gestured to the spread before us. "Am I right in assuming that this is the result of a talk with your parents last night?"

"Yes," he said through a mouthful of eggs.

"How did it go?"

He swallowed. "Pretty good. Mom couldn't hide her disappointment after she heard we were good friends and nothing more. She says you're prime daughter-in-law material."

"Tell her I'm already jealous of the woman who will have her for a mother-in-law." I tore off a piece of caramel roll and popped it in my mouth. Oh my gosh, it was so good! "It's the one thing I regret about becoming your partner in crime."

"Do you mind rephrasing that last part? As a sheriff, I'm duty bound to protect my reputation."

I rolled my eyes like I did when Jeff made unreasonable demands. "Okay, fine. Your partner in fighting crime. Are you satisfied now?"

"I will be once you pass me the rolls."

"Promise to leave some for me."

"You have my word."

After breakfast, Rick started in on the construction again. The racket made by his power drill set my teeth on edge. Silence returned forty five minutes later, and my ears rejoiced.

"Can you bring me a lightbulb?" he hollered from the other room.

"A regular one or the red one?" I hollered back.

"Regular for now."

I took it to him. He screwed it into a special socket hanging from a hook protruding from high on a stud of a wall he'd not yet paneled. The socket plugged into an extension cord that ran up the same stud. The cord was held in place by bent nails pounded along its width and exited the darkroom through a gap between the studs.

"Would you plug the other end into the wall outlet to see if it works?"

I did, and it did.

Rick gave a satisfied nod. "Now I can see what I'm doing."

"Anything more I can do?"

"Can you unpack the darkroom equipment? I'd like to measure it before cutting boards for the counter."

I laid out the equipment on a lab table. Rick started the drill, and I escaped to the kitchen where I pulled out the mixer to make a batch of chocolate chip oatmeal cookies. It was my version of dueling power tools. If deliciousness determined the winner, victory would be mine, I thought while creaming the eggs, brown sugar, and butter. After I finished the dough and slid it into the refrigerator to cool, I did laundry and cleaned my apartment. Around noon, I was fixing sandwiches and quartering oranges when Rick came into the kitchen.

"Your timing is impeccable." I pointed to the cupboard where my dishes and glasses lived. "Wash your hands and set the table."

He ambled to the sink. "Are you always this bossy?"

"Pretty much."

During lunch I asked how much remained to be done.

"Not much. We need to install the equipment and switch out the regular lightbulb for the red one. If all goes well, you'll be developing film by evening."

Soon we were stringing clothesline near the darkroom ceiling and mixing water and chemicals in gallon jugs. I labeled the jugs while Rick looked for the red lightbulb.

"Where will I find it?" he asked.

"In a little box on the top shelf of the closet."

He returned with the bulb, screwed it into the socket, and flipped the switch. Nothing. He blew out a long breath. "I think it's broken. Did you buy any extras?"

"That one was the last they had. Now what do we do?"

"I'll call the hardware store in Tipperary in the morning. If they don't have any, maybe Oscar Rumble can pick up a couple in Bowman and bring them to square dance class Tuesday."

"That's another two and a half days from now. Can't you drive to Bowman tomorrow?"

"Nope. I've got meetings all day." I opened my mouth to speak. He kept going. "And no, I can't ask someone else to get them for me. Around here folks think there's only two uses for those bulbs. A red-light district or a darkroom. I don't want either of those rumors floating around. Do you?"

"No."

"Well then, let's arrange the darkroom and lab the way you want them and call it good enough for now."

A couple hours later, cork boards and shelving lined the walls. The shelves held the equipment, books, and supplies Rick and I had purchased. Long tables sat beneath the shelves. My microscope occupied a place of honor in the center of the biggest table.

I surveyed the room and hugged myself. "It's an honest-to-goodness forensic lab!"

"The finest to be found west of the Little Missouri River."

"And the only one."

"Killjoy."

I looked at my watch. "It won't be dark enough for you to leave for an hour or more. Want to watch television?"

While he flipped between the two channels looking for something worth our while, I made popcorn and washed apples. He found an old black-and-white B movie. We were soon absorbed in a flick that was heavy on Amazon dangers and light on plot.

Rick turned off the TV after the bad guys landed in a South American prison. "At least our investigation doesn't involve tarantulas, quicksand, and piranhas."

"That's the advantage of twenty-below weather." I pulled back the living room curtain and peered out the window. "It's dark enough for you to sneak out undetected."

"Are you trying to get rid of me?"

Um, yes.

Saying that to Rick's face would sound ungrateful. I was truly grateful for his help this weekend, but I wasn't sure how to explain what I'd learned about myself this weekend. I liked living on my own, and I needed alone time to recharge for Monday morning. So I said something lame instead.

"More like sending you home to bed early so you have time to call Oscar Rumble before your meetings tomorrow. Do you really think he can get us a red lightbulb?"

"I have no doubt." Rick opened the door and left without elaborating.

Oscar must have a darkroom, I thought, as I picked up *Whose Body?* by Dorothy Sayers. The book had been a Christmas present from my sister, and I'd been waiting for a chance to dip into it. I sat on the couch, spread the granny afghan over my legs, and opened to the first page. Two sentences in, the phone rang.

Chapter 11

I snapped the book shut, threw it on the couch, and worried on my way to the phone. Had someone seen Rick leave? Had someone noticed we both skipped church? Was Dad in the hospital?

Bringing the receiver to my ear felt like slow motion. "Hello?"

"Hi, Jane, it's Mom."

Oh my gosh. Either Dad was sick, or Betty and Velma had told Mom about Rocko.

I braced myself for what came next.

"Do you know, your dad and I settled down with popcorn to watch the news and 'Harold,' I said, 'I forgot to ask Jane how her first square dance lesson went.' And do you know what he said?"

I relaxed. She didn't know about Rocko. "What?"

"He said, 'Hang the news, Doris, and give her a call.' So that's what I did. You'll need to talk really loud. I'm holding the phone so we can both hear."

I started by describing Oscar Rumble and then

explained how he taught us to circle right and left, alle-mande in both directions, and do-si-do.

Mom interrupted me. "I learned those steps in physical education class at college. Only the professor referred to them as 'square games.' "

"Why on earth did he do that?"

"The prof was a she. And the college was affiliated with a church denomination that didn't allow dancing."

"But they did allow games?"

"Card games, no. Board games, yes."

"Because board games are generally square also?"

Mom giggled. "It doesn't make much sense does it?"

"Dad, did you learn square games in phys ed too?"

"Negative." He slurred the word slightly. "Football players didn't have to take phys ed."

Mom interrupted. "That's enough about our lives in the dark ages. We want to hear about you. Are any other single people taking lessons?"

Aha! She had jumped on Dad's suggestion that they call so she could get a list of Tipperary County's eligi-ble—or perhaps most desperate—men. That was more good news, confirmation of Betty's reluctance to tell Mom about Rocko's death and further assurance that my parents hadn't yet heard about it. It was no big deal for Dad. He would encourage me to look into Rocko's death just as he'd done when Edgar Running Horse had died after Thanksgiving. As for Mom, the longer she remained blissfully ignorant about Rocko, the better.

"A few." I waited to see how long her patience would last. It was a short wait.

"Good grief, Jane! We deserve to know their names as payment for forking out half the lesson fee."

That brought me up short. My parents had shelled out money they didn't have in order to present me to Little Missouri's high society. They would be eating hamburgers instead of steak every Sunday dinner for a month to make up the difference. Their routine when they got home after church had been the same for as long as I could remember.

Mom, all five feet one and a half inches of her, lifted all five feet eleven of Dad from the car and swiveled him into his wheelchair. Then she wheeled him into the kitchen as he recounted the conversations he'd had in the Fellowship Hall after church. Still talking, he parked himself at the kitchen table, licking his lips as he antici-pated his favorite meal of the week.

When he stopped to draw a breath, Mom asked the same question she asked every week. "How do you want your steak, Harold?"

"Black on the outside, bloody on the inside, and still kicking."

Mom laughed. "Jeanette! Jane! Jeff! You kids get in here and help get dinner on the table."

We hurried into the kitchen. Mom didn't take kindly to dawdlers. Jeanette went to the basement to fetch a bucket of ice cream and a quart of the home-canned green beans we'd put up the summer before. She then chopped bacon into small bits and fried it in a saucepan before adding both the meat and grease to the green beans. I spread garlic butter on slices of French bread and put them in the oven to toast. Jeff squirted lighter fluid on the charcoal piled in the Weber grill.

Mom supervised from the patio door. The grill had

*been a gift from Dad the previous Christmas, and it was
her pride and joy.*

*"Go easy on the lighter fluid, Jeff," she scolded. "It's
expensive."*

*Once the coals were lit, she cut the apple pie Jeanette
had made into pieces. I set the table. Less than an hour
after church had ended, we sat down to Sunday dinner.*

*Dad said grace and then watched Mom cut his
T-bone into bite-sized pieces. With his fork, he stabbed a
piece of steak and put it in his mouth. He closed his eyes
and chewed, his expression rapturous. Mom smiled at
him, delighted by his joy.*

My parents had sacrificed weeks of their joy on the
altar of my social life. Teasing Mom now felt tawdry.
Unappreciative. They deserved an almost full report.

"Rique DuPeuss was there."

"That state trapper who lives in his camper and
offered you his homemade dewormer?"

"One and the same."

Dad hooted with laughter.

Mom did not. "Whatever square he ends up in, you
hustle to a different one."

"That's my plan."

"Who else was there? Anyone I've met?"

"Rick Sternquist."

"The sheriff? He's the last person you should be
dancing with. You are done with criminal justice, Jane
Newell. Don't let him do-si-do you into one of his investigations without a second thought."

That ship had already sailed, but this was not the best
time to encourage Mom to wave bon voyage. Instead, I

did my best to divert Mom's attention from the gang-
plank to the train station. "Dick Phillips was there, too."

"Oooo! Is he as nice as Betty says?"

How to put the man who'd been the worst date of my
life in a positive light? Hmm.

"He's so shy it's hard to tell."

"Shy? How?"

"He blushes more than he talks."

"There's nothing wrong with being fair-skinned. Be
nice to him. Are there any others?"

Other than Rocko? No. "That's the lot of them."

"Well then, you just show that Dick Phillips your
best side. You can be very witty and charming when you
want to be."

My mother had no way of knowing that the world
did not contain enough charm and wit to penetrate the
rock that was Dick Phillips. Since my primary goal was
to keep her fixated on my social life and oblivious to
my partnership with the sheriff, I agreed to amp up the
charm and humor.

"Thank you, Jane. You're a good daughter. And I
wouldn't mention this except that your father and I have
called you twice this weekend, so it's your turn to phone
next Saturday so it goes on your bill. Fair is fair."

Obviously, I'd inherited my charm and wit from
Dad's side of the family.

"Bye, Mom. Bye, Dad."

"Bye, Janie-Jo," Dad slurred.

"Good-bye, Jane." Mom hung up.

I returned to the couch and to Lord Peter Wimsey,
the protagonist of *Whose Body?* The more I read, the
more his considerable wit and charm grew on me. I real-

ized that even if Lord Peter added his abundant supply to my meager one, and even if we threw the whole lot at Dick Phillips, the man responsible for the worst date of my life would remain silent and immovable.

Still, I would honor my promise to beam my wit and charm in Dick Phillip's direction. When Rocko's death hit the Sioux City news channels, and it would, I'd need every bit of skill gained while practicing those attributes on the impervious Dick Phillips to calm Mom down. She would resist my efforts, but with Dad's help, we would do it.

Knowing that the worst date of my entire life might have a good purpose shone like a tiny pinprick of light against the darkness of Rocko's death and gave me hope. Lord knows I needed it.

CHAPTER 12

Beau Kelly lined up first when he heard the school bell on Monday morning. He led his classmates indoors, removed his ski mask, and sniffed. "Do I smell cookies?"

Tiege unwound his muffler. "I smell them too. Sugar cookies."

Elva inhaled. "With almond extract."

There was no pulling the wool over the eyes of this pack of hound dogs when it came to sniffing out baked goods. I hadn't planned to debut them until later this week, but I saw the value in using what was right under their noses to divert their parents' attention from what Rick and I were up to.

"Shhh!" I held a finger to my lips. "I don't want your parents to know that we're using cookies for an assignment later this week. They might not believe it."

That unleashed a cascade of questions.

"What day?"

"What subject?"

"All the grades or just one?"

"How many do we get to eat?"

I refused to answer. Their excitement ran high all morning. By lunch time I questioned my decision to let the cat out of the cookie jar. Then again, my students would tell everyone they saw after school that Miss Newell had spent her weekend baking. The town would soon be buzzing about how that new teacher from Iowa used cookies to teach school rather than speculating about why she and the sheriff weren't at church on Sunday. I was good with that.

Though the outdoor thermometer refused to go higher than fifteen below zero, Liv phoned to say she was taking the kids outside after lunch. "They gotta blow the stink off."

The minute the last kid waddled onto the playground, I dashed to the phone and asked Betty to connect me to Mrs. Dremstein at her office in Tipperary. "Tell her it's an urgent matter."

Betty responded with glee. "Should I caww the ambu-wance or a parent once you're connected?"

"Not that urgent. But it is confidential, so please hang up once Mrs. Dremstein is on the line."

"Hmph."

The principal answered on the first ring. "Mrs. Drem-stein. How can I help you?"

"This is Jane Newell in Little Missouri. I'm wondering if you'll be in your office after school?"

"I will. Why?"

"There's something I need to discuss with you in per-son. As long as the weather holds, I'll be there between four thirty and five."

"I'll be waiting for you." She paused. "At the risk of sounding like your mother—"

Was she part of Mom's spy ring too?

"—would you call before you leave? I don't like leaving anything to chance in this cold."

Not a spy. Just sensible.

"I'd be happy to. See you after school." I set the receiver in the cradle and lifted it to ring Betty a second time.

"Hewwo," she snapped.

"Would you connect me to Lacey Jo at her beauty shop?"

"Hmph."

"You can stay on the line this time."

"I'ww put you through immediatewy."

Lacey Jo's phone rang twice before she answered with a voice that exuded competence and friendliness. "Dyed and Gone to Heaven Beauty Salon. How can I help you?"

"Hi Lacey Jo. Is there any chance you have an opening around four thirty or five this afternoon?"

"Let me check my book." Short pause and the sound of pages turning. "Yes, I can squeeze you in between a perm and a color around five. What's the name?"

"Jane Newell."

Long silence.

Had she forgotten who I was? "The teacher. From Little Missouri."

Longer silence. Awkward too.

"On second thought, working you in isn't fair to the gals who already have appointments."

"Okay. Do you have anything after school next week?"

"I'll check." One second pause. No pages turning. "Nope. They're all spoken for."

"What about next Saturday?"

This time she didn't pretend to consult her appointment calendar. "Nope. Good-bye."

She slammed down the phone down so hard I winced.

Betty cleared her throat. "How'd you wand up on her bad side?"

I tucked a strand of hair behind my ear. It refused to stay put. "I wish I knew. I really need a haircut."

"How come you don't caww Winter Skye's mom?"

"She's a hairstylist?"

"Uh-huh. She'ww get you right in."

The recess bell rang. "Gotta go, Betty. The kids are coming. Thanks for the tip." I hung up and went to collect my students.

Liv hollered from the landing outside her classroom, "It's too cold to go outside again today. Let's do afternoon recess indoors."

The icy air was already making the skin on my cheeks prickle. I gave her a thumb's up. Thanks to the cold and the sunshine, the children came in rosy-cheeked, runny-nosed, and stink-free. Removing and hanging up their winter gear took them twice as long as getting ready to go outside. These kids knew how to use winter to their advantage. Thankfully, the fresh air, exercise, and cold had taken the edge off the morning's cookie mania. They were soon applying themselves to their assignments. I took advantage of the calm to correct papers and review the kindergarten lessons for the next day.

A few minutes before afternoon recess, I took out the easy jigsaw puzzles—all of them featuring horses of one variety or another—that I'd found at thrift stores during

Christmas break in Iowa. I set the puzzles on drafting boards, also thrift store finds. When recess started, the puzzles captured the kids' attention as intended. Once I showed them how to put the puzzles together on the drafting boards, I snuck into my apartment and called Galva Swensen.

"Galva, this is Jane Newell. Betty said to call you about a haircut."

"She said you might be calling. Come out right after school tomorrow if you want."

"You have time before square dance lessons?"

"Sure do."

"Can I bring your girls with me and save you a run into town?"

"It's a deal. See you when you get here."

I returned to the classroom where the children were quietly talking and fitting pieces into place. "You have a few more minutes of recess left."

The room resounded with groans, protests, and the occasional wail.

"Just five more minutes? Please?"

"This one's about done."

"Don't make us take them apart!"

"You won't have to take them apart. At the end of recess, you'll leave your puzzle on its board and slide it next to the wall. The next time it's too cold to go outside for recess, you can pull them out and finish."

Now cheers, hoots, and an occasional whistle filled the room.

The afternoon calm continued until the end of the day. Not one vestige of the morning's cookie craze reared its much-needed head. Well, I knew how to fix that.

"Remember," I sang as the children spread out in a long line, claiming floor space in the entryway and the classroom to wiggle into their winter garb, "not to say anything about cookies once school is out."

"But my mom's name is Cookie!" Tiege sprang up, his left foot protruding from one leg of his snow pants while his right foot aimed for the other. "I gotta tell her stuff." His right foot clipped the empty pant leg, and he toppled against Beau. Beau's arms windmilled before he tumbled into Elva. From there, the children went down like dominoes. The floor was littered with them.

I tickled their funny bones with an enthusiastic "That's the way the cookie crumbles!" as they picked themselves up, zipped their coats, and waddled for the door.

"Get it?" Renny's voice rose above the shouts of children climbing snow drifts as they crossed the playground. "Miss Newell made a joke. 'That's the way the cookie crumbles.' I'm telling it to my parents soon as I get home."

I hummed my favorite spy show theme song—*Dun dun dundun, Dun dun dundun, Dun dun dundun*—while I watched the children disperse, shouting at the top of their lungs about Miss Newell and the cookie assignment—*DA DA!*

Mission accomplished.

CHAPTER 13

Once the playground was empty, I rang Betty and asked her to place a call.

"Tipperary Schools. How can I help you?" the secretary asked.

"Would you tell Mrs. Dremstein that Jane Newell is about to take off for Tipperary?"

"Will do." She popped her gum. "Do you have an emergency kit in your car?"

I ticked off the items stored in my back seat. "Two blankets, candles and a tin can to set them in, matches, and chocolate bars. And I've got a jug of water ready to bring with me."

"Gas tank full?"

"Yes."

"Well, haven't you learned a thing or two since you and that silly little car of yours were stuck in a snowbank a few months back?"

I closed my eyes and prayed for something more compelling than the perils of city slicker Jane Newell and her trusty red Beetle to capture the interest of Tipperary County's citizens. A burst of gum-snapping roused me. My eyes flew open. It was time to be on my way. "See you soon."

"Drive carefully." Snap.

She waved me into the principal's office a half hour later. "She said to send you on in." Snap and pop.

"It's good to see you, Jane." Mrs. Dremstein came around and sat in one of the two chairs in front of her desk and gestured for me to take the other. She folded her hands in her lap. "Now, what brings you here today?"

I told her about the part-time position Rick had created, my true role in the investigation of Rocko's death, and the ruse we were using as cover. She had a few questions, which I answered, providing enough details to satisfy her curiosity without compromising confidentiality.

She leaned back in her chair, pursed her lips, and stared at me for an eternity. Or at least ten seconds. "First of all, thank you for inviting me into your confidence. I'll be able to control the damage more effectively now. We both know it will snowball the longer the investigation drags on. Can you venture a guess as to how long it might take?"

I shook my head. "We won't know if there are any leads to follow until the negatives are developed and the pictures I took are printed."

"And who's doing that?"

"Um, me."

She smiled. "That's something I've always wanted to learn. Where is the darkroom?"

Say it, Jane. What do you have to lose?

My job for one thing.

I resisted the urge to squirm and looked Mrs. Dremstein square in the eye. "In the guest bedroom of my apartment."

A muscle twitched on the right side of her mouth. Whether from amusement or anger, I couldn't tell. The next ten seconds spanned an eternity far greater than the previous one. That might be a mathematical impossibility, but with my job on the line, it was more than possible. Trust me. I know what I'm talking about.

The muscle in Mrs. Dremstein's cheek twitched again. "I take it you subscribe to the it's-better-to-ask-for-forgiveness-than-permission adage?"

"Not completely. Otherwise I wouldn't have driven twenty-five miles in this kind of cold to let you know what's going on." I felt a muscle in my cheek twitch.

"There is that." It was her turn to twitch. "And the sheriff's department is contracting with you to fulfill a service of benefit to our county. The school board will be in favor of that. They'll be far more likely to approve of your, ahem, enthusiasm and initiative if there's some way to use the darkroom to enhance student learning. Is there a way you can do so?"

Now my cheek did the twitching. "What if I photograph my students and print pictures the second and third graders can use when they write a history of the school year? I could also print photographs of kindergarten and first graders to make calendars they can give their moms on Mother's Day."

With that, our twitches leaped onto our lips, and we both smiled.

***

All systems were now go for my fake romance with Rick to go public. I initiated the operation by asking the secretary for the phone book.

"I haven't memorized Rick's work phone number. Not yet anyway." I dialed and waited until the sheriff's secretary picked up. "Is Rick back from his meetings?"

"He just got here. Can I ask who's calling?"

"Tell him that Jane Newell is stopping by in a few minutes." I hung up and primped in front of the small mirror in the secretary's office. I smoothed my hair, adjusted my barrette, and touched up my lipstick. Then I turned to the secretary, whose gum was popping like machine gun fire, and thanked her for the use of her phone.

When I arrived at Rick's office, I shut the door, took a seat in the chair across from the desk where he sat, and told him what I'd done.

"You sure don't let any grass grow under your feet, Jane."

"When there's a foot of snow on the ground, it's pretty easy. Did you make any progress today?"

"On a couple fronts, yes. Oscar Rumble will bring more lightbulbs tomorrow."

"Good. What else?"

"I interviewed Dan Barkley and Scott Gibson about Rocko's position at the Forest Service. They said he'd been an intern a couple years ago when he was still in college. He got a job at the fish hatchery in Spearfish after he graduated last summer. Dan ran into him there in September. Rocko said the job wasn't what he'd

expected and asked Dan to keep him in mind if anything opened up in Little Missouri. A month or so later,
several dead cattle were found on government land that
ranchers rent from the Forest Service. The animals had
been brutally killed. Dan and Scott looked into it but got
nowhere. The ranchers thought they were stalling, and
tempers started running hot. Dan appropriated funds so
they could hire someone to look into it. It was just a temporary position, but when Dan offered the job to Rocko,
he jumped at it."

I waited for him to go on. He didn't, so I asked, "Did
he find anything?"

"When I asked that question, they got mighty tight
lipped."

"Did you press them on it?"

"I did, and they agreed to fill me in. On one condi-
tion."

"Which was?"

"That I keep what Rocko had discovered to myself
until—and if—his death is ruled to be murder."

"But I'm your partner. You said you wouldn't hold
anything back."

"You're right." He leaned forward. "I don't want to
keep this from you, but it was my only chance to inch
the investigation forward."

I wanted to pound on his desk and yell, "You good-
for-nothing jerk! How am I supposed to trust a guy who
pulls something like this?"

Then again, if I did that, the secretary on the other
side of the door would hear my outburst, and the rumors
about the sheriff and the Little Missouri teacher having a
thing for each other would die a swift death. I swallowed

my hissy fit and pretended to be a grown-up. "Did what Dan and Scott told you provide any insight into our investigation?"

"Not yet. For now, the crime scene photos are our best bet."

"Well, then." I rose, threw open the door, and turned my voice sweet and silky. "You want to stop by my apartment after tomorrow's square dance lesson? We can continue this conversation then."

Rick stood, put his palms on his desk, and leaned forward with a wink. "It's a date."

His secretary caught herself a split second before she fell out of her chair.

I shed the sweet and the silk on the short walk to my car. Rick had talked a good game over the weekend before push came to shove. But when the push came, he shoved me aside quicker than snot running down a kindergartener's nose. I refused to wait for whatever scraps he chose to throw my way like I'd done in the past. I climbed in my car and smacked the steering wheel with a palm. Pain shot up my arm. My funny bone howled. I grabbed my elbow and came back to my senses.

This investigation is different, Jane. Rick needs your forensic skills. Do you really believe he'd hold anything back unless it was the only way to make progress?

I wiggled my fingers and flexed my elbow until my arm felt normal. Then I went to the grocery store for a few things and used their phone to let Betty know I would be home in a half hour.

"If I don't hear from you in forty-five minutes, I'ww send a search party. By the way," she threw in as if on a whim, "a wittwe whiwe ago, the secretary at the schoow in Tipperary had me connect her to the Sternquists. I overheard her ask Cookie if you and Rick is dating."

"And?"

"I disconnected immediatewy because it was none of my business."

"I appreciate your professionalism, Betty. Bye."

I loaded my groceries and drove west toward Little Missouri. Right about now, I was certain Betty was letting her prime operatives know that the sheriff and the schoolteacher were an item. Our sham romance would be the talk of the town with lightning speed. That part of our plan was a complete success. Its continued success depended on the sheriff honoring his pledge to hold nothing back unless doing so was his only option and on Oscar Rumble's red lightbulb delivery tomorrow night.

It was a twenty-four-hour eternity I didn't think I could endure. Then again, what choice did I have?

CHAPTER 14

The next morning, when less than twelve hours of eternity remained, my students whooshed through the door on a gust of teeth-chattering wind. The older children greeted the kindergarteners as though they had been apart for four weeks rather than four days. The second and third grade helpers once again swooped upon their kindergarten charges.

Tiege yanked at Jeremy's boot with unbridled zeal. "Hold onto your boot loops while I pull." Jeremy's left foot was soon bare of boot and sock. Panic gleamed in his eye.

When Tiege reached for Jeremy's other foot, I stepped between them. "Do you take off your own boots at home, Jeremy?"

"Uh-huh."

"Okay. You take this one off by yourself. Tiege, you make sure he sets them on the newspaper once he's done."

A series of similar fires waxed and waned throughout

the day. Cora wrote Winter Skye's name on the majority of the younger girl's seatwork. Elva started to unbraid and re-braid Keeva's mussed up hair after lunch recess. Renny cut out the shapes for Grace on her fine-motor-skills assessment. I wrote a memo to talk to the older children tomorrow about where their jobs ended and the responsibility of the kindergarteners began.

Fire management demanded my full attention and whittled down the remaining eternity to a doable three hours. Before long, my students were on their way home, and I was untangling the Beetle's seatbelts so Summer Rose, Spring Day, Autumn Breeze, and Winter Skye Swensen could buckle up for the drive. With four girls and three belts among them, the two youngest had to share one. The two oldest assured me this was standard practice in their family.

Summer Rose, the oldest of the four, sat in the front and directed me to their family's ranch west of town about two miles across the border into Montana. Their double-wide mobile home and a large pole building, easily four times the square footage of their house, clung to the south face of a rise toward the Long Pines.

"Mom said to park over here." Summer Rose pointed to the pole building. "She should be waiting for you in her shop."

I pulled in next to a metal pole with two small signs bolted to it. The top one said Swensen's Style Shop with an arrow pointing toward a standard-sized door to the left. The bottom one read Swensen's Taxidermy and had an arrow pointing toward another standard door and the oversized garage door next to it.

The girls tumbled out of the car almost before I was

parked. "Thanks for the ride," they chorused over their shoulders as they ran toward the house.

Despite the signs, I opened the left door with a great degree of trepidation. A week ago, I'd stumbled over a dead human and had no desire to stumble into a menagerie of dead animals, stuffed or otherwise. The aroma of permanent-wave solution and peroxide entered my nostrils. That, and the lack of taxidermy decor above the shampoo station, hair dryers, and laundry area, calmed my nerves. I was in the right place.

"Hi, Miss Newell!"

I heard Galva but couldn't see her.

"Hang up your coat on the rack and take a seat at the shampoo sink." She straightened, pulled a load of towels from the dryer, and set them on a folding table. "I'll clean out the lint filter and be right with you."

I took care of my coat and sat down. She swiveled the chair until I faced the mirror and finger combed my hair. "How long's it been since your last cut?" she asked.

"Early November, I guess. Long enough for it to turn into this mop." I pushed my bangs out of my eyes. They pushed back. "Can you make it behave?"

"Sure can." She whipped a cape around me and fastened the collar. She tipped the back of my head into the wash sink, adjusted the water temperature, and thoroughly baptized my disobedient hair. "Is Winter Skye behaving herself at school?"

"She is, and the other kindergarteners, too. That could change when the honeymoon's over, but I doubt it. They're good kids. Eager to learn."

"Whatever you're doing, she likes it. She talks my ear off all the way home. It's 'Miss Newell' this and 'my

friend Cora' that. The first day she was so tired, she
fell asleep eating supper." She squirted shampoo in her
hands and worked it into my hair.

"All-day school is a long haul for five-year-olds.
They're determined to keep up with the older kids, but it
has to wear them out."

"She's getting used to it. Last Thursday she had spunk
enough to help her daddy with the deer head he's doing
for Scott Gibson."

Warm water gushed over my scalp. I waited to
respond until after Galva rinsed away the soap bubbles.
"Winter Skye does taxidermy?"

"Oh yeah." Galva slathered conditioner on my hair.
"When she was little and I was busy cutting hair, Garth
took her to his shop and watched her. She paid attention to everything he did. Soon as she could walk, she
was handing him tools. Me and Garth don't spread it
around, but she's got a knack for it. Last fall, she bad-
gered her daddy until he showed her how to mount the
six-foot rattler he killed behind the house. You oughta
see it."

I oughta not.

"With square dance lessons tonight, there's just not
time."

She rinsed my hair again, wound a towel around my
head, and eased me upright. She untangled my mane
with a pink hair pick. I considered the state of childhood in Tipperary County. A seven-year-old drove a
pickup truck and welded windmills. An eight-year-old
baked apple pies. All manner of children rode horses
twice their heights. And a five-year-old did taxidermy.
What would be next? A nine-year-old pulling calves?

A six-year-old shearing sheep? A ten-year-old driving a snowplow? Better them than me.

Galva picked up her scissors and began snipping away. "That business with Rocko was terrible, wasn't it? Me and Garth woulda gone to the funeral if it was gonna be here. But it's back in Iowa where his family's from. That's a long drive."

"Don't I know it?"

She laughed. "I guess you do." Her smile faded and regret remained. "Rocko was the nicest guy. Everybody liked him. Well, most everybody did."

Interesting. "I only met him once, but I can't fathom anyone not liking him."

"He was real popular when he was an intern a few years ago and when he first came back a few months ago." She bit her lip and concentrated on trimming my bangs before continuing. "Then I heard that he doesn't get along with Scott Gibson. Scott is about as close-mouthed a piece of milquetoast as they come. His wife Linda, now she's not happy about living in Little Mis-souri. Used to mention it every time I did her hair. Her last appointment she went on and on about her new job at the newspaper. Then she moved on to how Rocko and Scott were at odds. She said they can't stand to be in the same room together. I figured she was exaggerating. She's real good at that. Then when me and Garth were at The Bend, Trudy said she heard the same thing at the Methodist church. I didn't know they went to church."

"The Gibsons?"

"Oh for heaven's sake, no! Everyone knows they're Catholic. I mean the Bertholds. Can you see them sitting in a church pew?"

Never had. Didn't think I ever would. I raised an eyebrow.

"Fishy, right?" She reached for the blow dryer. "I brushed it off until Iva said something at the grocery store."

She turned on the dryer, pointed it at my head, and turned it on. Had Rick heard this rumor already? I would ask him after tonight's dance lesson.

Galva worked my hair over with a brush and the blow dryer for several minutes. Then she turned it off and twirled my chair until I faced the mirror. "Your hair looks a little better than it did last week."

My eyes widened. She'd persuaded my flyaway curls to relax into soft waves. "It looks great."

She whipped off the cape and pointed at my blue wool sweater and trousers. "Will you do something for me? Wear what you've got on now to the dance hall tonight. Or if you got to change out of school clothes, at least don't wear that god-awful sweatshirt you showed up in last time."

It was an easy promise to make. Tonight, I didn't want to look like something even the cat wasn't willing to drag in. I wanted to look like a woman transformed by her new relationship with a great guy. Rather sickly sweet and clingy for my taste, but it was for a good cause.

I grinned at my reflection. "Can I get on your regular schedule?"

Galva grinned too. "You've got the kind of hair that needs to be shaped every four weeks. Does Wednesday after school work for you at least until dance lessons are over?"

"Wednesdays are good."

She wrote it in her appointment book and on a card she handed to me. "Maybe you can stay for coffee next time?"

I signed my name on the check and handed it to her. "I'd love to."

"And Winter Skye will give you a tour of the taxidermy shop. She knows as much about it as her dad."

"She's a marvel." I said a quick farewell and ran to my car before Galva tacked something else onto the end of my next appointment. I would enjoy sipping coffee in a cozy kitchen. The same could not be said for the taxidermy tour. Still, I would ooh and ahh about every hide, hoof, and whisker in the building because Winter Skye was my student, and I would do anything for her. Make that almost anything. I drew the line at touching, petting, or cuddling the disgusting, hairy things she and her dad created. That was never going to happen. Not ever.

Chapter 15

Two hours later, I stood in my entryway waiting for Rick and squinting at my reflection in the window. Had I gone over the top by adding lipstick to my new hairstyle and the honest-to-goodness grown-up clothes I'd promised to wear tonight? I pursed my lips and turned my head in one direction and then the other. No, it was not too much. Rick and I wanted to make a big splash when we walked into the dance hall together, and this look would do it.

A pair of headlights came from the north along Main Street and turned onto the street south of the school. It had to be Rick. As I picked up my plate of cookies, locked the door, and headed down the sidewalk to where he was parked, my heartbeat sped up—from excitement rather than nervousness. Our charade was about to divert people's attention so we could start investigating in earnest.

Rick reached across the cab and pushed the door open. "Climb on in."

"You're going to have to do better than this at the dance hall." I buckled my seatbelt as he backed onto the street.

"As in—"

"As in, you park near a streetlight so you're seen when you come around and open the door for me. That'll get a few tongues wagging."

"Aye aye, Captain." He gave a mock salute and drove to the hall. He pulled into a well-lit parking spot and helped me out like a true Cowboy Charming. I glanced over my shoulder and saw a curtain twitch in Velma's trailer across the street. I slipped my hand into Rick's and gazed adoringly at his face. Let the tongue wagging commence!

When we reached the entrance, Rick opened that door for me too. We stood awash in a pool of light, and his eyes widened. "You look like a million bucks!"

"Anything for the investigation, right?" I waved the compliment away and set the cookies on the snack table. When Dick Phillips and Rique DuPeuss came out of their man den in the corner, they looked as stunned as Rick. Darn. The lipstick *was* too much.

Rick came over and helped me out of my coat. Oscar Rumble slinked over and stood far too close to me as he held out a wrinkled paper sack to Rick. "The lightbulbs you wanted."

Rick handed over a five-dollar bill and took the bag. While he took our coats to the row of theater chairs lining the wall, Oscar snaked an arm around my waist and held tight. Only after Rick laid down the coats and turned around did Oscar loosen his grip, though not before his hand traveled south and pinched my tush.

That settled it. No more lipstick!

Rick hadn't seen a thing, not even Oscar's leer as he smoothed his pompadour. At that moment, the door flew open. Tiege Sternquist barreled into the room, followed by his parents, the Swensens, and their four girls, as well as the Gibsons and Jeremy.

"Miss Newell!" Tiege hurled himself across the dance floor with Winter Skye and Jeremy close behind. Oscar slithered silently away.

Tiege skidded to a stop in front of me. "What happened to your hair? It looks weird!"

"Kapow!" Jeremy added.

A disgusted Winter Skye put her hands on her hips. "Stop being mean to my mom. She cut Miss Newell's hair and made it all pretty."

The three children wandered off bickering. I scanned the hall for Oscar. He was on the stage fiddling with the dials on the record player and amp. He and his scaly arms could stay there all night as far as I was concerned.

Rick approached, guiding Gus Yarborough and a short, slightly built woman through the crowd toward me. "According to Betty," Rick said when they arrived, "this is the first time you two have met in person."

She extended a hand, and I did my best not to stare at the scar on her face. It ran from below her left nostril to her lip. The skin around the scar was stretched tight. When she smiled, a mass of crooked, unevenly spaced teeth peeked out. Her gray hair appeared to have been cut with fingernail scissors and curled in a style decades out of date. She wore a faded flannel shirt, high-water blue jeans, and tennis shoes. Her clothes looked like cast-offs from the 1950s television show *Leave It to Beaver*, but

I warmed to her. We were the only adults in the room sans cowboy boots.

I clasped her outstretched hand in both of mine. "What a treat to meet you face-to-face, Be—"

"Now that you've met her, do you agree with me?" Gus interrupted.

My forehead wrinkled. "Agree with you about what, Gus?"

"What I told you about my Betty when I come to your house in August to hook up your phone." He put an arm around her shoulder and beamed with pride as his face bent toward hers. "She is the most beautiful woman in Little Missouri."

Betty met her husband's unseeing eyes, her smile as lovely and devoted as my father's whenever Mom walked in the room. My heart swelled and my eyes grew moist.

"I agree with you and then some," I quavered, fighting to keep tears and snot at bay.

Rick shifted the conversation. "Who's running the switchboard tonight?"

"Scott and Winda Gibson vowunteered their girws. I trained them aww day Saturday. Stacy, she's a senior, caught on reaw quick. She's in charge tonight and the younger girw—now what's her name?"

"Tisha," said Pam Barkley who had wandered over.

"Tisha"—Betty didn't miss a beat—"is watching and wearning."

"They are nice girls," Pam confirmed. "Competent, too. Did you hear that their mom Linda got a job at the Tipperary Times?"

I remembered what Galva had mentioned earlier "Is that the name of the newspaper?"

Pam took me by one arm and Betty by the other and walked us away from the men. "Do you mean to say you don't subscribe to the paper? It's the best place to find out what's going on in Little Missouri and everywhere else in the county. Outside of our switchboard operator, that is." She winked at Betty.

Betty winked back. "They awways pubwish a few things I haven't got wind of yet."

The paper sounded like an investment worth making. "How do I subscribe?"

"Just talk to Linda," Pam said. "She goes to Tipperary after she drops off Jeremy at school. She can take your check to the newspaper office and save you a stamp."

Betty lowered her voice. "I been wondering if Winda's job is hard on Scott."

My investigation antenna quivered. "What do you mean?"

"He used to be very powite on the phone, but anymore he about bites my head off."

"You know," Pam looked thoughtful, "Dan's mentioned the same thing more than once lately. He thinks it's because Scott was turned down for a transfer. That was over a year ago, but Dan says Scott was easygoing until Rocko came. Now that he's dead—"

"Ladies and gents, it's time to circle round!" Oscar's voice came over the loudspeaker.

I cursed his timing under my breath. What had Pam been about to say? I reluctantly shifted my attention to Gus and Betty. She guided him to the circle and held his right hand. Cookie Sternquist came over and took his left one. As Oscar reviewed last week's steps, Gus listened intently. When we began moving through them,

I noticed how Betty and Cookie applied subtle pressure to Gus's hands. He executed each command with confidence and precision. His flawless performance continued as Oscar explained one by one how to execute the night's new steps—right and left grand, promenade, and swing. Still in the circle, Oscar took us through the steps several more times.

We were flushed and laughing when he declared, "You're doing just dandy. Let's take a break."

"Want to get something to eat?" Rick asked.

What I wanted was to get far, far away from Mr. Rumble. "No, but I could use something to drink." I stuck close to him while he grabbed several chocolate chip oatmeal cookies.

He held one out to me. "You could sell these, you know."

"Thanks." Oscar approached. I moved so Rick created a barrier between Oscar and me. I stayed there until he went to the stage and announced that the break was over.

"Now, ladies and gents, find three other couples and make a square."

I grabbed Rick's hand and dragged him toward the square his parents, the Gibsons, and the Yarboroughs were forming. I clipped Dick Phillips' shoulder as we ran roughshod through the square where the Barkleys and Gibsons were pairing him and Rique DuPeuss with Spring Day and Summer Rose. Dick blushed.

I blew past him, intent upon claiming the fourth spot in the Yarborough's square. We arrived and slid into place, crowding out Axel and Liv McDonald who'd been aiming for the same position.

Rick acted like a tornado had blown him from Kansas to Oz. I pulled his head close to mine with what I hoped was a smitten expression. He didn't look so much smitten as stunned. Oh, well.

"Keep an eye on Scott," I hissed. "I'll explain later."

With Rick thus dispatched, I turned my attention to Oscar and our square. Oscar explained that the couple facing the caller and the couple with their backs to him were the heads. The other two couples were the sides.

"Heads, raise your hands."

The Sternquists and the Yarboroughs did so.

"Now the sides."

The Gibsons raised their hands in unison with Rick and me.

Then Oscar started the music, using the same song as the week before. As he mixed new calls in with the old ones, the members of our square became Gus's eyes with a mere touch on his elbow, a gentle hand on his shoulder, and a soft whisper in his ear. Eventually, I entered into their delicate dance. When the final chorus neared, Oscar's voice rose above the music. "Now, sing the chorus to your sweetheart like you mean it."

The Gibsons, the Sternquists, and the Yarboroughs gazed at their spouses and joined in. Rick grinned at me and sang loud enough to turn heads. If he ever gave up law enforcement for a new career, country music wasn't for him.

My gaze moved from one person in our square to the next. The devotion of the couples made my heart swell and my eyes grow misty. I sang softly to them rather than to Rick "Yeah, yeah, there's somethin' 'bout you, baby, I like."

Chapter 16

Pam Barkley's voice rose above the buzz of conversation, coats being zipped, and snow boots being pulled on after the lesson ended. "Hang on a second, Jane."

Rick and I paused our quick dash to the exit. He leaned down and murmured, "So much for going straight to the darkroom."

Pam's eyes widened as she took in our heads close together, his hand on my shoulder. "A bunch of us are going to the café for pie. Do you two want to join us?"

"Oh"—I shifted away from him slightly—"I wish we could, but I have work that has to get done tonight. Maybe next time?"

"You get her home safe, Rick. And don't stay up too late"—She wiggled her eyebrows and gave us a knowing smile—"working."

He put a hand on the small of my back and steered me out the door. "I'll make sure she doesn't."

My giggle turned into a gasp with my first breath of

frigid air. We ran for Rick's pickup truck. Its interior was as cold as outdoors. We shivered in silence during the short drive and raced into my apartment. There, we gave in to fits of laughter.

Rick took a handkerchief from his pocket and wiped at his tears. "The look on Pam's face . . ."

"Want to make an educated guess about who they're talking about at the café at this very moment?"

"Could be us." Then he sobered. "Or it could be Rocko."

"Hey, would you like get coffee and pie at the café with a fellow Iowa transplant?" I heard Rocko ask. I closed my eyes and saw his body slumped beside The Bend's back door.

My laughter turned into a sob. "It's been a week since he died, and we've been spinning our wheels ever since." I grabbed the paper bag with the lightbulbs and unlocked the lab. "Let's not waste another second."

* * *

Over the next few hours, I developed the film, Rick used my blow dryer to speed the drying process, and I began making prints from the negatives. While I did that, Rick turned the forensic lab into a darkroom extension. He covered the tiny window with cardboard, screwed a red bulb into the overhead bedroom light fixture, and strung clothesline rope from wall to wall every which way. The second the prints were ready to handle, he hung them up to dry.

Eventually I came out of the darkroom proper and surveyed what he'd done. "Did you find out why Oscar had these red lightbulbs?"

"No, and I don't intend to until and unless I can confirm the reason."

"Did you know he made a pass at me while you took care of our coats?"

Rick frowned. "I figured he'd behave himself now that he thinks we're an item. I'll keep a closer watch from here on out."

"I won't let him get that close to me from now on. Next time he tries any funny business, I'll raise a stink he won't soon forget."

"I can't wait." He eyed the drying prints. "What do we do next?"

"We shouldn't handle them until they've dried a few hours. I say we call it a night and reconvene tomorrow after work."

"Unless something comes up, I'll see you then." With that, Rick cracked the door open and we slipped through, letting as little light in as possible.

I walked with him to the entryway and told him what Galva, Betty, and Pam had said about Scott Gibson's odd behavior. "Did you see anything odd about the way he acted tonight?"

"No, but he bears watching." As he put on his coat and gloves, he asked, "When you get a chance, would you type a report about the Scott scuttlebutt for the case file?"

"Sure can. If you don't make it tomorrow, I'll have Dale Cunningham put it and any prints of interest in the next day's mail."

"Good. Now we want to be sure that anyone who's still awake at this late hour will see me leave." He flipped on the porch light, stood in the doorway, and blew me kiss. "That should do it."

The cold rushed in as he rushed out. I watched him jog along the sidewalk. Once he rounded the corner, I locked the door and switched off the porch light. Little Missouri was shrouded in darkness except for where the streetlights poked holes in the gloom. A bright square appeared a block or so to the south not far from The Bend. The window-sized light disappeared just as I pinpointed its exact location. Velma Albright's trailer.

Most likely, she would keep spying until my lights went out. With that bright hope in mind, I stood close to the living room windows and waved in her direction. As I did so, a pickup truck turned from the street that ran beside Velma's house onto Main Street. The truck crept past the school. The driver slowed further until he was directly in front of my apartment. I knew he was a he because the sickly yellow glow of the streetlight illuminated his face.

I gave the driver a jaunty wave and yelled at him through the window glass and the darkness. "Not a good color for you, Dick Phillips." Then I closed the living room curtains with a snap, shut off the lights, and went to bed.

Chapter 17

My alarm clock rang in the middle of the night. I cursed the noisy ne'er do well and brought it almost to my face. What? It was six thirty! I dragged my bleary self to the shower. The stream of hot water did little to perk me up. I dressed and plodded into the kitchen for breakfast. I guzzled cup after cup of liquid caffeine before my students arrived.

Their enthusiasm—teacher jargon for "they never stop moving or talking"—along with my desire to examine the photographs hanging in the lab pushed me through the day.

The phone rang shortly after school began, and I hurried to answer. "Hewwo, Jane."

"Good morning, Betty."

"I have a message for you and Wiv from Mrs. Dremstein. She says the forecast for today's high of twenty bewow and a stiff wind from the north means aww students in Tipperary County should stay inside for recess today."

I hung up and muttered, "Start another pot of coffee, Jane. You're going to need it."

Did I ever. By dismissal time, my students were quivering with pent-up energy as they ran outside. My quivering matched theirs, but mine was caffeine induced. I watched from the window until the children were off the school grounds. Then I ran to the lab. There was much to do before my caffeine buzz wore off.

I removed the prints from the clothesline, spread them on a table, and used a magnifying glass to study them. Next I went through them again, making a pile of the ones that stood out. Then I went through that pile a third time, paying special attention to the dark shape captured in all of them. It protruded from under the north side of the landing.

At first, I thought it was a shadow. But it was in every shot of that side, regardless of the differences in lighting or angle. It wasn't a shadow. It was a . . . hmm . . . maybe a shoe?

I went into the darkroom to make two enlargements of the prints in question. Once they were drying in the darkroom, I went to my classroom, rolled a mimeograph master into the typewriter, and typed the report Rick had requested. I ran two copies on the school's mimeograph machine, put one in the crime lab file for our investigation, and slid the other into a manila envelope.

Next, I returned to my classroom and readied it for the next day. My caffeine buzz began to wane when I sat down to correct math papers. I carried on until the sum of forty-six plus ninety-seven eluded me. Was it one hundred thirty-three or one hundred forty-three?

Lay your head on the desk, Jane. Take a cat nap.

A soft snore woke me, and I sat up. A puddle of drool graced Elva's precisely rendered math paper. I mopped her paper dry with a tissue and surrendered my red pen. The rest of the correcting could wait until morning.

I dragged myself into the kitchen and dumped another container of Mom's frozen bean soup in a saucepan. While it heated, I went to the darkroom to see if the enlargements were dry. They weren't. I ate supper, put on my pajamas, set the alarm an hour early, and fell into a deep, delicious sleep before the clock struck seven.

I woke the next morning ready to go. Before the half hour was up, I was dressed for work, eating breakfast, and organizing the enlargements into two piles—one for Rick and one for me—between sips of coffee. That's when I realized Rick hadn't stopped by the previous evening. Or else I'd been dead to the world and hadn't heard him knock. In that case, Velma had already called Betty about me breaking up with the sheriff after a one-night stand in the school apartment, and the news was blanketing the town like a January blizzard.

Either way, I had to get the report and the photos in the mail. I tucked one set of enlargements into the manila envelope with the report for Rick. I added a note asking him for his thoughts about the shape beside the landing and sealed and addressed the envelope. The post office opened after school started, but I could call the postmaster in—I glanced at my watch—about fifteen minutes and arrange to drop it off at his house before my students arrived.

In the meantime, I corrected papers—the sum of forty-six plus ninety-seven was one hundred forty-three—and recorded grades. I took sugar cookies out of the freezer to thaw for art class and reviewed the lesson plans for kindergarten.

At seven thirty on the dot, I picked up the phone and asked Betty to ring the postmaster at his home. He answered immediately.

"Dale Cunningham here. What do you need bright and early on this Thursday morning, Miss Newell?"

I explained the situation. "Can I drop this off at your house right now?"

"I can do you one better. You get it ready, and I'll pick it up on my way to work."

"You're a gem, Dale. Thanks."

"Happy to help. I'll be there toot sweet."

He arrived as I rang the school bell and Tiege waved goodbye to his mother. Dale nosed into Cookie' spot when she pulled out. Tiege galloped across the playground, hurtling over snowbanks and sliding into line behind Stig and Elva. Dale exited his vehicle and marched along the sidewalk until he reached my students and took his place with military precision. The children squirmed like litter of rambunctious puppies. He stood as erect and still as a soldier, though his lips twitched when Jeremy Gibson tripped over Cora's feet and pitched into Renny. Renny then beaned the younger boy's head with his book bag.

I gestured for the children and Dale to come inside. Dale assisted children in the entryway while Renny, Jeremy, and I had a heart-to-heart in the classroom. In the end, Renny not only apologized but offered to play with the younger boy at recess. With the first crisis of the day averted, I retrieved the envelope from my desk and gave it to the postmaster.

He inclined his head one inch. No more. No less. "Miss Newell, I do admire how you talk to those boys. I intend to call every member of the school board and tell them to raise your pay."

"That's quite the offer. Thank you. How much do you need for postage?"

He balanced the envelope on his upturned palm and closed his eyes briefly. "It's four ounces. Seventy-seven cents ought to do it."

I rounded up and gave him a dollar to be on the safe side.

He waved it away. "I prefer exact change."

"But I don't want you to come up short when you weigh it."

He straightened his already erect posture and inhaled while looking down his nose at me. "I won't come up short."

He put the envelope under his arm. I counted out the exact change and gave it to him. He pocketed it, bade me an official goodbye, and executed a heel-clicking about-face. I decided not to wait up tonight for the school board to call and offer me a raise.

The children went to their desks. After the pledge, I announced that the kindergarteners would go first for show-and-tell. Each one took command of the room like they'd been doing it all their lives. In my opinion, their confidence outstripped their content. Winter Skye went up after Jeremy. I listened with one ear while calculating the earliest Rick might call after receiving the envelope. Then again, he might reply by mail or drive over this evening—

"—Jeremy's dad ran past my bedroom window—"

Wait. What?

"—And I got my dad, and he got on his boots and went after him, and I spied out my window 'cause I'm good at it 'cause I spy on my big sisters a lot."

Get on with it, girl.

"But I only saw my dad, not Jeremy's dad."

Rats!

"At lunch my dad said he found Scott." Here, she paused and wrinkled her nose at Jeremy. "Is your dad's name really Scott?"

Jeremy kapowed before he replied. "Yup."

Winter Skye crossed her arms. "Scott is not a cowboy name. My dad tracked your dad into the Long Pines and found him poking around where them cows been getting killed. Mom said that sounded sudpicious, but Dad said no. Jeremy's dad was just doing Forest Service stuff."

"He's always doing Forest Service stuff," Jeremy blurted without raising his hand.

The older students gave me looks that said, "Do something!"

"Go on, Jeremy."

The first, second, and third graders stared in horror, their mouths gaping. Tiege teetered on the edge of his desk.

I ignored the peril. "What kind of Forest Service stuff, Jeremy?"

"I heard him tell Mommy that Rocko was a troublemaker, and he didn't want to clean up after him"—Jeremy shook a finger as he bellowed the next three words—"one more time."

"No fair." Winter Skye stomped her foot as youngest children are often forced to do in the pursuit of justice.

"This is my turn for show-and-tell. Jeremy already had his."

What I wanted to do was call Rick with the latest show-and-tell report. Instead, I restored Winter Skye to the limelight and wrote a note to talk to the older students the next morning about how expectations for kindergarten hand raising weren't the same as for them.

Later, when every child was, by what I assumed was divine intervention, occupied with seatwork, I scrawled a note in my memo book. In red. In capital letters. With plenty of exculmation marks

CALL RICK ASAP!! IF NOT SOONER!!!

Chapter 18

At eleven thirty, Liv phoned and said the temperature had risen to a balmy ten below zero. "You up for lunch recess duty?"

What I was up for was a phone call to Rick. But Liv had taken the children outdoors after lunch the last time the weather had cooperated. Now it was my turn.

"Wait until noon to send them out so I can put on more layers."

Despite the extra layers, my toes and fingers were tingling when the bell rang at the end of recess. They didn't warm up until I explained penmanship lessons for all four grades—lowercase cursive "r" for third graders, an entire print alphabet review for second, uppercase manuscript "M" for first, and lowercase manuscript "L" for kindergarteners.

I reminded the children to fill both the fronts and backs of their papers. Then I dashed into the entryway and put an envelope with my Tipperary Times subscription check in Jeremy's backpack. I toyed with calling

Rick while the children completed their penmanship lessons.

No. The kindergarteners had a habit of finishing assignments in half the time I expected. Sure enough, they were staring out the window, their pencils nowhere in sight, when I re-entered the classrooms. I waited to call until afternoon recess rolled around and Liv would be on duty.

Once the children were sufficiently bundled, I booted them onto the playground and ran for the phone in my apartment. Rachel put me through to the sheriff's office while I mentally composed a coded message, one that would shift Betty's news network into overdrive and let Rick know we needed to talk without delay.

"Sheriff Sternquist here."

"Hi Rick." I pitched my voice low and sultry. "It's Jane."

"Are you catching a cold?" Rick asked.

So much for sultry.

"Just a frog in my throat." I coughed and tried a new angle. "Did you get my letter yet?"

"Uh-huh."

"Did you like what it said?"

He whistled. "Oh yeah."

Now you're cooking, Jane.

"Are you free tonight? I have something new to show you." I giggled like a smitten teenager.

A loud gasp came down the line followed by a snort.

"Are you choking, Rick? Did you swallow something?"

"No, I was about to ask you the same thing."

Betty's ears had to be burning. I poured on the gasoline.

"How soon can you get here? I want to make every minute of this evening count."

"Me too, Jane. I won't keep you waiting long."

We hung up. I returned to my classroom and laid out the materials for art class. In the five minutes it took me to set the sugar cookies, tinted frostings, and other decorating supplies on the back table, I guessed Betty had relayed the conversation with Rick several times over. An hour later, when I dismissed my students—smeared with frosting, high on sugar, and toting plastic containers filled with art masterpieces to share with their families—I assumed Mrs. Dremstein was fielding complaints.

Rick arrived and surveyed the blobs and smears of frosting coating every desktop, the back table, and the floor. "Miss Newell," he said as he set his hat on the frosting-free zone that was my desk and draped his coat over the back of my chair, "I do believe Velma will have your hide when she sees what your students have done."

I filled a bucket with warm, soapy water. "I'm hoping she won't see it." I wet a rag and attacked Cora's desk.

"Can I help?"

I pointed to a putty knife. "Use that to scrape frosting off the floor."

For the next hour he scraped, I scrubbed, and we discussed what Winter Skye and Jeremy had said during show-and-tell. By the end of the hour, we had eliminated all traces of the frosting tornado and were still trying to untangle what the kindergarteners had said.

"Do we dare give credence to the observations of a

couple of five-year-olds?" Rick asked when we went into my kitchen.

I poured coffee into mugs and set a plate of the remaining sugar cookies on the table. "Not word for word. But there's usually a seed of truth in what kids say, so we shouldn't totally discount them. Also, it corroborates what Galva and Betty said about Scott and Rocko not getting along. We at least have to consider that dynamic."

Rick dunked a cookie into his coffee and took a bite. He pronounced it delicious, though, as he had made clear before, not as good as chocolate chip oatmeal. "You're right, but we have to look for a link that connects what's come to light so far."

"But I don't like waiting."

"Don't I know it?"

"You didn't have to agree right away."

"But it's true. You don't like waiting."

"Well, I can't sit here and twiddle my thumbs."

"Then get out your set of enlargements and we'll look at them together. We may notice something we missed while studying them on our own."

Much later, when the cookies were gone and the coffeepot was empty, we agreed that the strange shadow was shaped like a shoe. But we could identify no details—not the outline of a tongue, the tip of a shoelace, the glint of a metal grommet—to confirm our suspicions.

I shoved away from the table and stood. "What a colossal waste of time. I'd offer to fix supper, but I have a mountain of papers to grade yet tonight."

Rick rose. "I'll call The Bend and pick up supper while you attack that mountain."

"You've got a deal." I went into my classroom and got to work.

When Rick returned with two grease-stained white paper bags, the mountain of papers had shrunk down to a hill. "Where do you want to eat?" he yelled from the apartment.

"In the kitchen," I yelled back.

"I'll set the table and holler when it's ready."

I whittled the hill into oblivion as cupboard doors banged, silverware jingled, and dishes clattered in the kitchen. When Rick yelled "Come and get it," I laid down my pen and joined him. We talked and laughed as we downed our salads, burgers, and fries. I confessed my uncertainty about how to manage the kindergartners during their first every other Friday, which started tomorrow morning. He described the challenge of being sheriff in the county where he'd been raised. Not once did we mention Rocko or shoes, dead livestock or the Forest Service. After supper, Rick cleaned up. I returned to my classroom and set up kindergarten centers. He tried to sneak out without disturbing me. A squeaky hinge gave him away, and I hurried to the door and hugged him.

"What's that for?"

"To thank you for supper and to keep the rumor of our romance alive."

He pulled away. "Do you think anyone's swallowing our act?"

"I know at least one person is."

"Who?"

"Dick Phillips." I pointed to the truck creeping along Main Street. The glow of the streetlight illuminated his face as he passed under it. "His skin has a yellow cast, don't you think?"

He descended the steps, winked at me, and waved at the truck. "Or is he just green with envy?"

The dim, the dark, the yellow, and the green couldn't hold a candle to what happened next. Dick Phillips blushed bright red.

Chapter 19

Keeva McDonald and Grace Berthold gripped each other's hands and tiptoed over to my desk during morning recess on Friday. The temperature had sunk to twenty-five below overnight, so we were confined to the great indoors. Again. The little girls gazed at me with the adoration unique to kindergarteners who believe their teacher knows everything. I returned their gaze and wondered if this was the day when their faith in me would be shattered.

Keeva spoke first. "Miss Newell." She fell silent, her courage apparently exhausted by the effort required to say my name.

Grace squeezed Keeva's hand tighter. "Me and Keeva got a question for you."

"What is it?"

Keeva's confidence returned. "Rosalie—she's my big sister. Do you remember her?"

In the five months I'd lived in Little Missouri, Rosalie had baked and served apple pie for dessert after a meal with her family, made blueberry pancakes for breakfast after a sleepover at my apartment, monitored her mother's mental health after Rosalie and Keeva's older brother Brock was arrested for murder, and presented evidence that moved a judge to dismiss the charges. The girl was unforgettable.

"I remember Rosalie."

"Well. We was looking at the calendar together, and she said Valentine's Day is in one month. I counted the days and it made thirty-one." Keeva's next words were pure Rosalie. "That may seem like a long time, but it is not."

"Not a long time for what?"

Keeva and Grace exchanged disappointed glances. I'd let the cat out of the bag. Their teacher didn't know everything.

Grace answered, "For us to make Valentine's presents for our mommies and daddies."

"No need to worry, girls." I smiled and tapped on the open page in my lesson plan book. It contained not a mention of Valentine's presents. Since Keeva and Grace couldn't read yet, my secret was safe as long as inspiration hit by afternoon recess. "Valentine's Day preparations are on the docket for this afternoon."

While the third graders constructed pinhole cameras during science class, inspiration hit. I would use my camera to snap photographs of the children. They could use them in the valentines they would make for their parents and classmates. I grabbed the camera at the beginning of afternoon recess and took candids of them playing board games and doing puzzles. Then I had them strike their favorite poses for individual shots.

I tried to capture the spirit of each child and couldn't wait to see how they turned out. I went straight to the darkroom after school and developed the negatives. Then I returned to my desk and made a file of worksheet masters to run off at Mrs. Dremstein's office in Tipperary tomorrow. She'd reserved a Saturday for every country schoolteacher in the county to drive over and make copies on the new Xerox machine the school had purchased. She said the copies were as good as the originals, though the claim sounded too good to be true. I spent the next few hours making a list of students who still needed a good photograph, grading papers, and writing lesson plans. My stomach growled louder the longer I worked, but I didn't leave my desk until it was clear of papers.

I shivered when I finally stood up. Icy fingers of cold snaked through the door and window frames as I went into my apartment for supper. I switched the menu from peanut butter and jelly to bacon, eggs, and toast slathered with the wild plum jelly Mom had tucked in my Christmas stocking. After supper I taped a note on the phone.

Call Mom tomorrow and thank her for the jelly.

Saturday morning, I opened the living room curtains, and sunshine poured through the windows. Cold burned my fingertips when I traced the frost patterns on the glass. Only then did I check the outdoor thermometer. Thirty-five below!

Taking a page from my mother's book, I boiled water for tea and made a pot of oatmeal. I could hear her saying, "Hot cereal on a cold morning will get you going." A half hour later, fortified by oatmeal sprinkled with brown sugar and a generous splash of Snippy's creamy milk, I went to the darkroom and made prints from the negatives of my students. Once they were drying on the line, I showered and dressed. Then I put on my coat and went outside to start the Beetle. It would need time to warm up before I drove to Tipperary. When I turned the key in the ignition, the car chugged, groaned, whimpered, and finally succumbed to the cold.

I climbed out of the car, intent upon kicking a tire. A gust of biting wind turned the cold into a carnivorous beast and brought me to my senses—not out of pity for my trusty Beetle, which had spent the night at the mercy of the elements, but because I was afraid kicking a frozen tire would break my toe. I stumped down the sidewalk and into my apartment where I slammed the door and sank into a chair. Now what?

I picked up the phone receiver, tore off the note, and stuffed it in the pocket of my coat. Then I barked into the receiver, "Where's Rick?"

Betty countered with a cheerful, "Good morning, Miss Neweww. He stayed with Bud and Cookie wast night. Would you wike me to connect you?"

"Yes, please."

Rick answered, and I explained my predicament. He offered to pick me up on his way to Tipperary. "You can work at the school while I finish some paperwork at my office. I'm helping Dad check cattle again tonight and can drop you off on the way."

He arrived ten minutes later. The wind freshened on the drive to Tipperary. Hypnotic swirls of snow scuttled from one side of the road to the other. "Maybe it's a good thing my car didn't start this morning. Is it as hard to drive in as it looks?"

"Worse. You got no business driving alone when it's this cold and windy."

"You'll get no argument from me. Riding in a vehicle with a radio unit is reassuring in this kind of weather."

"Pseudo-dating a sheriff has its advantages." A gust rocked the vehicle. Rick fell silent and concentrated on the road until he reached Tipperary's city limits. Then he relaxed. "How long do you think you'll be?"

I eyed the thick folder of master copies. "Two or three hours."

He pulled up in front of the school and let me out. "Call my office when you're done. We'll eat at the Nine Pins before we head back."

The janitor let me in. I figured out how to operate the Xerox machine. The copies it made were every bit as clear as Mrs. Dremstein had promised, and I called Rick an hour sooner than expected. "This new machine is fast. I copied two months' worth of worksheets in no time."

"Will wonders never cease? I'll be there soon."

A few minutes later, we walked into the Nine Pins. The waitress took a break from filing her nails. "Most people have the sense to stay home when it's this cold. Sit wherever you want."

We chose the booth farthest from the entrance. If any other fools rushed in to take advantage of the Saturday special—chicken-fried steak and mashed potatoes with two sides and a drink for three ninety-five—we hoped our booth would be warmer than the rest. By the time Rick mopped up the last drop of chicken-fried gravy with his dinner roll and I finished my chili and corn-bread, a goodly number of fools had indeed shown up.

The café was three-quarters full when Rick paid our bill and we went outside.

A ferocious wind slammed into us. The cold made my eyes water and my teeth ache. I bent my head and fought for breath on the way to Rick's vehicle. When we got inside, I looked up and saw clouds of snow rising and swirling. They reduced the visibility to almost nothing.

Rick shook his head. "Ground blizzards are nothing to sneeze at. Unless it lets up between now and dusk, you'll be staying in town with me tonight."

"That'll set Little Missouri's phone lines on fire."

"Your reputation is about to take a direct hit."

"Ah well." I tried to sound nonchalant. "This too shall pass."

"It's what will happen until then that concerns me."

"Think of it this way. Tonight there will be time to thoroughly review the evidence and analyze our suspects."

"When did you become such an optimist? I'll stop by my office for my case file." He turned on the ignition. Before he inched into the fog of snow, he met my gaze. "And just so you know, if you have to stay overnight, I call the couch."

Chapter 20

Rick's back door opened into a small kitchen. When I pocketed my gloves, my fingertips brushed against a wad of paper. I pulled it out and saw my own note.

I showed it to him. "Do you mind if I phone my mom? Let me know what the charges are, and I'll pay you back."

"Want to hang up your coat and use the restroom first?"

I said yes to both. He took my coat and pointed me toward a small bathroom. He was hanging up the receiver when I returned to the kitchen.

"You can use this phone if you want. Or there's one down the hall in my office if you want some privacy."

"This one's fine." The phone rang before I reached it.

Rick picked up. "Sheriff Sternquist here." He listened and glanced at me, his eyes bright with amusement. "Here she is."

My mother? I mouthed.

He nodded, handed me the receiver, and beat a hasty retreat.

"Hi, Mom."

"Hello, Jane. I was going to call this morning, but your Uncle Tim insisted on showing Harold how the snow had drifted during that last storm. Wanda and I went along for the ride, and before we knew it, Tim drove your father all the way to Le Mars for Vander Meer's doughnuts."

Oh no! She heard about Rocko when they were there.

"Anyway, we got home a few minutes ago. I called your apartment, but Betty said the sheriff had taken you to Tipperary."

She knows about Rick. Prepare for a grilling.

"She said you and Rick are getting thick. Her exact words were 'thick as thieves.' Him being at your apartment until all hours of the night. Meals at the café together. Holding hands at square dance lessons. And now you're at his house! What do you have to you say about yourself?"

"Can I talk to Dad?"

The mention of her husband was guaranteed to calm Mom down. She rarely denied him the joy of conversation with friends, family, neighbors, and complete strangers. She sputtered into the receiver and then handed it to Dad.

"Dad." I kept my voice low so Mom couldn't hear me. "Listen up. Rick Sternquist—do you remember me telling you about him? He's the sheriff in Tipperary County."

"Affirmative."

"Okay. We are officially partnering on a murder

investigation. That's still not common knowledge, and we're pretending to be a couple as cover for the time we're spending together. Rumors are flying, and none of them are true. I don't want Mom to know yet for fear she'll say something to Betty. I'll call you next week when Mom's at work and fill you in. But can you keep this under your hat for now?"

"Affirmative."

"Thanks. Now, you can either hand the phone back to Mom so I can thank her for her wild plum jelly, or you can hang up and pass the message along."

When his receiver crashed into its cradle, I knew clumsiness hadn't caused him to drop it, though Mom would assume it had. Dad had done it to let me know he was committed to keeping my secret. At least for now.

Rick looked up from where he was arranging the contents of the case file on the kitchen table. "Has your mom heard about us yet? Did she give you an earful?"

I sank into a chair. "Yes on both counts. She's going to come unglued when she hears about me staying here tonight."

"Well then, you'll be relieved to know that while you were in the bathroom, I called my neighbor and arranged for you to sleep in her guest room. She even volunteered to tell Betty what's going on."

"This neighbor sounds like she's got gumption, taking on Betty and welcoming a total stranger into her home. Who is she?"

"Your boss."

"Mrs. Dremstein?"

"One and the same."

What was with Rick and his penchant for arranging

slumber parties for me with school personnel? First with Velma in the trailer where she chain-smoked when she wasn't cleaning the school or arranging my social calendar. Now with the school principal. Could I possibly fall asleep in the guest room of the woman who wrote my performance reviews?

"Does she smoke?"

"No. But she's big into preventing fires."

"There aren't any fires to prevent in the middle of winter."

"If you stay overnight with me, she'll be putting out fires for months. And you could still lose your job."

Well, when he put it that way . . .

"What time does the party start?"

"After supper."

In the meantime, we combed through the case files. We reread Rick's notes about Rique DuPeuss's analysis of the animal prints and the conversations with Forest Service personnel. We reread my notes of my conversations with Galva, Betty, and what I'd gleaned from show-and-tell at school. We studied the enlargements of the crime scene photographs.

Rick summed up the fruits of our intense labor while we washed dishes after a late supper. "Our best lead is a shoe-shaped shadow. Whatever cast the shadow was carried off by dogs after Dick Phillips fell asleep guarding the crime scene. Now he drives by your house late at night. Rocko and Scott Gibson didn't get along, and Scott's behavior has been erratic lately. Which makes Dick and Scott our prime suspects, but we have no evidence against them and won't unless one of them shows up at square dance lessons wearing only one shoe."

I wrung out the dishcloth and draped it over the faucet. "In other words, this investigation is going nowhere."

"But you're going to Mrs. Dremstein's. I'll walk you over." Rick put on his coat and helped me into mine.

The wind howled during the short tramp next door. Mrs. Dremstein let me in quickly. Rick pivoted and hurried home.

"Thanks for doing this," I said as she hung up my coat. A great gust of wind slammed into her house and threatened to blow it off its foundation.

"You're not the first stranded teacher I've put up for the night. I rather enjoy it." She showed me the guest bedroom, the bathroom, and the kitchen. "Would you like a hot drink or anything?"

"No, thank you. It's been a long day, and I'm ready to turn in."

This was a half-truth. The day had been long and eventful, but the prospect of making small talk with my boss was too intimidating to consider.

"Okay, then. I'll see you in the morning."

I went into the bathroom where Mrs. Dremstein had set toothpaste and a toothbrush still in its package on the vanity. In the guest room, she had laid out a nightgown. Next to the bed was a bookshelf full of mysteries by American and English authors. She had what looked like complete sets of Agatha Christie and Dorothy Sayers paperbacks. I curled up in bed with *Whose Body?* and read until I was ready for sleep.

I burrowed under the covers and was soon dreaming. The strangest dream was about square dance lessons. Wild dogs sat outside the hall, a single shoe dangling from the mouth of each one. Every man inside the hall was missing a shoe, and their shod feet pounded unevenly in response to Oscar Rumble's calls. My confusion mounted as the calls came faster and the footfalls grew louder.

Someone shouted my name once. "Jane." Then again and again. "Jane. Keep up, Jane. Keep up!"

Wait. What was being said? I clawed away the covers from over my head and listened intently. The pounding resumed.

"Wake up, Jane," Mrs. Dremstein called through the door. "The wind died down in the night, and Rick wants to get you to Little Missouri before it starts up again."

I was dressed in five minutes, and we were on the road in ten after bidding Mrs. Dremstein a hasty good-bye.

"I let you get a few extra winks while I got ready for church," Rick explained as he dodged the drifts the ground blizzard had left as calling cards.

"You're going to church?"

"You too. We want to make sure everyone knows you stayed at Mrs. Dremstein's house and not mine. It's also a chance to observe our pitiful list of suspects. Who knows? One of them may let his guard down."

"When did you become Mr. Optimistic?"

He didn't answer, and conversation languished as he navigated the maze of drifts on the road.

He broke the silence when we reached Little Missouri and he parked beside my Beetle. He put the box of worksheets I'd copied in my classroom, then came into the kitchen and said, "I'll make breakfast while you get ready."

I checked the outdoor thermometer. Thirty below. I took a wool pantsuit into the bathroom, showered, and changed.

Rick hurried me through a gourmet breakfast of cold cereal and coffee. "We should get to church early so we can watch Dick and Scott come in. Watch for stiff body language. Refusal to make eye contact. Stilted conversation. Anything that seems a little off."

His description described Dick Phillips's normal behavior. I wasn't expecting any revelations from that quarter and decided to concentrate on Scott Gibson. When we arrived at church, I settled into an unobtrusive corner and kept an eye on the door. Scott and Linda Gibson came in with their four kids and a flurry of clumping boots and dropped mittens. Scott acted like every other dad who wants his kids to behave at church.

Several families followed the Gibsons into the foyer. I didn't see when Dick Phillips entered but did see him go straight to a back pew without glancing at anyone. He looked as guilty as sin when he took a seat. Nothing new there.

If the foyer was noisy before Tiege Sternquist burst through the door, the volume doubled when he bounded over to me. "I hear you stayed at the *princible's* house in Tipperary last night. Was it fun? Did you watch television or play games?"

Conversation ceased and heads swiveled in our direction.

Thank you, Tiege, for your public service announcement.

I matched Tiege's volume and upped it a decibel. "Actually, it was boring. I brushed my teeth and went to bed."

Heads swiveled away and conversations resumed. Shortly thereafter, Pastor Petersen arrived, and congregants drifted into the sanctuary for the service.

I looked at Rick and Tiege. "I'm ready to go into church. Are you?"

Rick guided us to the back pew where, instead of paying attention to the sermon or the service, we watched Scott and Dick.

"What a waste of time," I told Rick when he chauffeured me to my apartment after church. "We'd have been better off listening to the sermon. What do we do now?"

"Widen our pool of suspects."

I reached for the door handle. "Let's get to it."

"Not today. I promised my deputy the afternoon off."

"You're a nice boss. Thanks for the ride." I hopped out of his truck and made my way along the drifted sidewalk. When I entered my apartment, I decided to take a break from the investigation. Instead, I would look over the photographs of my students.

After supper, I looked at the pictures drying in the darkroom. I'd documented Cora's fairy sparkle, Winter Skye's spunk, Jeremy's kapow, Beau's grave sweetness, Elva's teacher expression, and even Renny's longing for approval. In the next week or two, I was sure to capture Tiege's zest for life, Bennan's love of learning, Stig's little-boy earnestness, and the growing friendship between Keeva and Grace.

If only, I thought as I crawled into bed that night, I was equally confident about increasing our pool of suspects. With every day that went by, the trail of Rocko's killer grew fainter. Before long, I feared, it would disappear.

CHAPTER 21

During the night, the temperature rose to ten below. It was an improvement, but not nearly enough to melt the top layer of snow into a crust and stop the constant drifting. Rick didn't stop by on Monday or Tuesday, and I imagined our investigative trail drifting shut with cold, depressing finality.

"Goodbye, Miss Newell!" Elva hollered after school on Tuesday. She scaled a drift in the playground and slid down the other side. "See you tonight."

"See you there!" I stepped onto the landing and waved. Unless I was mistaken, it was no longer below zero. Had our cold snap ended? I wheeled the television into my classroom and flipped it on in hopes of catching the weather while I corrected papers.

The news didn't come on until after the television was back in my apartment, and I was fixing supper. The forecast was for continued warmer temperatures—*Yay!*—and eight to ten inches of snow tonight—*Boo!*

The weatherman gazed through the camera lens.

"The front will move through western South Dakota around midnight, so as long as you're home and safely tucked in bed by then, you'll be fine."

I switched off the television and readied myself for the evening's lesson. Now that Rick and I were an established as a couple, I put on comfortable jeans and a sweater. I fluffed up my hair to signal that our romance was alive but didn't apply lipstick so Oscar would know he was dead to me.

By then it was six thirty, and I hadn't heard from Rick. I couldn't wait much longer. I put on my winter things, grabbed my purse and plate of cookies, and went out to start the Beetle. I was surprised to see that the day's drifts on the sidewalk and behind my car were gone. Who had done that?

I wasn't sure the car would start, but the engine caught on my second attempt. I waited while it warmed up, alternately cursing Rick's lack of communication and hoping he would show up so I didn't have to fend off Oscar Octopus on my own. At six fifty-five, I was shifting into reverse when he pulled up beside me.

I was out of my vehicle and into his faster than Oscar could make a pass at a woman. "I was beginning to think you wanted me to face the consequences of our sleepover alone."

"Sorry. I should have called." He rested his head on the seat back and exhaled. "Me and my deputy have been pulling cars outta ditches pretty much nonstop since Sunday night."

"But I thought people around here knew how to drive in winter."

"The ones who grew up in Tipperary County do. I'm

talking about the crazies who aren't from around here. They take off in any kind of weather. They have as much sense as a duck in a desert. Driving too fast. No emergency kits." He put his vehicle in reverse and backed out. "At least the folks at the dance hall know better."

I chewed the side of my cheek. "I'm not from around here."

"True. But I am, and you're with me. So I'm your free pass."

"One of the many advantages to being a pseudo-couple."

"Sure is. And when this case breaks loose, Rocko's killer won't notice what we're really up to." The dance hall was ringed with vehicles, so Rick parked by Velma's trailer.

"It looks like we're the last ones here." I grabbed his hand and pulled him across the street. The second we entered, Tiege hurled toward us. He ran into me. I toppled into Rick. Rick caught me before I hit the floor. Bud and Cookie ran over and waded into the confab.

Tiege shouted, "Hi, Miss Newell!"

Bud collared him. "You gotta watch where you're goin', Son."

Cookie knelt beside Tiege. "You go sit on a chair and think about what you did and what you can do to make it right." She got up, engulfed me in a hug, and whispered, "You okay?"

"I'm fine." She gave me an extra squeeze as a gaggle of children surrounded us. She moved away to make room for them.

Elva put her arms around my waist. "Are you hurt, Miss Newell? Do you need a Band-Aid?"

That unleashed a swarm of hugs and questions from the other children. Only when I assured and reassured them that I was fine did they run off to play. Only when they were gone did Tiege approach me.

He spoke without meeting my gaze. "I'm sorry I runned into you, Miss Newell. I don't always watch where I'm going."

"Apology accepted." We shook hands, and he careened across the room to join his friends. Just then Oscar Rumble's amplifier squealed, and I turned toward the stage. Oscar adjusted a knob. As he straightened, he wiggled his eyebrows at me and leered like we were alone in the room.

I shuddered. The man creeped me out.

He picked up the microphone and spoke into it. "Let's circle round, folks, and review what we learned last week." He ran us through several steps and added a few more. Once we mastered those, he told us to form squares and choose a head couple.

Bud and Cookie joined us. They brought along Gus and Betty, as well as Rosalie McDonald. In short order, they recruited Rique DuPeuss to complete our square. When Oscar was satisfied with our progress on the night's new moves, he announced a break. Most of the crowd gathered around the snack table. The smokers and spitters, along with those who needed the bathrooms, grabbed their coats and went outside. They returned a few minutes later, their shoulders dusted with snow.

"It's coming down very hard." Rique brushed snow from his coonskin cap and turned to Oscar. "You better leave now, or you won't get home."

Oscar waved Rique's concern away. "I've got a bed

in my Suburban for this very reason. I've stayed in it before."

A crowd gathered at the door and took stock of the storm. Tiege led several children on a mission to squirm their way to the front of the group.

"That kid's a holy terror," Oscar Rumble said quietly. He stood close. Too close. His breath tickled my ear, and his hand pressed into the small of my back like I belonged to him. "I hear you and the sheriff got cozy over the weekend. I can do you one better tonight. The bed in the backa my outfit sleeps two." His hand wandered south until it rested on my hip.

I grabbed his fingers, squeezed them as tight as I could, and flung them away. "Touch me again, and you'll discover who the holy terror really is. I'll kick you where it hurts and inform the sheriff. Got it?"

"Oh, the teacher's feisty. I'm into feisty." He leered and sauntered toward the stage. He climbed the stairs and picked up his microphone. "Form those squares again, folks, and get ready for the music." He started the familiar record and called the dance.

Our square executed the steps flawlessly. I circled Rick and found myself facing Oscar as he smoothed his pompadour, looked directly at me, and mouthed the words to the title—"There's Somethin' 'Bout You Baby I Like."

I didn't join in.

Chapter 22

The snow was falling fast and thick as Rick drove me home. He laughed harder than I thought the retelling of my conversation with Oscar the Octopus warranted. Even so, I asked Rick if he wanted to come in, but he declined. He and everyone else who'd been at the dance hall needed to get home before the snow piled up. Or the wind picked up. Or the temperature plummeted again.

That exact weather trifecta hit Little Missouri sometime in the night. Mrs. Dremstein phoned before my alarm rang on Wednesday morning.

"The roads are drifted shut, and the wind chill is thirty below. The entire county is shut down, and I've called off school. Will you let Liv and the parents know?"

I got a hold of Liv, and we divvied up the families between us. I quickly discovered my efforts were superfluous. Every parent said Betty had already let them know. No surprise there.

My alarm went off as I crossed off the final name

on my list. I thought about going back to bed, but I was wide awake now. So I ate breakfast—oatmeal with Snippy cream and coffee with another dollop of Snippy cream—and stuck to my usual workday routine. My only concession to the weather was trading the wool pantsuit I'd laid out for a heavy sweatshirt and blue jeans. With long johns under both.

The furnace struggled to keep the cold at bay, and I decided to help it along by baking something. I was thumbing through my recipe box looking for one with ingredients I had on hand when a knock sounded.

What kind of fool would pop in to visit in this weather? The door refused to open more than a crack. I blew on the frost-covered window to create a peephole, put my eye up to it, and saw Rick Sternquist knee-deep in snow. His coat and hat were covered with snow. His face was snow white. I fought off the temptation to offer him a poison apple. Instead, I shouted for him to clear away the snow and come in.

"How did you get here?" I asked once he stood in the entryway.

"Snowmobile."

"You look half frozen. Can I get you some coffee?"

"Can you put it in a thermos and come with me? There's a situation that needs checking, and I'd like to have a witness along."

"In this cold?"

"Trust me. You wouldn't want to miss this even at fifty below."

I filled a thermos with what was left of the morning's coffee and put on extra socks, a thick sweater, and lined jeans. Over that get up, I layered my usual winter wear and pulled on my boots. Finally, I took the afghans from my couch and tucked them under one arm.

"What are those for?" Rick asked as we left.

"In case I get cold."

Rick waded through the snow ahead of me, got onto the snowmobile after me, and grumbled as he wedged the afghans between us.

"Is this official business?" I yelled in his ear as we sped down Main Street.

He didn't answer until we were parked in front of Round the Bend. He got off, grabbed the afghans before they toppled into a snowbank, and grabbed me before I did the same. When had he become familiar with my signature move? He gestured for me to follow. We slogged through the snow and stopped at the southeast corner of the building.

He peered around the corner, and I did too. There sat Oscar Rumble's Suburban, its engine idling, and its windows steamier than the Amazon rainforest.

"This is why you dragged me out in the cold?" I hissed. Not an easy feat while my teeth chattered, but I crushed it. "Oscar said he planned to sleep there."

"That's so. But I had a call early this morning from Clarice, Lacey Jo's grandma. Seems that Lacey Jo drove over to The Bend yesterday and didn't come home last night. I called the Bertholds to see what they knew. Glen said Oscar and Lacey were mighty chummy right up until he chased them out and closed the bar early." Rick pointed at a blue Ford Bronco parked beside The Bend. "That's Lacey's outfit. It's stone cold, and she's not inside. So where might she be?"

"Oscar told me that his vehicle sleeps two." I studied the Suburban. "Do we ring the doorbell or what?"

The words were barely out of my mouth before the door behind the driver's seat swung open, and Lacey crawled out. Her makeup was smeared, her hair tangled, and her clothing askew. She tottered toward her Bronco, shivering, coatless, and oblivious to our presence. Her platform sandals were useless in the snow. Any minute she was going to wipe out.

I waded toward her and held out an afghan. "Lacey Jo, wrap this around your shoulders."

Her gaze was cold and ungrateful. When a spasm of shivers engulfed her, she snatched the afghan. She turned away and headed for her Bronco again. Two steps later, her foot shot out from under her.

I grabbed her elbow and we both went down. I'm not sure how we righted ourselves, but once we did, I escorted her to her vehicle. "Is your coat in there?"

"No." She climbed inside, started the engine, and wrapped her upper half in the afghan. "I left it in the Suburban."

I held out the other one. "Tuck this around your legs while the car warms up. Is Oscar still in the Suburban?"

"Nope."

"Where'd he go?"

"Don't know. Don't care. The man's a beast."

I went back to Rick, who was shining a flashlight around the interior of the Suburban. "You can't search without a warrant, can you?"

He stepped away. "No, I can't. But if Lacey sent you to retrieve her things, I'm happy to watch."

"She needs her coat."

Rick grinned. "Have at it."

"The last thing I want is for Oscar to show up and find me in his vehicle. Wait right here."

"I will."

I went to the back of the vehicle and opened the double doors. Light illuminated Oscar's sleeping quarters. He had replaced the dome lights with red bulbs, and they cast a seedy glow. Mirrors lined the ceiling. A leopard skin bedspread lay bunched to one side of the mattress, a pile of clothing on the other. Shuddering, I climbed inside and searched for Lacey Jo's coat. I found one shoe, shirts, pants, and underthings, at which point I thanked God that I was wearing gloves. I crawled out and went around to the back passenger door where a woman's coat and one men's dress shoe lay on the floor.

Every fiber of my being wanted to leave the Suburban and never enter it again. But the shoe compelled me to take a second look. I held up the shoe. Its shape was familiar. I pocketed it and left the Suburban for good.

Rick drew closer. "Find anything?"

"Let me take Lacey Jo's coat to her. Then I'll tell you."

I went to the Bronco and knocked on its window. She opened the door but didn't invite me inside for hot cocoa. I handed her the coat. She threw the blankets at me and slammed the car door in my face. Before I could turn around, she put her outfit in reverse and backed into a snow drift.

"I did what I could," I told Rick after returning to where he waited. We stood together and watched her tires spin. We waited for her to surrender to the weather and accept our help. Eventually my feet grew numb.

"I'm going home." I hefted the afghans and smiled at Rick. "She's all yours now."

Chapter 23

He headed for Lacey Jo. I headed for the tracks made by Rick's snowmobile. When I turned onto Main Street, a bundled-up Velma burst out the café's entrance and began shouting at me.

"You and the sheriff gotta put an end to your funny business before you get run out a town on a rail."

"Will the sheriff be run out with me?"

"What does that have to do with the price of beans in China? You're gonna get yourself fired."

"No, I'm not."

She waded over to me, her eyes sparking and her voice shrill. "Oscar Rumble is in the café right now bragging about how he's gonna lure you into his Suburban sex den after the next square dance lesson."

"Trust me when I say that I will never set foot in Oscar's Suburban."

"It's mighty hard to trust you now that you're shacking up with the sheriff."

"Velma Albright, I thought we were friends. Why

would you believe a bunch of rumors instead of me?"
I drew closer until we were nose to nose. "If you ever
repeat that lie about Rick to my parents, our friendship
is over."

With that, I trekked toward home, thinking about
Lacey Jo the entire way. I didn't know why she had
turned against me, but we had one point of complete
agreement about Oscar Rumble. The man was a beast.

I marched into the schoolyard and along the sidewalk to the cadence of a single phrase—the *man* wuzza
beast—over and over until I halted at the base of the
landing.

Wait a minute!

I looked back at the sidewalk and then at the stairs
in front of me. Someone had shoveled the snow again. I
was too curious about the shoe in my pocket to care. The
mystery of the stealthy snow shoveler would have to wait.

I went inside and dropped the afghans on the entryway rug. For a few seconds I stood there enjoying the
waves of delectable warmth washing over me. Then I
took the shoe from my pocket and laid it on the rug, too.
Next, I removed one layer of clothing after another. By
the time my sweatshirt and jeans came into view, I was
sweating. Finally, I carried the afghans and every item of
clothing that had touched the inside of Oscar's Suburban
to laundry room, tossed them into the washing machine,
and turned on the sanitize cycle. When dealing with a
beast and his den, a person can't be too careful.

With the Oscar threat contained, I got a pair of latex
gloves from the forensic lab and retrieved the shoe. I
took it into the lab and dusted the leather Oxford for fingerprints. It was covered with them. I photographed the

prints up close and then the shoe from every conceivable angle until I'd used the entire roll.

I took a break to transfer the laundry to the dryer. That should cook to death any Oscar germs that might have survived drowning in the washer. After turning the knob to its hottest setting, I got busy in the darkroom. My stomach began to growl while I secured the tops and bottoms of the negatives and unleashed my blow dryer on them.

I ignored my hunger, unclipped the dried negatives, and began making prints. Once they'd been hung up, I took the photo of the shadowy shape from the case file. When I compared it to the shoe, a shudder that had nothing to do with the cold ran up my spine.

I set them on the table and ran to the phone. "Betty, do you know where Rick is?"

"He just ordered wunch at Round the Bend. Griwwed cheese and tomato soup, I bewieve."

"Got it!" I replaced the receiver, hurried to the dryer, and pulled out my de-Oscared winter gear. My fingers flew as I buttoned, zipped, and snapped everything securely into place. I pulled on my boots, took my purse from its hook, and plunged into the arctic cold. I followed the cleared sidewalk to the cleared parking area where my Beetle sat buried in a massive drift. I said a silent thank you to my kindly snow-removal genie as I climbed the berm left by the snowplow and trudged along Main Street. The north wind blew me to The Bend.

I reached the café entrance and fumbled with the knob. I leaned a shoulder against the door and gave a mighty push. It flew open, and I stumbled inside, scattering snow in every direction. It was an entrance worthy of Edward Shackleton. From what I'd experienced of winter in Little Missouri, Shackleton and his men would have benefited from a winter training here before their Antarctic expedition.

Rick sat in the toasty booth closest to the kitchen. He flicked a blob of snow from his grilled cheese sandwich before dunking the golden triangle into his tomato soup and taking a gargantuan bite.

"Mm-mm-mm-mm-mm."

I think he was referring to the food and not me.

"Coffee," I gasped. "Trudy, I need coffee. And an order of what Rick's eating."

"Comin' right up, Miss Newell." Her head popped over the partition that separated the dining area from the kitchen. Then she raised her voice. "Renny and Grace, you get over here and hang up your teacher's coat and such."

They scampered from the bar to the café on unwilling elf feet. From what I gathered, their mother's command had interrupted a hot game of pool. They did as she had asked and scampered back into the bar. Soon the smacking of pool balls and bickering of children filled the air again.

The noise was good cover in case Trudy tried to listen in while I brought Rick up to speed regarding my morning's work. By the time my soup and sandwich arrived, he wanted to bag up my meal and head straight to the crime lab to see the shoe and the photographs.

I curved a protective arm around my plate and bowl. "You got to eat your food while it was hot, and I do too." I enjoyed my meal while he paid the bill and made small talk with Trudy. Then he stood by the door impatiently tapping his toe until I used the last bit of sandwich to sop up the remaining drops of soup in the bowl. So good. So, so good.

With the gallantry of a man who wants to move from one thing to another without further delay, Rick collected my winter things and brought them over while I drained my coffee cup. He helped me into my coat—what a guy!—and then picked up a paper grocery sack from the bench where he'd been sitting. It clinked when he shifted it to the crook of his elbow.

I arched an eyebrow. "Are you stealing restaurant crockery again?"

"Keep your voice down." He shot a quick glance toward the doorway to the bar and hurried me outside. "Oscar and Lacey Jo have been cuddled up in the bar for the past hour. They seem to have reconciled their differences. I told Trudy to bring their coffee cups to me, and I don't want them to find out."

"Knowing Trudy, she's already broadcast the news."

"Nope. I told her it has to do with the official investigation into Rocko's death. She and Glen feel like he died on their watch, so she'll keep quiet."

"You want the cups dusted for prints?"

"Right after you show me what you found."

We climbed onto the snowmobile. I stuffed the bag of crockery inside my coat, and we roared off. In my apartment, we went into the lab. I pointed him to the shoe and the photograph on the table.

Rick whistled when he laid the shoe on top of the shadowy shape. "It's a perfect fit. Assuming the shoe belongs to Oscar, we've got ourselves a new suspect. He's in town. I'm in town. Seems like the right time to pay him a neighborly visit, don't you think?"

He must have been asking a rhetorical question because he bundled up and left before I thought of an answer. I watched from the window as he mounted the snowmobile and sped off. I shuddered. Once again, it wasn't because of the cold. It was because Oscar Rumble was in town, and I couldn't imagine one good thing coming from him being here. Not one.

Chapter 24

For the rest of the afternoon, I alternated between working in the lab and my classroom. I started by dusting the confiscated cups for prints, photographing them, and developing the film. While it dried, I bagged and labeled the cups. After that I made prints from the negatives of Oscar and Lacey Jo's fingerprints and hung them up. Then I made a chef's salad for dinner and invited Sir Peter to eat with me. I had just finished my second chapter when the phone rang.

I bookmarked my page and answered it. "Hello, this is Jane."

"Hi, Jane," Mrs. Dremstein said. "Are you enjoying your snow day?"

"Very much." Though probably not in the same way other teachers were.

"Good. Say, the plows have cleared the roads, but there's supposed to be significant drifting during the night. Would you let your families know there's a two-hour delay tomorrow to be on the safe side?"

After Mrs. Dremstein hung up, Betty said, "I can teww Wiv if you wike."

"That would be great. I'll start with Burt and Iva Kelly. Could you connect me to them?"

She did. A half hour later the calls were finished, and I went into my classroom to adjust lesson plans for tomorrow's shorter day. The kindergarteners would be coming, so the process took longer than expected. Finally I returned to the darkroom, grabbed a magnifying glass, and began to compare the fingerprint photos. I found a few prints on the shoe that matched those from Lacey Jo's cup and many more that matched Oscar's. I typed up my analysis, labeled the photos, and sorted them into two piles. Then I put the photographs in two envelopes, one for me and one for Rick, along with a copy of the report for each of us. I locked everything in the filing cabinet, then left the lab and locked the door.

It was late, so I picked up *Whose Body?* and apologized to Sir Peter for abandoning him earlier. Then I got ready for bed, crawled under the covers, and read until my eyes refused to stay open any longer.

The next thing I knew, my dreams were interrupted by a metallic scraping sound. I put a pillow on my head and was drifting off again when my alarm clock rang.

Enough already! I threw back the covers and got out of bed to investigate the incessant scraping sound. It was louder in the living room, so I parted the curtains an inch or two and peered through the window. Between the brightening eastern sky and the streetlights, I saw someone clearing the sidewalks. I recognized the camouflage ski mask, the coat, and the thick, hand-knitted mittens. Dick Phillips. I let the curtain drop and went about my business.

Once I was dressed and ready for school, I brewed a pot of coffee and took a carton of eggs from the fridge. The scraping of Dick's snow shovel persisted. Guilt stirred within. I opened the curtains and watched him for a few seconds. He'd been shoveling since before dawn's early light and had to be cold and tired. Probably hungry too.

Would it kill you to make him a couple eggs, Jane?

It would not. I went to the door and poked my head outside. "I'm fixing eggs for breakfast. Care to join me?"

He shook his head and bent deeper over the shovel.

"Please. You'll be doing me a favor. Merle brings eggs faster than I can eat them."

The head shaking increased. The shoveling decreased.

"I fry the eggs in bacon grease. And there's coffee."

He straightened, stuck the shovel in a drift, and spoke to the ground. "You talked me into it."

Five words! Half again as many as on our date. I stood frozen in place, my head out in the cold, the rest of me in the entryway.

He climbed the landing stairs and stared. "You want me to eat out here?"

Twelve? A new personal record for the man!

"Come inside where it's warm." I let him in and pointed to the rug. "Set your boots there and hang up your things. Have a seat at the table once you're done."

I turned on the burner and spooned a dollop of bacon grease into the frying pan. When the fat began to sizzle, I cracked eggs into the pan. "Do you take cream or sugar in your coffee?" I waited for a reply.

None came.

I spoke again, louder this time. "Cream or sugar?"

"Neither, thanks."

Fourteen! Wait a second.

Why did Dick sound like Rick? I washed raw egg off my hands and went to the entryway. There I found the sheriff standing where I had left Dick a spoonful of bacon grease and half a dozen cracked eggs ago. "What did you do with Dick?"

He turned up his palms in a gesture of innocence. "When I came in, he went out."

I went to the living room window and saw Dick throw his shovel in the bed of his pickup truck before he climbed into the cab. "Did he say why?"

"Not a word. I'm on my way to Tipperary and stopped to see if you have any fingerprint results. I didn't mean to interrupt you or upset him."

"Don't worry about it. Maybe he used all the words he had and went to find more."

The eggs sputtered in the pan, and I hurried to the stove. "You can tell me about your visit with Oscar while we eat breakfast. There's plenty for both of us. I'll send a fingerprint report with you."

"I don't have much to tell," Rick said as I filled his coffee mug. "Oscar swears up and down that he was loading his equipment into his Suburban during the time Rocko was attacked. By the way, he refers to the Suburban as his traveling love den."

"Gross."

"He also said he's missing a black dress shoe."

"Did you tell him that I have it?"

"Why would I do that? As far as he's concerned,

you're my girlfriend and have nothing to do with the investigation. I'll return the shoe if and when he's cleared of suspicion."

"And if he is the guy?"

"The prison will issue him shoes." He checked his watch and stood. "I better get going. What do you have for me?"

I got his envelope from the lab and handed it to him.

He held it up. "Thanks for this. And for breakfast. Once we wrap up this case, I'll make things right between you and Dick."

"That could be an awkward conversation. He may not have enough words for it."

"In that case, I'll do the talking." He bopped the top of my head with the envelope and left.

The children began arriving while I was washing dishes. The cold, wintery air carried their high-pitched laughter across the playground and into my kitchen. I dried the frying pan and put it in the cupboard. As I passed from my apartment to the classroom, someone pounded on the door. I opened it and found Tiege and Renny on the landing. Tiege waved a snowy mitten or scarf or stocking cap back and forth under my nose.

"Miss Newell, me and Renny found this by the street."

I grasped his wrist to stop the motion and pushed his hand back a few inches. I recognized the thick hand-knit mitten at once. "Where was it?"

"Over there." Renny pointed to the spot where Dick Phillips had parked his truck earlier that morning.

"I know who it belongs to."

They relinquished it with the speed of children eager

to squeeze in the maximum amount of playtime possible before school. My intention was to ring Betty and ask her to tell Dick where to pick up his mitten. But when I laid it on my kitchen counter to dry, its outline was unmistakable. I took it into the lab, tucked the thumb under the mitten's hand, and laid it on the enlargement of the shadowy shape at the crime scene. The mitten matched the shape of the shadow as perfectly as Oscar's shoe did.

That could explain the increase in Dick's weirdness since Rocko's death. His silence at the café could have been the result of a guilty conscience. Maybe he kept driving by my apartment and shoveled my snow to ease his anxiety regarding the sheriff's movements. And he might have left this morning to get away from Rick and avoid doing something to implicate himself.

I locked the mitten in the lab and smiled. When placed next to the photograph, it had spoken in Dick Phillip's language, screaming "Suspect!" without uttering a word.

CHAPTER 25

When the students came inside a few minutes later, Jeremy yelled, "Kapow!" and flew over the threshold in a single bound. That proved to be the high point of the day for him and his fellow kindergarteners. They were shocked when I announced we were skipping show-and-tell because of the late start.

Winter Skye recovered first. "No show-and-tell? But I brought what me and Dad made in his shop."

My appreciation for school delays that cancelled show-and-tell rose a notch. The kindergarteners had the opposite reaction. They went pale when instructed to open their seatwork folders and start their assignments.

Keeva opened her folder and held up the paper where she was to trace and then practice her name. "Rosalie makes me write my name when we play school. I'm already real good at it."

Grace's disillusionment grew as she worked on a dot to dot. "It's gonna be a cat. How come I gotta finish it?"

Stig replied with lofty, first-grade wisdom, " 'Cause school is your job."

His impression of me was uncanny.

Bennan piped up next. "Jobs are hard work some-times."

Whoa! These upperclassmen were a hard-nosed crowd.

The kindergarteners hunched over their desks, four downtrodden Oliver Twists all in a row. Not one of them held out their seatwork folders and asked, "More, Sir? Can I have some more?"

When lunchtime arrived, they rallied and tore through their food. The day was calm, bright, and above zero. The children fidgeted in their desks until I finished eating and took them out for recess. Liv's students came out at the same time, and the children joined forces to construct snow tunnels.

My mind wandered as I paced the sidewalks Dick Phillips had shoveled. I needed to make a strong case to Rick about why Dick should be named as a suspect. The sheriff held Dick in high regard, but seeing the photo-graph and the mitten placed side by side would give Rick pause. But he was bound to interpret Dick's behavior differently than I did.

Before broaching the matter with Rick, I wanted to talk it over with someone older and wiser. Someone who lived far from Little Missouri, who wasn't chummy with Betty Yarborough and Velma Albright, and who possessed an uncanny ability to detect signs of his kids' guilty consciences. By next recess his afternoon nap would be done, he would feel refreshed, and Mom would still be at school. It was the perfect time to call.

The kindergarteners returned to the classroom, their show-and-tell outrage forgotten. They rolled up their sleeves, paged through old magazines, and cut out pictures to glue on sheets of butcher paper labeled with the consonants they'd learned.

Arming five-year-olds with scissors and glue held numerous inherent risks. However, the time the activity required gave me a chance to take the other students through their social studies lessons. Granted, Grace Berthold squirted glue in her hair more than once despite being coached to point the bottle at the paper instead of her head. On the bright side, no one lost an eye or lock of hair.

When I saw horse pictures—and there were many, many horse pictures—glued beneath "b," "g," and "r," I wondered if the kindergarteners had learned anything since they started school.

"Shouldn't the horses be on the "H" paper?" I asked.

The children exchanged glances. Keeva took up the reins as spokesperson. "B for b-b-brown, g for g-g-grey, and r for r-r-roan."

Less than a month into her school career, and the kid had elementary education major written all over her.

I swallowed a laugh. "I see."

Keeva pointed to the clock. "Do you see what time it is?"

I thought about letting her make the announcement. However, she didn't have enough education to student teach yet, and I didn't have enough experience to supervise her. I did the honors. "Get ready for recess."

The children took forever—at least it felt like forever—to get dressed and go outside. Once they were gone, I raced into my apartment and rang Betty. "Call this number, please."

"Your mother won't be home from schoow yet."

"I'm calling my dad. We're planning a surprise for Mom."

"Weww, I'ww get off the wine after you're connected. What I don't know, I can't repeat."

How often could I use this tactic before Betty got suspicious?

Dad picked up after a few rings. "Harold Newell here."

His clear, crisp speech confirmed that he was rested and alert. "Dad, it's me. I only have a few minutes. Can I ask you a question?"

"Shoot."

"How did you know when Jeanette and Jeff and I were hiding something? You seemed to have a guilty-conscience antenna."

"Are you saying I'm a gnat or a fly?" He chuckled. "Or heaven forbid, a mosquito?"

"Not at all. But it stung when you sussed out the truth."

He laughed again.

"Seriously, Dad. How did you know?"

"My days got a hundred percent more interesting when you kids came home after school. Since I didn't have a job or chores to do or hobbies because of these darn shaky hands of mine, I could watch your expressions and listen to your stories without being distracted. I noticed things like when you did and didn't meet my eyes. The pitch of your voice. A change in posture. The slant you put on a story so you were in a good light and the other person wasn't."

"Anything else?"

"Blushing. Evading questions. Being at a loss for words. Those kinds of behaviors speak volumes."

"How many of those did you need before you suspected we weren't telling the truth?"

"That depended on who it was. You talked all the time, so when you went silent, I knew you were hiding something. Jeff blushed. Jeanette's voice went up an octave. Still, I gave all three of you the benefit of the doubt until the telling details began to add up."

The recess bell began to ring. No! I had more questions.

"My students are coming inside. I have to go."

"So I have to wait for another call to find out what this is really about?"

"I'm afraid so."

"Your voice just went up a notch, Janie-Jo."

"That's Jeanette's tell, not mine."

"And you're not at a loss for words. That's in your favor. Are you blushing?"

"Goodbye, Dad." I hung up and hurried to collect my students.

As I helped Stig work free a stuck coat zipper, Dad's final question reverberated in my thoughts. I wasn't a blusher, but Dick Phillips was. Rick refused to take that behavior seriously. A few of the other tells Dad had mentioned—not meeting my gaze, change in posture or voice timbre, slanting stories—came straight from the Dick Phillips playbook. They had to be things Rick watched for when interrogating suspects. By leading with those when I mentioned Dick to the sheriff, he might come around. I would call after school and invite him to supper. While we ate, I would make my case for adding Dick to the suspect list.

"Miss Newell?" Stig asked. "Please let go."

Let go? Of what?

I came back from the future and discovered my hands still clutching Stig's no longer stuck zipper. I released my grip.

"Sorry, Stig. You caught me in a daydream."

His eyes grew wide as he hung up his coat. "I thought only kids did that kind of stuff." He put his hand in mine as we entered the classroom.

"Lots of grown-ups do too."

"Was your daydream happy?"

"I won't know for sure until later today." I steered him to his desk and announced it was time for science class. To make the time go faster, I took photographs of the children as they did science experiments in small groups.

An hour later, school ended and the children put on their things and went out the door.

Finally, I could call Rick. But a glance out the window sent me in search of my coat and hat instead. The country kids were milling around the playground and their parents' outfits were nowhere to be seen. I put on my winter things and went outside to supervise until their parents arrived.

A wind gust snatched my breath away. Snow swirled around the playground and swept across the street. If it was this bad in town, it had to be worse in the country. No wonder the parents were running late. And if they didn't make it to town, their kids would have to stay with me tonight. Then I would have to tell Stig that my daydream hadn't been happy. What I wouldn't mention was that it was terrifying.

CHAPTER 26

Cookie was the first to show up almost ten minutes later. She pulled up beside the snowbank on the edge of the street and rolled down her window. "Visibility is terrible. It's gonna take people a bit to get here."

In a single breath, I cursed the weather for interfering with the investigation and thanked God for deliverance from what would have been the worst indoor camping adventure ever.

Tiege shot across the playground faster than an Olympic luge athlete. "Can I drive home? Dad said it's 'bout time for me to learn how to drive in snow."

"This ride's gonna be plenty interesting without you at the wheel. Now get in the passenger seat and fasten your seatbelt."

After she and Tiege left, I prayed for Elva, Stig, and Winter Skye's parents to remain safe on their way to collect their children. God answered in his own sweet time. Once the playground was empty, I sent Keeva to her mom's classroom. Then I slogged inside and asked Betty to connect me to Rick.

"He and his deputy got their hands fuww keeping foows off the roads. They'ww be at it from now untiw morning. Is it an emergency?"

My heart said you're darn tootin' it's an emergency. But my brain said the bad weather was keeping our suspects, even those who blush, from going much of anywhere.

"No," I whined. I hung up and cursed the weather. When that got old, I prepared for Friday and wrote lesson plans for next week. I wanted tomorrow evening to be free for my meeting with Rick, which was going to take place if I had to steal a snowmobile and drive it to Tipperary.

I talked myself down from that ledge before supper. Afterwards I made a batch of chocolate chip oatmeal cookies. If the sheriff didn't buy into my reasons for Dick becoming a suspect, maybe cookies would persuade him. It was worth a shot.

The next morning, the aroma of freshly baked cookies still lingered in my apartment. I hustled through my morning routine and opened the living room curtains to check the weather. Every now and then, a pickup truck rumbled by. The traffic moved faster than the previous afternoon. From the looks of things, the roads had improved.

I rang Betty. "Would you leave a message for Rick, wherever he may be?"

"You can count on me, Miss Neweww!"

"Tell him to call me at the school right away."

"Concerning what?" She oozed curiosity.

The school bell began to ring, and I blessed Liv McDonald's punctual heart. "Gotta go, Betty. The kids are lining up."

Rick called smack dab in the middle of the first graders' math lesson.

"Are you free tonight?" I asked as the children eavesdropped.

"I am," answered Rick as Betty and who knew how many people on the party line listened in.

"Can you come for supper?"

"When?"

"Five thirty."

"I'll be there."

The children were long gone when Rick arrived.

He gestured at the steady stream of traffic inching along Main Street. "What's going on tonight?"

"Us." I stepped onto the landing and waved like a homecoming queen.

He pulled me back inside. "You are incorrigible."

"They came for a show, and I want them to get their money's worth."

I set out supper while he hung up his things. He tried to discuss the case while we ate, but I insisted on waiting until afterwards. He would be more inclined to view my argument favorably with his belly full of spaghetti with marinara sauce and salad.

After the meal, we went into the lab. I set Dick's mitten and the photo enlargement side by side on the worktable, folded the mitten thumb under the hand, and laid it on top of the photo.

Rick rocked back on his heels. "Will you look at that? It's as good a match as Oscar's shoe. How long have you had it?"

"Since yesterday morning. The kids found it on the playground and brought it inside."

"Do you know who it belongs to?"

"I think Dick Phillips dropped it after he finished shoveling snow before school."

Rick spoke sharply. "Dick is not a killer. You're barking up the wrong tree, Jane."

"That may be so, but I had to show it to you. Otherwise I would be withholding possible evidence."

He rubbed his face and exhaled. "You're right."

"Should we continue this conversation over coffee and dessert?"

I waited to say more until we were seated at the kitchen table with mugs in hand and a plate of chocolate chip cookies before us.

I broke a cookie in two and dunked one half in my coffee. "How do you decide if a person you're questioning is telling the truth or holding out on you? What do you key in on?"

"Are you talking about witnesses or suspects?"

"Either."

He set down his mug and laced his fingers together. "Innocent people usually look me in the eye. I'm suspicious when someone doesn't."

"Anything else?"

"The classic stuff they teach at the academy. Watch a person's posture. Pay attention to the pitch, cadence, and speed of their voice. Look for deviations from how someone usually interacts. That kind of thing. Now, none of that amounts to a hill of beans without anything to support it."

"So Oscar Rumble is a possible suspect because of the shoe I found?"

"That, and he was in Little Missouri the night of the murder. He was also highly evasive when I questioned him."

"What about Scott Gibson?"

"Again, he was in town the night Rocko died. He couldn't hardly look me in the eye when I interviewed him and Dan Barkley. His feud with Rocko is well-documented, as is his odd behavior. All that combined warrants further investigation."

I put an elbow on the table and rested my chin on my hand. "Hmm. You know, Dick Phillips hasn't looked me in the eye since Rocko's death. He tracks my whereabouts at all hours, which is a change in his routine. And even though the two of you are friends, when you stopped by the other day, he took off for no obvious reason." I dunked the other half of my cookie and ate it. "Can I ask you something?"

"Go ahead."

"Did you ask him to keep an eye on me after Rocko died? Like you did after Edgar Running Horse was killed?"

"No."

"Then based on his recent actions and the evidence in the lab, why isn't Dick a suspect along with Scott and Oscar?"

He stared into his mug for a long minute before he stood. "Bag and label the mitten and write up your report. Then put everything in the case file and add Dick to the suspect list. I'll see myself out."

He left without a good-bye. I went to the lab and did as Rick had asked. When I locked the case file back in the cabinet, I felt no elation over besting Rick at his own game. Instead, I felt as though I'd won a battle that didn't need fighting and lost the war we needed to win.

CHAPTER 27

The next morning, I waffled between having oatmeal chocolate chip cookies dipped in milk or oatmeal drowning in chocolate chips and fresh cream for breakfast. My hand was lifting the lid from the cookie jar when the phone rang. I picked up and mumbled a distracted hello.

"Oh for heaven's sake, Jane! Speak clearly."

I plunked down the lid like a five-year-old caught in the act. The five hundred and fifty miles between us hadn't dulled her ability to guard the cookie jar. "Hello to you too, Mom."

"Oh. Hello. Your dad watched the KELOLAND News out of Sioux Falls last night. That weatherman said that northwest South Dakota had quite the snowstorm earlier this week."

I squinted at the scene outside the living room windows. The glitter of sunlight reflecting off the snow made my eyes water. "He heard right. I'll go outside with my camera later and take some pictures to send you. It kinda looks like the Arctic Circle out here."

Mom sniffed. "Well, you are practically in Canada."

"North Dakotans might have something to say about that."

"North Dakota. South Dakota. What's the difference? They're both a long way from us."

I moved on. "At least the snow waited until after Tuesday's dance lesson. Did I tell you that Gus and Betty Yarborough are coming?"

"You didn't, but Betty did. She explained how Gus does it, but I couldn't quite follow."

"I'ww teww you again." Betty co-opted the conversation for the next five minutes.

Once Mom caught on, she asked Betty to repeat it to Dad. "I could never in a million years explain it like you do, Betty."

I listened in, delighted by Dad's snorts and chuckles that increased in volume and frequency the longer Betty talked.

Eventually Mom cut Betty off. "Harold is laughing so hard he's crying again. I have to help him blow his nose. Goodbye, Jane."

"Bye, Mom. Tell Dad goodbye too." I hung up, quite proud of how I'd kept Mom from obsessing about the distance between Little Missouri and Sioux City. Feeling hungry again, I opened the cookie jar. The phone rang. I examined the lid for a hidden motion sensor before picking up the phone.

"Hi Mom."

"Miss Neweww, I'm fwattered to be mistaken for your wonderfuw mother."

"You're welcome."

"Doris doesn't know I'm cawwing." She barked her next sentence with the ferocity of a drill sergeant. "Everybody wistening in better hang up immediatewy." She waited until the flurry of receivers settling into their cradles ceased before continuing. "I have a confidentiaw matter to discuss with you and hope you take it the right way."

How had I evaded Mom's scrutiny only to be subject to Betty's?

"I hope so too."

"You know that your mother howds a poor opinion of Sheriff Sternquist."

She caught me off guard, and I replied with caution. "I do."

"You and the sheriff have been spending pwenty of time together since square dance wessons began, haven't you?"

Now I had an inkling of where she was going with this. Again, I replied cautiously. "We have."

"What many people of Wittwe Missouri consider to be an inappropriate amount of time?"

It was time to throw caution to the wind. "Why should it matter to them, and what does any of this have to do with my mother?"

"Because there's some people—and mind you I don't agree with them—who are tawking about running you outta this town unwess he puts an engagement ring on your finger reaw soon."

I retraced our conversation. Mom's opinion of Rick. My relationship with him. The gossip around town. A possible engagement. Then I circled around to Mom once more.

"You're worried about how Mom will react if Rick asks me to marry him?"

"Yes." Her single word was laden with relief.

"Stop worrying, Betty. My relationship with Rick doesn't include a marriage proposal be—"

"Then prepare to wose your job."

"Please let me finish." Leaving nothing out, I told her the truth about Rick's frequent visits and our late nights together.

The decision was a gamble made without consulting Rick. He had every right to consider what I'd done a breach of trust. But I didn't think he would. We knew we were the talk of Little Missouri and Tipperary County. We'd taken Mrs. Dremstein into our confidence so she could do damage control. Adding Betty to the team meant she could do the same.

There were other benefits to having Betty on our side, and they far outweighed any negative reaction Rick might have to my unilateral decision. As the switchboard operator, she could coax those who wanted me fired to stand down. As an insider, she was far less likely to let anything slip about me and Rick during her phone tête-à-têtes with Mom and Velma. Plus, Betty could relay messages between Rick and me as well as clear the lines when necessary. Really, I told myself while waiting for Betty's reaction to what she'd just heard, we should have recruited her sooner.

"It's a tough assignment. You can't tell anyone, not even Gus, what Rick and I are actually up to. And I'm not sure anyone can quell the rumbling around town. I understand if you don't want to become involved."

"You can count on me to manage the situation as wong as I'm needed, Miss Neweww. A murder investigation is not to be taken wightwy." The phone line crackled with solemnity and purpose.

Yes!

We talked strategy a few minutes. I volunteered to explain Betty's involvement to Rick in person tomorrow. She volunteered to confirm he would be attending church. We hammered out a few more details. When the call finally ended, I was ravenous and made oatmeal. The phone didn't ring when I removed two cookies from the jar and crumbled them on my hot cereal. I ate breakfast in peace.

Fortified by a healthy meal, I got ready to go outside, looped the strap of the new camera around my neck, and entered the wild blue and white yonder. I clumped around town, taking pictures of towering snowbanks and eerie drift formations set against a clear winter-blue sky. It was the perfect way to spend a Saturday morning until Dick Phillips and his pickup truck neared the intersection where I stood. He steered his outfit in the opposite direction, and I climbed on a drift to photograph the overhang of snow on Snippy's barn. I ignored Dick's second pass along Main Street, but when he did it a third time, I quickly shot the remainder of my roll of film and went home.

Dick drove slowly by while I stood on the landing and fished my apartment key from my pocket. Was he watching me or searching for his missing mitten? Whatever he was up to, it wasn't going to ruin my Saturday. I went to the darkroom and made negatives from the rolls of film I'd shot this morning and during science class earlier in the week. Later, as I made prints, I released my worries about Dick's behavior and how Rick would react when he heard that Betty was in on our secret.

Let tomorrow take care of tomorrow, I whispered while images of little children and towering snow sculptures emerged from the papers in their chemicals bath. *This is beauty sufficient for today.*

Chapter 28

Sunday morning dawned calm and clear and cold. On the way to my car, I raised my face to the sun and relished the feel of its feeble rays on my skin. The drive to church took longer than usual. The snow piles at the intersections were taller than the Beetle, so I crept into each one and beeped the horn to announce my arrival.

I parked and entered the foyer curious about the reception I'd receive. Betty's assignment was less than twenty-four hours old, perhaps not enough time for her to win over my detractors. My main item of business was to catch Rick and tell him what I'd done before he caught wind of it himself and started looking for the mole in our spy ring.

Cookie came up and wrapped me in a hug. "You picked quite the year for your first winter in Little Missouri. They're not all like this."

"Will Rick be here?"

"He should be. He stayed in Tipperary last night, but I think the roads are okay today."

"Hi, Jane!" Pam Barkley greeted me like a long-lost relative. "We haven't had you over for Sunday dinner since before Christmas vacation. Can you come next week?"

Her invitation revealed the hidden cost of my partnership with Rick. Keeping up our sham romance had taken the place of meals in my students' homes, non-skid pancakes and Snippy updates with Merle, and impromptu slumber parties at Velma's house. Okay, I could do without that last one, but I missed the others. I also realized that twenty-four hours had provided ample time for Betty to instigate a slow thaw, though I couldn't fathom her tactics. She'd vowed not to mention the forensic lab in the apartment, my official connection to the investigation, and the romantic hoax Rick and I were perpetrating. What did that leave her to work with?

Rick entered the foyer and stopped to chat with Dan Barkley and Garth Swensen. I accepted Pam's invitation, gave her a side hug, and caught his eye in the process. I tipped my head toward the kitchen and mouthed, "We have to talk."

He finished up with Dan and Garth and then sauntered into the kitchen. I chatted with Pam and Cookie until she excused herself and went to the sanctuary to begin the piano prelude. I told Pam to save me a seat while I hung up my coat—which I did—and visited the restroom—which I did not. Instead, I joined Rick in the kitchen and told him about Betty.

"I'm sorry I didn't run it by you first."

"I believe I've done the same thing to you now and then."

True.

He scratched his head. "Sometimes you have to act and hope your partner understands."

"And you do? Understand, I mean?"

"Uh-huh. Hey, should we take advantage of the break in the weather to drive up to Bowman for dinner and a movie? Maybe sniff out some Oscar scuttlebutt?"

"Sounds great. Pick me up at my apartment after church?"

"See you then."

I left for the sanctuary where Pam had indeed saved me a seat. Rick entered a few minutes later and sat in front of us with his parents. My attention remained focused on the service through the hymns and the prayers. It waned, as it almost always did, when Pastor Petersen began the sermon. So little of what he said seemed relevant to my life. I was midway through an embarrassingly wide yawn when Pastor Petersen read two verses that spoke directly to me.

"Jesus then said to the Jews who had believed in him, 'If you continue in my word, you are truly my disciples, and you will know the truth, and the truth will make you free.' "

Since I'd set foot in Little Missouri last August, I had come to believe that Jesus was real. Except for the twenty times a day when doubt crept in. Even so, I would continue to trust in him while looking for the truth about Rocko's death. Once Rick and I found that truth, justice could be done, and we could be truthful about the nature of our relationship. Knowing the truth and living it, I was beginning to believe, was good for the soul.

After the service, Rick took off without a backward glance. I left shortly thereafter and parked beside the sheriff's vehicle outside my apartment. Rick hopped out and motioned for me to roll down my window.

"Let's caravan to Tipperary. You can park your car at my house, and we'll drive to Bowman together. It'll save me some miles after our date."

I rolled up the window, he climbed into his vehicle, and we were off. I focused on Rick's rear bumper until my car was parked beside his house and I was in his passenger seat. Only then could I marvel at the white landscape stretching in every direction and the otherworldly snow formations in the ditches. They were mesmerizing.

I was disappointed when we reached Bowman's downtown and Rick pulled into a parking spot in front of the Silver Dollar Bar and Grill. It occupied a corner lot like Round the Bend. However, it was slightly larger and spiffier than that establishment. The vehicles surrounding it were slightly less battered than their Little Missouri counterparts. Perhaps because the streets around it were paved and plowed.

Rick held my elbow, and we minced across the snow-packed sidewalk. I glanced over my shoulder. "Is your vehicle going to scare away the clientele?"

"That's what I'm hoping." He held the door and then steered me toward a booth with a clear sightline to the formidable brunette behind the bar. "A small crowd means more opportunities to chat up the bartender and our waitress. I hear Oscar Rumble's burned bridges with both of them."

"Ah." I slid the menu out from under the ketchup and mustard bottles. "This could be interesting."

A young woman with flaming red hair set glasses of water in front of us. "Where you from?"

Rick smiled. "Little Missouri."

"You drove here in this cold? On a Sunday? What for?"

"Heard there's new movie at the theater."

"*Star Wars*?" She grew animated. "I've seen it twice, but some folks say it's sorta far-fetched. All them space cowboys and such."

"We're gonna take in the matinee as long as the wind doesn't come up."

"Then I better take your order so you get to the theater right on time." She pulled a pad and pen from her apron pocket and scribbled down the Sunday pork chop dinner special for Rick and a chef's salad with dressing on the side for me. Sunday penance for Saturday's cookie-laced oatmeal.

While we waited for our food, Rick sauntered to the bar and slid onto a high metal stool with a black vinyl seat. The bartender gave a happy yelp, hurried over, and clasped his hand in both of hers. She frowned. He gestured to me. She sized me up. Her frown deepened. I waved. She didn't. Rick said something more. She gave him an earful and glanced my way again. I extricated myself from our three-way exchange by staring out the window. I was looking at nothing when Rick returned and the waitress delivered our orders.

I picked up the little pitcher of dressing and poured a thin stream on my salad. "I see you and the bartender are pals. She had plenty to say."

"Her name is Barbara. She said Oscar's been talking up some young schoolteacher from Little Missouri who's taking square dance lessons and a lot more from him. He says the two of them have a thing going."

"What?" The pitcher in my hand tipped and flooded my salad. "The man is delusional scum."

"Barbara holds the same opinion. She says he's all hands and don't you dare get caught in a dark corner with him."

"Her concern is appreciated but unnecessary. I can handle Oscar Octopus."

Rick was taking a sip of coffee just then, and a tiny stream came out his nose when he coughed. Quite impressive. He recovered and went on. "She says he's famous for threatening to take out anyone who horns in on his latest love interest."

I looked at Rick. "Rocko and I were together a lot the first night. Oscar must have seen us. Do you think he . . ." My words trailed off.

"There's no way to know and every reason to investigate that possibility. We now have a motive for Oscar in addition to opportunity. All we need is a method and we can celebrate the end of this case." He picked up his water glass and clinked it against mine.

I picked up my fork and attacked my salad. "We better eat fast so we don't miss the start of the movie. I don't think it's going to be my thing, but who cares? Our trip to Bowman is already a success. Space cowboys, here we come!"

CHAPTER 29

"Wait a minute." Sunshine assaulted my eyes as we left the dim theater. The brightness made them water. I swiped the tears away with my glove as I left outer space and returned to the cold Dakota winter.

Rick passed over his handkerchief and zipped his parka. "The waitress got it right. Cowboys in space."

"Right down to Han Solo's Millennium Falcon." I gestured at the pickup trucks we were walking by. "It's as much of a beater as these are."

We discussed the movie all the way to Tipperary. He pulled up beside my car and waited until the Beetle's engine sputtered to life and turned over. I pulled out, stopped at the gas station to fill my tank, and drove home. When I entered my apartment, I stayed at the window waiting for Dick Phillips and his truck to make an appearance. The phone rang before he showed up, and I gave up my vigil.

My "Hello, this is Jane" collided with a wet, whistly schlep. I waited for Merle to speak. He waited for who knew what—divine intervention, for Betty to call him an old coot, for me to say I was hungry and would he fix supper—the possibilities were endless.

"You been avoiding me, Teacher?"

"Just keeping busy. Dance lessons and work. You know."

"You got any openings this week to eat non-skid pancakes with an old man?"

My stomach growled. I'd burned through my chef's salad while helping Princess Leah escape those stormtrooper guys in the weird white armor. "How about in a half hour?"

"Come on over." He hung up.

I made sure my classroom was ready for the next day. Then I went into the lab, typed up the bartender's conversation, and added it to the case file. I took a minute to review my notes on Scott, Dick, and Oscar. Merle liked to drop cryptic tidbits about people, and I wanted to be ready to take full advantage of them. Then I was off to Merle's house for non-skid pancakes, bacon, and a side of gossip.

Merle served up all three in rapid succession. I was pouring syrup on my waffles when he asked, "Them kind-ee-gartners behaving?"

"They are."

"Even that Gibson boy?"

"Yes." I bent over my plate so Merle wouldn't see my smile. He was making this easy. "His name is Jeremy, by the way. What about him?"

"We-ull." Merle bit the end off a strip of bacon and motioned with what remained. "His daddy's got a reputation as a hothead. I come upon him in the Long

Pines last fall. Heard him shouting before I seen him. He was going at that Rocko kid, cussing and threatening to remove certain parts of his anatomy. Didn't leave much to the imagination, I can tell you that. I know better than to poke a bear, so I stayed put in some brush 'til they cleared out."

"You should tell the sheriff what you saw."

"He's been a hard man to get a hold of since you got home after Christmas. Could you maybe pass it along when you see him next?"

I agreed. By the end of the meal, he'd passed along a pitcherful of juicy gossip. Garth and Galva Swensen were having money troubles. Dan Barkley had applied for a transfer to the Forest Service in the Black Hills. Somebody had been messing with the new trap lines Reek Dupee set out. The Sternquists had come upon one of their steers dead in the forest land near their ranch. Merle ran out of gossip, and my stomach ran out of room simultaneously. I helped with dishes, he loaded me up with two dozen eggs and a gallon of milk, and I went to my lab to add what he'd said to the case file.

For the next two days, keeping up with my students left little time for the investigation. Rick didn't call to say he was picking me up Tuesday evening. At about six thirty, I was arranging cookies on a plate when a loud knock sounded at the door. The unexpected noise sent me straight toward the ceiling. Heart pounding, I cracked the door open and peered out.

"Hi," Rick said.

"You scared me half to death," I snapped and then softened. "Merle said your folks had a dead steer at their place. What happened?"

"Another livestock killing. I asked Dad and Mom to keep that detail to themselves for now to give us some breathing room. Other than that, I've been following Oscar Rumble's dance lesson trail and calling law enforcement in every county he's visited in the last five years."

"I want to hear more about the steer and Oscar."

"Are you okay walking over to the dance hall since it's not too cold? I want you and nobody else to hear what they said. It's an earful."

"Sure."

He grabbed the plate of cookies, I locked the apartment, and he filled me in as we dawdled our way to through town.

Law enforcement officials in three states and dozens of counties had confirmed Barbara's story. On numerous occasions, Oscar had threatened violence against men who showed an interest in the women he was chasing. He got hauled in after the occasional fight, but very few of the women and even fewer men made a complaint. None had filed charges against him. Everyone interviewed believed Oscar had it in him to kill Rocko.

As we neared the hall, I passed along what Merle had said about Rocko and Scott. "Maybe we should skip the lesson, go to my apartment, and decide how to follow up on what we've learned."

"We do that, and we'll lose the goodwill Betty's been manufacturing. The best way forward is to go inside, dance like we're in love, and wait for the perpetrator to let something slip."

"In that case, let's keep the suspects close at hand. I'll invite the Gibsons to join our square. You ask Dick

Phillips. I'll observe them while you keep an eye on Oscar."

"That'll do."

We entered the hall, and I scanned the crowd to see who was there. Scott and Linda Gibson stood with Bud and Cookie near the stage. Perfect! I went over to chat with them, and then Oscar instructed us to form squares right off the bat. I invited the Gibsons and Rick's parents to join our square directly in front of the stage. Rick brought Dick over, along with young Rosalie McDonald, and we were in business.

Oscar ran us through every step he'd taught thus far. As he called the dance, I clasped hands with Rick, then Bud, then Scott, then Dick. Rick met my eye. Bud winked. Scott looked away and scowled. Dick did the same and added a blush. As the evening progressed, our square entered into an easy, shared rhythm. Except for Dick. He remained off-kilter, an interloper among us.

At the end of the lesson, Rosalie stood on her tiptoes and put her mouth close to my ear. "What's wrong with Mr. Phillips? He's acting like he killed Rocko Vander Meer."

Had her parents not come to collect her, Rosalie might have solved the case then and there. I hurried over to Rick, and we hurried to put on our coats and get outside, far from Oscar Rumble's long, lecherous reach.

On the walk home, I described Dick and Scott's behavior. Nothing new there. What he said about Oscar, on the other hand, was concerning.

"He watched our square almost exclusively. Ninety percent of the time, his eyes followed you and whomever you were dancing with. I held you kinda close now and then to see how he would react."

"And did he?" We climbed the steps to my apartment landing and stood in the glow cast by the overhead light.

"I'll put it this way." Rick scanned the darkness. His words came out low and tense. "If looks could kill, we'd both be dead."

Chapter 30

What Rick had learned from his inquiries, along with his concerns about Oscar's obsession with me put me on high alert for several days. I did several things to cope. First, I threw myself into teaching. When my students left, I locked the doors and distracted myself by creating the most inventive lessons and centers I could conjure. Then I locked myself in the lab and combed through the case notes and photographs looking for leads we might have missed. Any remaining waking hours were spent eating meals next to my window, where I watched for any indication that Oscar Rumble or Dick Phillips had me under surveillance.

Rick continued to pursue leads through official channels. I expected him to show up any minute with evidence in need of fingerprinting, photographing, and analyzing. Or to call with a cryptic update only Betty and I would understand. Two days later, I'd heard nothing. I gave him another day of grace, and then I was done waiting. After school on Friday, I picked up the phone.

"Would you connect me with the sheriff's office, Betty?"

"Rick's out of town on business."

"When will he be back?"

"From what I overheard . . . um, understand . . . he wiww return Saturday evening."

"Do you know where he is?"

"I bewieve he is meeting with some Forest Service bigwigs in the Bwack Hiwws." Her voice grew hushed. Confidential. "Is this rewated to our investigation? Wouwd you wike me to track him down and dewiver a message?"

In a split second, I composed one message after another in my head.

Why haven't you touched base since Tuesday? *Too desperate.*

When are you standing up to Dan and Scott and telling me their secret? *Too confidential.*

Why didn't you tell me about this big Forest Service meeting? *Too ignorant.*

Why are you not treating me as an equal partner? *Too whiny.*

I tossed my musing into the air like so much mental confetti.

"Thanks the offer, Betty, but no. There's too much risk of it falling into the wrong hands and jeopardizing the investigation."

"You are absowutewy right, Miss Neweww. Does the sheriff know what a vawuabwe partner you are?"

No, he does not, I thought, as I bade her a sweet and cheery good-bye. *Not at all.*

During the weekend, I put most of my energy into revealing nothing of substance to Mom during our Saturday morning phone call and putzing in my classroom. I wasted what little energy remained keeping watch at my window in case Oscar or Dick made an appearance. I abandoned my post after Dick Phillips crawled by in his truck for the umpteenth time early Saturday evening. If Oscar was around, Dick's presence would either scare him off or provoke a fight. In either case, my watchfulness was superfluous. I made sure that every exterior door was locked and then laid out clothes for church tomorrow and the work week. After that I made popcorn and spent a few minutes searching for something good to watch on television. When that didn't pan out, I picked up *Whose Body?* and escaped with Sir Peter Wimsey to London for the rest of the evening.

✳✳✳

The sun was shining and the thermometer read twenty degrees above zero when I stepped outside. I threw caution to the wind, of which there was not the tiniest whisper, and walked to church. The air as fresh and crisp as peppermint candy, and I breathed in great lungfuls of it. The beautiful day seemed to have the same effect on others, too. We greeted one another with giddy cheer and talked in the foyer until the prelude called us into the sanctuary.

Only Dick Phillips acted out of sorts. He watched out of the corner of his eye when I took my seat between

Cora and Bennan Barkley in the second-to-the-last pew. I watched out of the corner of my eye as he blushed and slipped into place behind us.

In my book, it was a good place for him. He was out of sight and at the same time created a human shield between me and Oscar, should he put in an appearance. A highly unlikely event, since "There's Somethin' 'Bout You Baby I Like" wasn't in the hymnal.

I didn't think of either man again until the service ended and the sanctuary emptied. Dick moved to a corner of the foyer and glowered while the Bertholds, Barkleys, Borgesons, and I visited. When I left with the Barkleys for Sunday dinner, Dick's glower was still going strong.

The aroma of pot roast hung in the air when we entered the Barkleys' mudroom and hung up our coats. All except for Dan who said he had to get something from his office and would be back in time for dinner. Pam went to the kitchen and pulled the roasting pan from the oven.

"How can I help?" I asked.

"Make the gravy?"

I'd eaten many meals with the Barkleys and knew how Pam arranged her cupboard. I took a Tupperware gravy shaker from a cupboard and added flour from the canister on the counter and water from the faucet. After securing the lid, I looked out the window above the sink and shook the mixture. Several official Forest Service pickup trucks were in the parking lot behind the office building. Tucked between two of them was the official Tipperary County Sheriff's Department pickup truck.

What was Rick doing there, and why was he doing it

without me? I shook the flour and water mixture and repeated the question in my head. With each word, I shook harder. At the word "me," the lid popped open. Flour water exploded everywhere.

"I'm so sorry!" I gasped and snatched the dishcloth from the sink.

Pam ran water into a bucket and grabbed another dishcloth. "No big deal. It's not a normal day around here without something to clean up."

A few minutes later, we'd mopped up the mess. I stole a glance out the window. Rick's truck was still in the parking lot. I mixed more flour water. The truck was still there. I made the gravy. Still there. I poured it into the serving bowl and set it on the table as the Barkleys' back door squeaked open and shut. Dan came into the dining room, and we all sat down to eat.

"Cora, it's your turn to say grace," Pam prompted.

We bowed our heads, and Cora began. "Dear God, thank you for my princess dress and for Daddy's safe trip to Rapid City with the sheriff yesterday and for glitter shoes and Miss Newell eating with us." She paused.

"Bless the food," muttered Bennan. "I'm hungry."

"Bless the potatoes and gravy and pie for dessert," Cora sighed. "Amen."

Pam picked up the meat platter. "Have some pot roast, Jane. It's hot on the bottom so hold it on the side."

I took the platter as instructed and forked a tender piece of meat onto my plate. When I passed the platter to Dan, he looked at it and not at me. I held onto it until he met my gaze. I raised an eyebrow and smiled. "Anything new happening at work?" Then I surrendered the platter. "The underside of this thing is hot. Watch what you're doing."

He ignored my warning and touched the bottom with his bare hand. "Ouch!" he yelped.

Served him right.

Chapter 31

Dan made himself scarce while Cora, Bennan, and I played several hands of Uno. When the game ended, they presented me with a stack of pictures they'd drawn. That hatched an idea.

"Do you have a piece of scrap paper? And a dark crayon?" Adhering to the strict childhood code of justice, the first request went to Cora and the second to Bennan. I scribbled a note for Rick to please call or stop after his meeting. I returned Bennan's crayon, shouted a quick thank you to Pam, and made a quick getaway. My stroll home detoured through the Forest Service parking lot. Rick's vehicle was still there. He'd been inside for two hours at the least. How much did they have to talk about? I stuck the note under the driver's side windshield wiper where he couldn't miss it. I didn't think he'd have the gall to ignore it.

I was wrong. Rick didn't show up before I went to bed at ten. He didn't call during school on Monday or when he knew I was available in the evening. The man had an abundance of gall.

By Tuesday morning, my temper was running hot. I can't say for certain that it directly influenced Tuesday's weather, but it might have. The temperature hit freezing at lunchtime. By the time I supervised afternoon recess, the mercury had reached forty degrees. I stomped through a puddle of slush and checked my watch. Two fifteen and time for the kids to go inside. I took the school bell from the pocket of my parka and rang it. Thinking about Rick's silent treatment made me ring it harder and faster.

"Jeesh, Miss Newell." Renny gave me a wide berth as he lined up. "You're gonna hurt somebody with that."

At least I think that's what he said. The bell was ringing too loud to be sure. I motioned for Elva, who stood first in line, to hold the door as her classmates filed in. I followed the children inside. Still fuming about Rick, I slammed the door.

"My hand!" Elva snatched it away and covered it with her other one. Tears sprang to her eyes. "Why did you do that, Miss Newell?"

"I didn't . . . I . . . let me see." Gently, I coaxed her good hand away from the injured one and examined the damage. The tip of her index finger was discolored and beginning to swell.

"Tiege, get the ice cube tray from my kitchen freezer and the dishtowel beside the sink." While he fetched them, I eased Elva's arm out of her coat and told the other children to color at their desks once their coats and boots were put away.

Tiege returned with the tray, took an empty sandwich bag from his lunchbox, popped a couple ice cubes into it, and handed it to me. I wrapped it in the dishtowel and showed Elva how to hold it in place.

Tiege spoke solemnly. "That'll make it feel better, Elva. So will the horse I'm gonna draw for you."

"Make it a paint," she said before obeying my request for her to flex her fingers and show me her palm.

When I was certain her injury was limited to her index finger, I settled her at her desk and called her mother. "I wasn't paying attention," I told Mary. "It's all my fault."

She brushed away my confession. "Don't beat yourself up. I'll be there quick as I can. Keep ice on it."

Between when she hung up and when she arrived, I'd freshened Elva's ice pack once and beaten myself up more times than I could count.

Mary swept in and examined her daughter's finger. "No permanent harm done and no need to take you home early. I'll splint it so it's protected, but you'll be good as new in a day or two. I'll wait in the truck until school gets out."

My guilt went into remission, and I was able to focus on our science experiment about water and surface tension. I handed out jars of bubbles so the kids could observe the phenomena. Elva rallied and abandoned her ice pack for a bubble wand.

When the children left and the classroom grew quiet at day's end, my guilt returned. I replayed the moment when the door slammed. In the worst way, I wanted to blame the incident on Rick's silence. Had he called as he should have, I wouldn't have become angry, and the incident wouldn't have happened. He really did bear partial responsibility. Only really, he didn't. The children were my responsibility during the school day. So was controlling my own emotions.

That's not my strong suit, I confessed once I quit hoping beyond hope that the God who saw all things had been too busy to notice me earlier in the day. *I can't do it myself. Will you help me? Forgive me?*

As my mind calmed, I realized that the consequences of my failings didn't mean excusing Rick's lack of communication. We needed to talk about why he'd avoided me for an entire week. I would insist on hashing things out after square dance lessons tonight however long that might take.

I sat down at my desk and stayed there until everything was ready for the next day. There was a good chance I would need to sleep in later than normal tomorrow morning.

***

When Rick didn't arrive to pick me up by six fifty-five, I hoofed it to the dance hall. He wasn't there either. I trotted over to where the Yarboroughs and Gibsons were engrossed in conversation and tapped Betty's shoulder. "Will you save a spot for us in your square? Bring the Gibsons and drag Dick Phillips along if you can."

"Absowutewy." She scanned the room. "Rick said he's coming."

How nice of him to tell Betty and not me.

I waited by the door until he ambled in at seven-oh-one and matched him step for step as he took care of his coat. "I don't know where you've been, but don't think about leaving town until after you tell me why tonight." I turned and led him to our square where we danced in snarky silence the whole night through. He went one way during the short break, and I went another. There had to be a country western song about our situation, but I didn't know what it was.

Scott Gibson seemed to be ignoring Rick as diligently as I was. That was new. Dick, whose partner was the finger-splinted Elva, blushed in time to the music and met neither my eye nor Rick's. Betty and Gus danced flawlessly and were the only couple in our square who acted like they were having fun.

After the lesson ended, I grabbed Rick's hand and didn't let go. Except for when we put on our coats. Then I stepped on his foot to keep him from sneaking away. After our coats were on, I took his arm and pushed him outside where he tried to pull away. I applied what I like to think of as non-liquid surface tension and held on tight.

He gave up. "What's gotten into you?"

"You're the one who's been avoiding me for days. Don't bother asking me questions until you explain what you've been doing since last Tuesday."

"Can I start by saying I'm sorry?"

Surprise loosened my grip. "It's a good place to start. Just don't end there." I reestablished my grip, clinging to him like a lovestruck teenager on the walk home. Once in my apartment, I thought about handcuffing him to the stove until he came clean. But no. One scratch on the oven door, and Velma would be all over it.

I motioned for Rick to sit in the kitchen chair farthest from the exit, turned on the kettle, and thumped a plate of cookies in front of him. "Now, tell me what you've been doing."

He downed a cookie before he began. "Dad found another dead steer last Wednesday when he checked stock."

"Was it like the one he found before?"

"Exactly the same. The only difference between these two killings and the ones that came beforehand was where they happened. The others took place on Forest Service land. These last two occurred on privately owned land. I spent most of Thursday trying to track the bastard who did it. Between the cattle trampling the snow and constant drifting, I quit trying and photographed the area instead."

He dug in his pocket and set a roll of film on the table. "I was gonna give this to you on Friday so you could make prints over the weekend. Late Thursday night, Dan Barkley called and threw a wrench into the works. The Forest Service higher-ups in the Hills had called a hush-hush confab, and he'd been ordered to get me there by eight on Friday morning."

The kettle whistled, and I rose to make tea. "Why did you have to be there?"

He held up a finger. "I'll get to that in a minute. First you should know that Dan and I were in the Hills Friday and Saturday. We came back late Saturday night. I spent Sunday in more meetings at the Forest Service office here. There was a bad accident on Highway 85 Sunday night, so me and my deputy had to deal with that. Monday I was on the phone about Oscar Rumble. Today I directed traffic on Highway 20 while ranchers rounded up cattle that had wandered onto the road because the snowdrifts were covering fence lines."

I put a mug of tea in front of him. He dunked his cookie and ate it in one bite. "Now ask your questions."

"Why didn't you call from the Hills on Friday evening?"

"Dan and I shared a room. I didn't want him listening in."

"Why didn't Dan go to the Sunday meetings with you?"

"I can't tell you quite yet. I can tell you that I made a case for bringing my partner—who I may have led them to believe is a part-time deputy—into these discussions."

"Did they go for it?"

"Yes. They need a few days to go through official channels. Realistically it'll be more like a week since it's the federal government. Can you wait that long?"

"Do I have any choice?"

"Not really. But we don't have to sit around twiddling our thumbs. You can develop the film. I can write up a report on Oscar Rumble and mail it to you. You may see something I've overlooked."

"Along that line, could you also mail a list of everyone who was at the first dance lesson or at Round the Bend around the time Rocko was attacked? Maybe we've overlooked someone."

"Consider it done."

He polished off the cookies and left. I turned off the porch light after he turned onto Main Street and toward the dance hall where his pickup truck was parked. Seconds later, I watched Dick Phillips drive by slowly. As he inched past, I finally thought of something positive to say about his presence. At least he wasn't Oscar.

CHAPTER 32

Wednesday was unremarkable, but Thursday began with Stig Borgeson dawdling in the entryway until the other children went into the classroom. He looked up, his face as glum and grey as the sky. "Is this Balentine's Day?"

"No. It's February second."

He brightened.

"Valentine's Day is two weeks away."

He burst into tears and wailed, "But I'm too young to get married!"

I crouched down and looked into his troubled eyes. "Who said you're getting married?"

"The big kids. They said there's gonna be wedding bells in our room on Balentine's Day."

Oh, for pity's sake. What was wrong with big kids these days?

I took his hand. "Stig, I promise that our Valentine's Day party"—emphasis on the "v" because opportunities for impromptu phonics lessons shouldn't be ignored—

"will have games and goodies and Valentine cards, but no weddings." I started to get up.

He wrapped his skinny little arms around my neck. "Wanna know why I don't want to get married?"

"Why?" I croaked as his forehead pressed against my Adam's apple.

He let go and whispered in my ear, " 'Cause when I'm old enough, I wanna marry you."

My heart melted into a big, slushy puddle.

"Stig, what a nice thing to say. But you were right to say you're too young to think about getting married." I stood and squeezed his hand. "How about we have lunch in ten years to talk it over again?"

We entered the classroom together where I announced that there would be no wedding bells on Valentine's Day in our classroom. After all, if one kid feared becoming a child bride or groom, the others did too. A palpable aura of relief invaded the room, and the children attacked their schoolwork with great vigor, perhaps because the pressure was off, but more likely because they knew their work had to be done before they could decorate their Valentine's mailboxes.

The previous evening, I had transformed an ordinary shoe box into my own glitzy Valentine card mailbox out of red, pink, and white construction paper, glue, glitter, and paper doilies. Then I used cardboard and pink construction paper to make a large heart and wrote "Valentine's Day, 1978" on it with red glitter. It remained hidden on a high shelf until the children dove into their art projects.

They worked on their creations with the enthusiasm, though not the skill, of Olympic champions. My challenge for the afternoon was prying them away from their artistic endeavors, handing them the cardboard heart I'd made, and getting them to stand still long enough to snap their pictures.

When dismissal time arrived, eleven studies in red and pink graced our classroom shelves. Eleven students stood admiring them with open-mouthed awe.

Gracie Berthold spoke for them all when she said, "Balentine's Day is the beautifulest day of all."

Once the awestruck artists were on their way home, I called the post office. "Dale, this is Jane Newell. Did I get a large envelope from Rick Sternquist today?"

"You did at that, Miss Newell."

His precise speech and military cadence had its usual effect on me. I stood straight and maintained that posture on my march to the post office. My box was stuffed with Rick's envelope, a bunch of bills, and the latest issue of the Tipperary Times. I flipped through my mail and went to the window.

"This one's addressed to Rique DuPeuss." I handed a postcard sporting a strange, garish illustration to Dale.

He beat a military tattoo on the counter with his palms and accepted the postcard. "I'm off my game by one. Rique's box is next to yours."

I executed a civilian goodbye and returned home. I opened Rick's envelope and pulled out the report. Much as I wanted to put life on hold and pour over its twenty single-spaced pages this evening, I couldn't. Tomorrow was a kindergarten Friday, and I'd promised to have pictures ready to add to Valentine boxes. That meant an evening in the darkroom. While I was at it, I would develop Rick's film too.

I developed both rolls and hung up the negatives.
While they dried, I did schoolwork and ate supper.
Then I went into the darkroom again and began making prints. Watching the children's gap-toothed smiles,
bright eyes, messy hair, and freckled noses emerge was
pure magic. I pinned them to the line with their faces
toward me to enjoy while I processed the other roll. The
children's innocence was a total contrast to what Rick
had photographed.

Images of the mutilated body of a steer lying on snow
stained red with blood emerged in the chemical baths.
They were sickening, and I hung them facing away from
me. Something about the mutilation gave me pause.
Reluctantly, I turned the photos around and studied
them again but couldn't pinpoint what I was searching
for.

I would wait until Rick stopped by to study the
disturbing, destructive images any further. I couldn't
imagine what brand of irrational logic moved a person
to treat an animal with such cruelty, much less to do it
repeatedly. I turned the prints toward the wall again, left
the lab, and locked the evil away.

In the morning I took down the photographs of my
students and gave them to their owners. The children
glued them to their boxes at the end of the day, declaring
them to be masterpieces.

Between the children's departures and church on
Sunday, my time was devoted to reading Rick's report
about Oscar and studying the list of people who had
been either at dance lessons or Round the Bend the night
Rocko died. Nothing screamed murderer, but I did find
several things to discuss with Rick. My stomach was

growling, and I was seeing double when the phone rang. I checked the time. Six o'clock?

Oh boy! How had I spent the entire day on the case and forgotten to call my parents? I was in for it now. I hurried to the phone. It rang before I got there.

I snatched the receiver. "Hi, Mom. Sorry I didn't call."

"Apology accepted."

Not Mom. "Rick?"

"Disappointed?"

"More relieved. Do you have news?"

"I do, but can we wait until tomorrow after church? It's private."

A collective intake of breath came down the party line.

Time to play things up. "Before or after?" I purred.

"Both." He matched me purr for purr.

I waited a beat until a deeper, collective gasp died down. We decided to meet in the foyer at nine fifty. Having done our part to boost church attendance and guarantee worshipers would arrive early, we said good-bye and hung up.

I made it to church at nine forty-five and walked into a crowded foyer. Conversations faltered and people glanced everywhere except at me. I pretended I'd left something in the car and went outside to wait for Rick.

When he arrived, I wove the fingers of our gloved hands together. "Follow my lead." I led him inside, through the foyer, and into the kitchen where I shut the door.

I kept my voice low. "What couldn't you say on the phone?"

Rick replied in kind. "You're to come to the Forest Service after school tomorrow."

I raised the volume and squealed, "Yes! I've been waiting a long time for this."

"You and me both," Rick boomed. Then he whispered, "Can we go over the photographs this afternoon?"

I spoke loud and clear. "Let's celebrate with dinner out and a drive"—I stepped close and murmured—"so I can see for myself where the cattle were killed."

"Great idea!" He went toward the door.

"Wait!" I hissed before touching up my lipstick, planting a sloppy kiss on his lips, and wiping away all but a small smudge. I looped my arm through his and grinned. "Now, let's meet our public."

We made our slow way through the foyer and down the center aisle to the second pew from the front. We sat as close to one another as we dared. Cookie finished the prelude, rose from the piano bench, and dropped a note in my lap as she went to sit with Bud and Tiege. I unfolded the note to see what she'd written.

You two are incorrigible!

I handed the note to Rick and snuggled closer.

Yes, we were.

CHAPTER 33

My incorrigibility took a nosedive when Rick parked in a pasture access a mile or so south of the Sternquist's lane. Snowdrifts littered the landscape, and I was not excited about tromping through them after we finished our sandwiches. This wasn't the celebratory dinner we'd led the eavesdroppers at church to believe we were going to enjoy. Rick had packed our picnic in my kitchen while I changed clothes. He had insisted we get going to take advantage of the sunshine and calm winds.

At least the cab had been warm, I told myself as I scaled a drift on the way to the snowmobile on the other side of the fence. Rick aimed the machine toward the herd of cattle about a hundred yards to the west. Hay lay scattered on the snow near the watering trough and the windbreak surrounding it. Engrossed in their meal, the animals barely noticed us passing by.

Rick parked about twenty yards west of the trough and got off. "Dad found the first steer right there." He pointed to where several gnarled cottonwoods ran along a little draw.

From what I could see, they were the only trees in this section of the pasture. I shaded my eyes and squinted at the pines darkening the butte that rose beyond the fence line to the west. "How far to that fence from here?"

"About a mile."

"And from the fence to the pines?"

"I dunno. Fifty yards or so."

"Who owns that land?"

"Forest Service."

"Hmm."

"Let me know when you're ready to check out the other site."

"Now's fine."

Rick steered the snowmobile north and a little west. The cattle, the bales, and water trough where we'd just been were still visible when he came to a stop. We dismounted and he pointed to the top of a rise.

Again I blocked the sun with a hand. If only it would block the wind, which was picking up. "I recognize this area. It's in the photos you took. Does it seem weird to you that the killer chose such an open spot? And it's close to the water trough and the hay. Why not somewhere more secluded?"

"It almost feels like the perpetrator wanted the second steer to be discovered immediately."

"Or like he's taunting your parents. But why would anyone who knows you're the sheriff do that? Unless it's because you *are* the sheriff. That doesn't make sense." A gust blew hair into my mouth. I spit it out.

"We better go before the wind whips up a ground blizzard. It's easy to get disoriented real quick out here."

We left immediately. The wind was howling by the time we got into the truck. When we reached Little Missouri, dark clouds were piling up in the west. We decided it would be best to wait until after the Forest Service meeting tomorrow to go over recent developments. Rick took off for Tipperary before the weather grew worse.

I was no sooner in my apartment and out of my winter things than the phone rang. It was Mom.

"Shouldn't your father and I be the first to know you're engaged? And to the sheriff, no less. I told you to stay away from him."

Betty wouldn't have passed that along to Mom, which left only one snitch. "Have you been talking to Velma?"

"It's true then?"

"It is not."

"Will it be true in the future?"

"It will not."

"That's what your father said, but when Velma told me what happened at church—"

"You realize she's passing you second-hand information? She doesn't attend church."

"Oh. Maybe I should have listened to your father. He said I was all worked up about nothing."

"He's right. Now, let's talk about something else. How was your week?"

Dusk was falling when I hung up a half hour later. Fresh snowflakes swirled beyond the window. Wind whistled through the cracks in the trailer. I fixed a bowl of cereal and ate it while trying to predict the purpose of tomorrow's meeting at the Forest Service. I gave up, put the empty bowl in the sink, and sat down to finish *Whose Body?* A couple hours later, I shut it with a satisfied sigh and wrote myself a note to ask the bookmobile librarian for the next Peter Wimsey mystery. After that, I went to bed and had a weird dream about Bud Sternquist finding a dead steer with pince-nez in his bathtub.

The weather righted itself by morning, though two inches of fresh snow had added a layer of sparkle to the tired drifts below. When I rang the school bell, first Elva and then Cora ran up and grabbed my left hand. Disappointed, they dropped it and pouted through math class. The engagement gossip had affected the girls more than the boys, who bopped through their lessons without a wisp of unrequited love dragging them down.

After work I rushed to the kitchen and slid the casserole I'd made before school into the oven. A honk sounded, and I went to the window and saw Rick pulling up. I grabbed my coat and met him outside.

"Wanna drive or walk?" he asked.

"It's not blizzarding." I put on my hat and gloves. "We better exercise while we can."

Cold seeped through my coat as we walked the few blocks to the Forest Service office. Had it been any further, I would have regretted my decision. When we went inside, Dan and Scott led us to a cozy conference room and brought in a pot of coffee.

Dan got straight to the point. "We gave Rick permission to tell you that we hired Rocko to look into the cattle killings. What he didn't have permission to tell you until our superiors granted us clearance is this. The person behind the killings either works for the Forest Service or some other government agency housed in this building."

I blinked. "Such as?"

Dan reeled off a list of possibilities. "Bureau of Land Management personnel, state trappers, temporary summer help. Heck, it could even be one of the town's volunteer firefighters or a Fly Ranch employee who supervises summer crews made up of kids from out there. More people are in and out of this office than you might think."

Rick spoke as he scribbled in his notepad. "Can you provide a complete personnel list?"

"Consider it done," Dan promised.

"We'll keep it between the two of us." Scott gestured to Dan. "The powers that be want the culprit to think no one has any idea that he—or she—comes from within. We had to insist Rick keep our suspicions under wraps until our supervisors were convinced they could trust you. Needless to say, we expect you to keep it confidential."

I set my coffee cup down on the conference table. "When did you tell them I'm the person working with you?"

"Not until the meetings in the Hills. They wouldn't budge until they vetted you."

"How did they do that?"

"By asking me to vouch for your professional skill and discretion."

"That was enough for them?"

"Not quite," Dan said. "Scott and I backed him up. And they called Mrs. Dremstein. She independently corroborated what we'd said."

I picked up my mug and took a deep sip. I wasn't all that thirsty, but I didn't want my smile of self-satisfaction to mar my aura of professionalism.

"Scott and I want to assure you that our wives don't know what you and Rick are doing," Dan said. "We will play along with, and maybe even play up, the romance angle until the two of you drop it."

"Might that explain why Cora inspected my ring finger this morning?"

Dan looked sheepish. "Maybe."

Scott cleared his throat. "Have either of you heard that Rocko and I didn't get along?"

Rick and I exchanged glances and then nodded.

"We cooked that up so people would think Rocko suspected me. We were hoping the real culprit would get sloppy. Now I wonder if the killer got tired of looking over his shoulder and decided to take Rocko out of the picture."

"Did Rocko leave any notes about what he'd learned?" Rick asked.

Dan sighed. "Not that we've found."

Rick directed the next question to both men. "Do you find that odd? Do you think Rocko hid his notes somewhere?"

They answered yes to both questions. Then the conversation dried up, and we all rose. Dan and Scott saw us to the door, where they shook our hands. Rick and I went outside.

He took my arm, and we walked through the deepening twilight. "What do you think?"

"I'm ninety-five percent sure they both gave us the full, unvarnished truth."

"And the other five percent?"

"It says that either Dan or Scott is telling the truth

and the other one killed the cattle, killed Rocko, and is hiding his notes."

"We know it's not Dan. He was in the dance hall from the time Rocko left until I found him. Scott's another story."

"He has more against him now than before. He wasn't in the dance hall at the time of the attack. He works for the Forest Service in the same building as Rocko and had access to Rocko's office."

I thought of Jeremy in his Batman cape, of Scott's wife Linda and his daughters. I began walking faster. "Come on."

"What's the hurry?"

"There has to be some evidence that points away from Scott. I'm going to find it."

I shook free or Rick's arm and raced toward home. He picked up his pace to match mine. He had longer legs, but I was more determined and got there first.

CHAPTER 34

I set the casserole and green salad on the table, and we ate quickly. Once again, I was done first. Rick finished the last of the casserole while I laid out the case file and evidence on the tables in the lab. When he joined me, I picked up the list of those who'd been at the hall or Round the Bend on the first night dance lessons were held.

"I checked the names on the list against where people were when Rocko was attacked. Would you go over it a second time? No one should be eliminated unless we are certain they couldn't have done it."

When Rick finished, several names remained. Several people had gone outside immediately after the lesson—Scott Gibson, Dick Phillips, Oscar Rumble, and Rique DuPeuss, along with Garth and Galva Swensen. Glen Berthold said he had hauled bags of trash across the street to the vacant lot where his garbage cans were hidden behind a tall, wooden fence during the time in question. Trudy said she'd used the restroom at Round the Bend around then also. A few couples had entered the bar and café together and left together. And Ruby York had stopped in the bar alone looking for her husband Hank.

I looked at Rick. "How did I miss Ruby's name until now?"

"After you asked for a list, I talked to Glen and Trudy again about who was at The Bend that night. Trudy remembered she'd been heading for the bathroom when Ruby came in and asked about Hank. Ruby was gone when Trudy returned, and the entire incident had slipped her mind. Glen had been emptying the garbage and didn't see her.

The addition of Ruby to the list made me uneasy. She and Hank lived with their horde of cats in a tar-paper shack behind the Methodist Church. Between Hank's World War II veteran's pension, their huge garden, and seasonal work for local ranchers, they were able to live independently. When I first met Hank, he proudly informed me of his deal with town hall to clean up the city dump. Later I learned that whenever he headed to the dump with his wheelbarrow, Betty alerted townspeople to drop off clothing, furniture, and lumber for him to find when he got there. He also had a temper, which I'd observed for myself. Until now, I hadn't known he frequented the bar.

"Is Hank a drinker?"

"For three hundred sixty-three days every year, he is not."

"And the other two days?"

"He goes on a bender. Usually Ruby finds him before he's in bad shape and hauls him home."

"Since his name's not on your list, can I assume Ruby didn't find him at Round the Bend?"

"That's right."

"So Ruby left alone."

"Right again."

"Where did she say she found him?"

"She swears he was in bed when she got back home. Knowing Hank's temper, I didn't press the issue. Now I may have to."

"Be careful, Rick. For Ruby's sake."

"For both their sakes. I'll start by interviewing the couples on the list and then move on to those who don't have anyone to vouch for them. Maybe that'll shake something loose, and I can leave Ruby and Hank alone."

Next, I picked up the stack of photographs Rick had taken of the second dead steer. "These are really good, though I don't know how you could stand being so thorough with the terrible mutilation staring you in the face."

"I didn't get all the pictures I wanted. My plan was to round up a crew to flip the carcass and photograph its other side. But I got called over to an accident east of Tipperary. When I finally got word to Dad to leave the carcass be, he and Mom had hauled it over to the burn pile and lit the match. That's their version of coyote control."

"Why did you want pictures of both sides? Other than the brand, one side of an animal mirrors the other, doesn't it? How many more shots do we need to prove whoever did this has a sick mind? There's got to be something to link this person to Rocko's death. The trick is to find it."

We went through the pictures one by one, sharing our impressions and concerns and taking notes. As had been the case when I made the prints, a detail, or perhaps an impression, gave me pause. When I tried to pinpoint what it was, it flitted away.

"Something about these pictures bothers me, but it won't hold still." I pushed them away and stood.

Rick rose too. "Maybe you're trying too hard. Or you could be tired or disgusted by what you've seen."

"All of the above."

"In that case, I think we should call it a night and start fresh in the morning. I'll conduct as many interviews as I can tomorrow. You continue shaping the minds of the next generation of Tipperary County leaders. I'll send a message through Betty if there's a breakthrough. Otherwise, I'll pick you up before dance lessons and we can talk afterwards."

The next morning, I did a terrible job of shaping the leaders of tomorrow. With only seven days until Valentine's Day, their young minds preferred love and the promise of chocolate over leadership. Such a surprise.

Since it wasn't snowing, blowing, or below zero Tuesday evening, Rick and I walked to the dance hall. I asked him how the interviews were going.

"I didn't punch any holes in what the couples from the café had to say, so they're in the clear. Most of what Galva and Garth Swensen said jived, but not everything. I don't know what's going on with them. Scott Gibson tells the same story no matter how I phrase my questions. I'm meeting with Oscar later tonight. That leaves Dick Phillips and Rique DuPeuss. Getting ahold of them has been a heck of a deal. I'll corner them during tonight's break and set up meetings with them."

"Maybe we should put together a square with the Gibsons, Swensens, Rique, and us and see what shakes out. We can concentrate on Oscar and Dick during breaks. What do you think?"

"It's gonna be interesting."

We entered the dance hall and were the recipients of a host of winks, elbow jabs, and wedding square-dance jokes. Part and parcel of being incorrigible, I guess. The absence of a ring on my finger made no difference. The teasing continued unabated.

"You deserve it," Cookie murmured.

I hurried past her and invited the Gibsons and Swensens to be part of our square. They accepted eagerly, as did Rosalie McDonald. She emitted major junior-bridesmaid-audition vibes. Rick brought Rique over. His vibe was more along the lines of the any-square-but-this-one variety. I couldn't tell if his discomfort was because he believed I'd jilted him or because he was our guy. I was none the wiser by the end of the evening.

Due to Rick's meeting with Oscar, I hitched a ride to my apartment with the Swensens. They hadn't done anything out of the ordinary during the lesson. The ride home was another chance to check them out.

Galva finger-combed my hair as I put on my parka. "Your hair could use some reshaping before Valentine's Day. It could be a big night for you and Rick." She wiggled her eyebrows. "I've got an opening at four this Thursday. Can you make it?"

I played along. "Oh, that's nice of you."

Then she whispered, "I've got news for you that's not fit for the party line."

"It's that titillating, huh?"

"Gossip about Oscar Rumble always is. I can't wait to tell you all about it."

Oh, Galva. Neither can I.

CHAPTER 35

Beau Kelly came to school the next morning with a paper bag clutched to his chest. "Is this the day for mailing our valentines?" he yelled when he lined up. "I brung mine!"

He was a day early. I gazed at the animated, excited boy. He was a far cry from the despondent, numb child I'd met in August soon after his mother had died. A bubble of happiness had slowly formed in him and expanded in the intervening months. Even so, he remained fragile. How could I tell him the truth without popping his balloon of burgeoning joy?

I felt my way along and prayed the answer would come to me. It did. "Bring them straight to my desk when you come in. You can store them in the file cabinet. I'll even show you how to lock the cabinet so they stay safe until tomorrow when the kindergarteners come. It'll be fun for everyone to deliver valentines at the same time." I motioned the children into the entryway.

Tiege tore off his backpack, nearly knocking Cora off

her feet. He pulled a sack from its outside pocket. "I got mine too, Miss Newell. See?"

"I do. Come along with Beau."

The boys arranged their sacks in the bottom drawer of the cabinet, and I showed them how to lock and unlock it. "I'm putting Beau in charge of unlocking the cabinet tomorrow."

"Aw, no fair," Tiege protested out of habit, though I could tell his heart wasn't in it. He had an intuitive compassion for Beau that brought out the best in both boys.

As for the other kids, the valentines hidden in the cabinet didn't bring out the worst in the kids, but they came darn close. The children ignored directions. They forgot to do their assignments. They turned every lesson into a prequel of the upcoming Valentine's Day party.

Stig looked up from the story during first-grade reading class. "Elva and me put chocolate hearts in our valentines." Beau and Bennan licked their lips.

"Mom bought the expensivest cards in Belle Fourche for me and Grace to hand out," Renny told Elva while they counted change together during math class.

Cora interrupted second-grade science class to tell Tiege, "Mommy's putting pink sprinkles on the cupcakes." Tiege invited himself over to help.

By dismissal time, I was partied out. "How am I going to make it until the actual holiday?" I groaned after they left. Between love-addled children, a wedding-obsessed town, and waiting for Rick to complete interviews and send his reports, I wasn't sure the world contained enough chocolate to get me through the next five days. That didn't stop me from dipping into the stash of chocolate chip cookies in the deep freeze. I wasn't a total pessimist.

Thursday began with an onslaught of children and their paper sacks bulging with Valentines, which more than doubled the silliness quotient among the children.

"Miss Newell." Elva marched up to me, her bag nestled in her arms, her tone decisive. "The boys from the big room are saying they're going to sneak to our entryway and steal our valentines."

An outraged din arose from the children still in the entryway as they confirmed her statement.

"Beau!" My words came out somewhere between a shout and a holler. "Beau, would you please unlock the file cabinet so the other children can put their cards in with yours."

His classmates swirled around the cabinet like snowflakes in a ground blizzard. When the storm passed, Beau locked the cabinet and handed over the key.

I put it in my pocket. "Now let's get to work so you're done with enough time left to deliver cards this afternoon."

Wonder of wonders, a calm fell over the room and remained until fifteen minutes before the end of the school day.

I stood, relishing the calm before the storm. Then I said, "Get ready to deliver your valentines." I handed the key to Beau.

He crooked a finger at me and stood on tiptoe as I bent toward him. "I want Tiege to have a turn. Is that okay?"

I nodded. Beau delivered the key to Tiege. Tiege hugged Beau. Beau beamed with happiness, and the best in both of them lit up the room.

Tiege opened the cabinet, the other children swirled

around it, and then stormed over to the mailboxes to make their deliveries.

"What do I do with this one?" Grace Berthold held up a card with "Mrs. McDonald" scrawled on the envelope.

"That's a good question, Grace." I said and then checked with the other kids. "Do any of the rest of you have cards for people in the big room?"

Several students raised their hands.

Keeva came up with the solution. "Put them on my desk, and I'll give them to Mom." She wrinkled her forehead. "I mean Mrs. McDonald."

After school several big kids brought cards for children in our room. So many big kids were taking their own sweet time that I feared I would miss my appointment with Galva. When I could wait no longer, I called Liv and asked her to check my room and lock up before she went home. With that, I skedaddled and made it to the appointment only five minutes late.

Galva fastened a cape around my neck after I sank into the chair. "I was about to give up on you. Thought maybe you were hiding out after all that razzing Tuesday."

"I'm tougher than that."

She swiveled my chair around and tipped it to the edge of the shampoo sink. "They're a bunch of fools thinking that Rick would propose this early in February. You and I know good and well that he's gonna do it on Valentine's Day. Maybe during dance lessons so we can all watch. Doesn't that sound scrumptious?"

More like sickeningly sweet.

"What's up with Oscar?"

"Well, me and Lacey Jo rode down together to a class

in Rapid City last week. When I said you are Winter Skye's teacher, she acted like you're first cousin to a rattlesnake." She toweled my hair and helped me sit up.

"Me? Why?"

"She says you steal her boyfriends." She untangled my hair with a comb and then picked up her scissors.

"What boyfriends?"

"Junior Wentworth, for one." She punctuated the revelation with a snip of her scissors. "And then Oscar Rumble." Another snip.

I shuddered.

"Hold still so I don't clip your ear."

"I have never been on a date with Oscar, and I never will."

"That's what I said. What with you and the sheriff getting engaged next Tuesday. I told her you aren't a threat, but Oscar told her that you can't keep your hands off him."

My head whipped around. "He's delusional."

She snipped my ear.

I yelped.

She staunched the bleeding with a tissue.

I bled. A lot.

Galva got back to my haircut several tissues and one Band-Aid later. I waited to resume the conversation until Galva put the scissors away and my blood supply was no longer under threat.

Our awkward silence broke after she finished with the blow dryer. "I'm not patting myself on the back or anything," she said as she twirled me around to face the mirror, "but you look pretty enough for a marriage proposal."

She was right. About the hair. Not the proposal. More awkward silence while Galva waited for me to agree with her. I tried to come up with a response that wouldn't encourage her to drive to the courthouse and help the registrar of deeds to fill out my marriage license.

Winter Skye, bless her determined little heart, burst into the salon and saved me. "Come see what me and Dad are doing, Miss Newell."

I ripped off my cape faster than Oscar Rumble had lied to Lacey Jo and followed the little girl into Garth's shop. She skipped over to a table where he was arranging several small grey animals into a row.

"What are those?" I stepped closer.

"Mice!" Winter Skye jumped up and down.

I reached out a hand, steadying myself against the table.

"She wants to learn taxidermy in the worst way," Garth explained. "Mice are cheap and don't take too long start to finish."

I inhaled and then exhaled, lying through my teeth. "They are kinda cute." I gazed at the far side of the table, my eyes searching for anything other than a mouse to focus on. What they found made me weak in the knees. I clutched the table with both hands until I could hold on with one and point with the other. "What's that?"

"This?" He picked it up. "I found it in the fence between us and the Long Pines this afternoon. A heifer or a steer musta caught its head in the barbed wire, tore free, and left this ear behind. Want a closer look?"

Garth set it in front of me. I looked at it from one angle after another. The outline of the shadowy shape Rick and I had been chasing since the night Rocko died wasn't that of a shoe. Or a mitten.

It was the outline of a cow's ear. That changed every-thing.

Chapter 36

I pushed the Beetle's speedometer past wise and into foolhardy territory on the way home. Then I raced into the kitchen and rang Betty. "I need to speak to Rick. Do you know where he is?"

"Wast I heard, he stopped a speeder on Highway 85 and recognized her as the suspect in a Bewwe Fourche robbery. She's in custody, and he's preparing to take her to the Butte County jaiw. Very exciting."

Her exciting was my frustrating. What were the chances of this happening when I'd discovered evidence that could break the case wide open? "Do you have any idea when he'll return?"

"Midnight at the earwiest. Do you want him to caww you when he can?"

"No, thank you." What I had to tell him had to be delivered in private. "Tell him I'll be at his office after school tomorrow, and he has to be there."

"Consider it done."

I fixed an egg sandwich for supper and ate so fast I

didn't taste it. Then I went into the lab and pulled out the enlargements of the mysterious shape from the night Rocko died. I flipped through the pictures of the dead steer. The detail that had stymied me for days was now glaringly obvious. My eye had recognized the shape of the animal's ear, but my brain hadn't processed it until I'd seen the one Garth had found.

I set the photographs aside and picked up the paper with the names of people Rick had interviewed a second time. The Gibsons, the Swensens, Dick Phillips, Rique DuPeuss, Oscar Rumble, and perhaps the Yorks. I ran a finger beside their names, looking for anyone with a connection to the Forest Service.

Not the Yorks. *Thank goodness.*

Not Oscar Rumble. *Even though he was my top candidate for bad guy.*

The Swensens? *Not that I knew of.*

Dick Phillips? *If he supervised the Fly Ranch summer work crews Dan had mentioned.*

Rick DuPeuss. *Yep.*

Scott Gibson? *Definitely.*

I crammed the paper and the pertinent photographs in an envelope and stuck it in my purse. Then I kicked off the twenty remaining hours of waiting until my meeting with Rick by watching *Fish* and *Barney Miller*. After that, I passed the time by getting a good night's sleep, putting in a full day with kids on Friday, and driving to Tipperary at foolhardy miles an hour. I flew up the courthouse steps and into Rick's office, where I slammed the door behind me and waved the envelope under his nose.

"It's a cow's ear!"

"Not a rabbit's foot?"

"Get a load of this, wise guy." I set the photographs on his desk and pointed first at the one from the crime scene and then at the dead steer in the pasture. "See?"

He studied them in turn. "You're right. It's a cow's ear. How did you figure it out?"

I told him what I'd seen in Garth's taxidermy shop, though I left out the mice. They didn't seem pertinent. And they were gross.

"How did I miss it?" Rick leaned on his elbows. "I've been looking at cattle all my life."

"Attached to their owners' heads, yes. But not lying on the ground like the one in the crime scene photo." I produced Rick's interview list and slid it over to him. "Now that we have more proof there's a connection between the cattle killings and Rocko's death, look through the names again."

Rick took the paper, marked it with a pen as he read, and gave it back to me. He'd crossed out Oscar Rumble and the Yorks, put a question mark after the Swensens, and circled Dick Phillips, Rique DuPeuss, and Scott Gibson. "These are the three we oughta concentrate on. They have connections to the Forest Service, and they know cattle."

"Did you interview Dick and Rique?"

"Yes, but I've got new questions for them and Scott in light of this." He tapped the photograph with his pen and picked up the phone. "Betty, would you connect me to Scott Gibson?" He covered the phone receiver and looked at me. "You free tomorrow?"

I nodded.

He spoke into the receiver again. "Scott, I need to talk

to you. At your office. Not at home. When can I stop by tomorrow?" Pause. "Okay, see you then."

He hung up. "I'd like you to come with me to talk to Scott. Can I pick you up at nine forty-five?"

"I'll be ready."

"Now, about the other two men. They don't know we're working together. Do you think we should tell them the truth so you can come to their interviews too?"

I wanted to go with Rick in the worst way, but not as much as I wanted to expose Rocko's killer. I dug up every speck of maturity I possessed and shook my head. "Not yet."

Before this, I hadn't known that making the right choice felt right, but it didn't feel good.

Rick looked skeptical. "You sure?"

"Our partnership is our best weapon. We shouldn't reveal it prematurely. Plus, Dick will talk more without me there."

"Since the two of us became an item, he doesn't say more than a sentence to me when he sees me."

"You get sentences out of him? I'm impressed." I closed my eyes and visualized Rique DuPeuss's trailer sitting next to where Gavin Wick lived with his family. Gavin, a student in Liv's room, had proved resourceful in the past. "Let me know when you'll be interviewing Rique. I'll round up my spy network and do some poking around while he's occupied."

"You have a spy network?"

"My lips are sealed."

"Want to go to supper at the #3 before you head home?"

The #3 was the best restaurant in Tipperary. My lips unsealed. "Yes!"

A couple hours later, after Rick and I devoured tender steaks and made googly eyes at one another for the benefit of the other diners, after we said goodbye, and after I made a quick stop at Tipperary's grocery store, I drove home. I found my yellow legal pad and outlined my weekend plan of attack. Once it was on paper, I went to bed.

Saturday morning, I rose early, went to the phone, and launched a preemptive strike.

"Good morning, Betty!"

"Good morning, Miss Neweww! How can I hewp you?"

"I'd like to call my parents, please." The words sounded like the lamest battle tactic in human history. However, tending to Mom first would eliminate some mother-induced potential disasters. Like her calling me at an inopportune time. Or her raising an alarm among her Little Missouri cohorts and sending out a search party when I didn't want to be found.

She came on the line, all breathless with worry and inordinate concern. "Jane, you're calling so early. What's wrong?"

"Nothing, Mom. Today's going to be busy, and I wanted to call before things get rolling."

"That's nice of you. What do you have going on?"

I glanced at the legal pad and reeled off my answer. "School stuff. Cleaning my apartment. Lunch with a friend." That friend being Rick, who didn't know we were going to Round the Bend after the interview with Scott.

"Man or woman?"

"Rick Sternquist."

"But you said you weren't—"

"We still aren't and never will be." I glanced at the clock. "Do you need to get to the grocery store?"

"Oh my stars! It opens in ten minutes. I have to go now, or the place will be a zoo. It always is on Saturday morning. I'll say goodbye and hand the phone to Dad."

"Goodbye, Mom. I love you."

"I know dear." Her voice faded. "Harold, you finish up with Jane. I have to go."

"Hi, Dad." I drew a line through Roman numeral one on my outline and moved to my Roman numeral two, which was a fact-finding mission. "Talk about the weather until Mom's gone."

"Affirmative, Janey-Jo." He ran through the area snowfall totals before saying, "She's gone. What's up?"

I brought him up to date with the investigation, ending with a description of the cow's ear. "You worked with cattle, and I'm wondering if this rings any bells for you."

"No cow bells." He snickered at his own pun and waited until after I chuckled to say more. "During the depression, some of my pals killed gophers and other pests. They cut off the tails and took them to the court-house to collect a few cents bounty. It doesn't seem like much now, but for some families, it meant they could buy a ham bone for their bean soup. Your mother makes a tasty bean soup. I wish I'd reminded her to pick up the ingredients."

I agreed with Dad, then guided him back to the severed critter tails. "Did anyone pay a bounty for ears?"

"Well, they could have, but why bring in two ears

instead of one tail since nobody was stupid enough to pay out for one ear. What you're talking about sounds more like he's collecting souvenirs. Mighty grisly souvenirs."

Soon after, we wrapped up our conversation. "Love you, Dad."

"Likewise, Janey-Jo."

I hung up and shuddered. Dad's take on cow's ears as souvenirs turned my stomach. I took out my legal pad and crossed out the second item on my outline. Then I wrote down my question for Scott at the interview. The answer I suspected he would give would clear him of suspicion, which would be a great relief to his son's kindergarten teacher.

I made oatmeal for breakfast and topped it with fresh, clotted cream, smiling at the thought of Snippy, Merle's faithful milk cow. Of all the cattle in Tipperary County, and there were thousands, she was the one who mattered to me. My fingers tightened around my spoon. Snippy was also the only cow I had the power to protect.

I got up from the table, threw on my coat, and ran over to Merle's. Pounding on the creaky door to the mudroom, I shouted, "Merle, it's Jane! Snippy's in danger!"

CHAPTER 37

Snippy may or may not have been in danger. With "not" being the more likely scenario. However the mere thought of his heifer being in peril would move Merle along faster than anything else. Faster being a relative term in light of his bad hip and his cats, who lived to arrange their bodies into a series of obstacles for him to dodge.

He shot into the kitchen before I could repeat the alarm. He plowed through the mudroom, cats scattering in every direction. He burst outside, wild-eyed and breathing hard, holding a shotgun.

"Them damn coyotes." He blew past me and aimed the shotgun at the barn as he gimped toward it. "Stand clear, Snippy! I'm coming."

"Put the gun down, Merle!" I shouted. "Nothing's attacking Snippy right now. We just need to make sure she's okay."

Merle lowered and disabled it. "Then how come you made it sound like my ol' Snip was under attack?"

"Have you heard about the latest cattle killings at the Sternquists?"

"'Course I have."

"It was the first time the culprit targeted the same rancher twice. It could indicate the killer is getting bolder."

Merle looked suspicious as he peered at me. "You're the one who's gettin' bolder, talking about patterns and culprits and such. How come you know all this?"

Oops! It was too late to backtrack, so I forged ahead. "I can't tell you yet. For now, let's make sure Snippy is alive and well."

"Come on, then." He went to the barn and swung the door open. "Here she is."

And there she was, ears twitching as she munched on hay. I went inside and scratched her ears. "Hello, old girl. Looks like Merle already milked you."

" 'Course I did. An hour or more ago."

I examined the barn door's latch. A padlock hung from the metal loop that the clasp fit over. "How often do you use the padlock?"

"Every night."

"Starting now, lock it during the day too." I shut the door and fastened the padlock. "Who else stops by to check on Snippy?"

"Scott Gibson when he come for milk and eggs the other day. Linda used to do it before she got that job at the paper. Dick Phillips is here real regular."

"Does he ever say anything?"

"Same as anybody else I guess. Can't hardly shut him up when he's talking' bout you."

There had to be another Dick Phillips in town.

"Anyone else?"

"Like who?"

"I don't know. Garth Swensen maybe. Or Rique DuPeuss. Dan Barkley?"

"Not Garth or Dan. Their wives take care of them. Reek comes real regular on Tuesday afternoon to use my bathtub and washing machine since square dance lessons begun. He don't ask about ol' Snip. Or you." He patted the shotgun dangling from the crook of his elbow. "I gotta put this away. You care to join me for non-skid pancakes?"

I pulled back my cuff and looked at my watch. Nine fifty. "Sorry, Merle. I have to be somewhere five minutes ago."

"With the sheriff?"

"How did you know?"

Merle smirked and pointed toward Main Street. "He's driving this way. And your poker face could use some work."

Rick parked beside the Beetle. I went into my apartment for my legal pad. I made sure the apartment and classroom doors were locked and hurried to back to Rick.

He started the engine. "I'm interviewing Dick this afternoon at two and Rique at four."

"Where?"

"Both at the dance hall."

Good. I could call Gavin and arrange to meet while Rique was tied up with the sheriff.

On the way to see Scott, I told Rick about Dad's souvenir theory.

"The idea has merit. But why hasn't anyone mentioned it before?" Rick countered.

I thought for a minute. "Well, some of the carcasses weren't found before coyotes and other scavengers got to them. Or the owners were like your dad and burned the carcasses right away."

"True."

"So if the killer always removes the ear facing down, it could go unnoticed. Unless a rancher noticed the damage and talked to someone who had observed the same thing, no one would be the wiser."

"I wonder if Rocko figured it out. That could explain his death. If he added his suspicions to his notes, that could be why they disappeared." Rick parked in front of the Forest Service office. "I'll take Scott through the interview questions he'll be expecting and a few new ones. Then I'm turning it over to you. You found the new evidence and should be the one to bring it up. Is that okay?"

More than okay.

Scott seemed a little nervous when he ushered us into his office, but not unusually so. He answered Rick's questions about the night in question, never straying from what he'd said in previous interviews. Had he been lying since the beginning, he couldn't have kept the details straight.

After about twenty minutes, Rick looked at me. "Do you have anything you'd like to ask, Jane?"

Scott's confidence had grown during the interview. He turned to me, his gaze unfaltering.

I returned his gaze with similar confidence. "Were you ever called out to the sites of the livestock killings?"

"Just the first one."

"When was that?"

"Sometime in November. I can get the exact date for you." He began riffling through the papers scattered across his desk.

"Let's finish up the questions first." I knew what to ask next but consulted my notepad for effect. "Did you notice anything unusual about the killing?"

He stared at the far wall for a few seconds. "Everything was unusual. The predator was a human who went onto Forest Service grazing land and stuck a butcher knife into a steer's gut. Who would do such a thing?"

"That's a good question, Scott, and you may have seen something that leads to the answer we're looking for. Take your time and think back to the scene. Could there be a small detail you saw in passing and didn't realize might matter?"

He rested his head against the back of his office chair, hands clasped over his small potbelly, and stared at the ceiling. After a few minutes, he sat up straight. "There was a big blood-soaked patch of dirt under the steer. The ground was half-frozen, but it hadn't snowed yet. The blood under the belly made sense, considering where the animal had been stabbed." He looked at me and then at Rick. "But there was blood under the head. Where did that come from?"

I heeded Merle's advice and worked on my poker face. "I don't suppose you lifted the head."

"No."

"Anything else?"

Scott thought a little longer. "That's it," he sighed. "Sorry I couldn't help more."

"You've been a great help." Rick stood.

I rose and gestured to Scott's desk. "Please call when

you find the date of the first killing. We'll let ourselves out."

"Sure." Scott picked up a stack of papers and paged through them.

I clamped my lips together to keep my thoughts from escaping before Scott was out of earshot. Dad had been right! The cattle killer was collecting ears for souvenirs, and we were finally getting somewhere!

CHAPTER 38

We walked out of the building and into the wind. "Let's grab lunch at the café and take it to my house." A gust snatched my words and sent them flying.

Rick squinted at the gray clouds. "Where did this come from?"

I spoke again, louder this time. "My house. For lunch."

" 'Fraid not." He wrenched open my door and held onto it until I was in the cab. "I need to head to Tipperary before this gets worse. I'll stop at Rique DuPeuss's to reschedule our interview since he doesn't have a phone. I'll wait and call Dick when I get to town."

He dropped me off at home. I hurried inside, my head bent against the wind and blowing snow. How did people in this county get anything done during the winter? At this rate, we might as well postpone our investigation until spring. I ate lunch with my legal pad, rearranging my outline. Then wind blew while I wrote a report of the interview with Scott, cleaned my apartment, and worked in my classroom. When my stomach refused to stop sending distress signals, I made popcorn and watched television to drown out the wind. It didn't work, and I had to put a pillow over my head when I went to bed.

The wind played itself out during the night. Fresh snow had fallen also. It was hard to tell how much because the wind had whipped it into drifts. The Beetle was drifted in, so I walked to church. Snowflakes sparkled and danced in a light breeze. After the service I went outside and found the sun shining like a benediction. The brightness made my eyes water. While I rummaged in my pocket for a tissue, Gavin Wick popped up from behind a snowdrift in his yard. I wandered over to see what he was doing. The middle section of the drift had been hollowed out, and he was stacking snow bricks across its opening.

I shot a quick glance north of the Wicks' house where Rique's camper sat on cement blocks, and then looked at Gavin again. "What are you making?"

"An igloo. I'm gonna sleep in it tonight. Mr. DuPeuss gave me his old down sleeping bag. He says if I wrap up in it, I'll stay good and warm."

"Did he help you build this?"

Gavin scooped up snow and packed it between the cracks in his bricks. "Nah. I knocked on his door this morning, but he's not there. He didn't leave a note taped to the window like usual either. I tried the knob, but the door was locked. I looked through the window, but all I seen was a bunch of socks and other stuff hanging from his clothesline. You wanna see?"

I thought he'd never ask!

Soon my nose was pressed against the window. The

grimy glass made the interior of the camper as hazy as a Monet water lily painting. I cupped my hands around my eyes to cut the glare. A clothesline ran from wall to wall similar to those in my darkroom. Unless I was way off, the things hanging from it weren't socks and stuff. I wasn't about to tell Gavin what I thought they were.

"He's got plenty of socks." I whistled and pointed to the igloo. "How long are you going to be outside?"

"All day. Except for meals. And I'm sleeping out here tonight, remember?"

"Could you do me a favor?"

"What is it?"

"Give me a call if Mr. DuPeuss returns."

"Okay." He went over to his igloo and hefted another icy brick into place.

I waded through the snow toward the church. Rick hadn't been there for the service, but Bud and Cookie had. Their pickup truck and several others were still there. I burst into the foyer like a wild woman, or so the expressions of those in the room led me to believe.

Bud was beside me faster than snowballs melt in the desert. "What can I do for you, Miss Newell?"

"I need to talk to you privately." We went outside, and I spoke with great urgency. "Do you know where Rick is?

"Far as I know, he's in bed. He and his deputy was up real late cleaning off a porch roof before it collapsed under the snow weighing it down."

"Is he at your ranch or in town?"

"Tipperary."

"Thanks." I returned to the foyer as dramatically as before and shut myself in the kitchen. Then I snatched the receiver and rang the switchboard.

"Betty, this is Jane. Grab a pen and paper and write down a message for the sheriff. It needs to be word for word."

"I awways have a notebook and penciw handy. Go ahead."

"Tell Rick not to be late for lunch at my apartment. The food is ready, and he should come now or what I've spent seven weeks preparing will be lost." I repeated the message and asked her to read it back to me. "That's perfect. He's at his house in Tipperary. He may be sleeping, so let it ring until he answers."

"You can count on me, Miss Neweww."

"Please call my apartment after you talk to him."

"Aye aye, ma'am."

I thanked her, clicked my heels, and struck out for home. When I got there, I slapped together grilled cheese sandwiches and a lettuce salad. For a celebratory touch, I opened a quart of Mom's home-canned peaches. Not quite chocolate chip oatmeal cookies, but who has time to bake when she's about to break an investigation wide open?

Betty called to report that she'd delivered my message and Rick was on his way. I brewed a big pot of coffee and presented him a steaming mug when he arrived twenty minutes later.

"You read my mind." He took a swallow, then handed it to me so he could remove his boots and coat.

I set his mug on the table and dished up the grilled cheese. While we ate, I told him what I'd seen in Rique's camper. "Gavin hasn't called to say that Rique has returned. Should we take a stroll that direction after dessert?"

"That's a fine idea. You should bring your camera and the telephoto lens. Maybe I can distract Gavin so you can get some shots through the window."

"The glass is very dirty. I don't think they'll show much."

"All we need is to show probable cause for the judge to issue a search warrant."

Soon we were strolling through town arm in arm, wearing our devious hearts on our sleeves. I took the occasional photo along the way. We stopped at Gavin's igloo and Rick quizzed him about its construction. When Gavin crawled inside his sleeping quarters, I raised the camera and took picture after picture until he emerged again.

I gestured for him to stand in front of the igloo. "Let me take your picture."

He lit up. "Would you take one of me pretending to sleep inside it?"

I took several pictures of Gavin. Once the roll was used up, I wished him a warm and restful night. Then Rick and I were off to my apartment where I developed the negatives. Rick combed through the case file, compiling photographs, documents, and evidence to present to the judge. The phone rang while I was agitating the film in the developing fluid.

A few minutes later, Rick raised his voice and spoke through the darkroom door. "That was Betty. The weather service has issued a blizzard warning for all of Tuesday, so Oscar is moving dance lessons up a day. Is there any way to finish the prints in the next hour?"

He was asking the impossible for all the right reasons. He needed to get the search warrant before Rique got wind of our suspicions and destroyed the damning evidence we'd seen. But the prints wouldn't be ready until tomorrow morning, and then only if I got up during the night to speed the process.

"How soon can you be here in the morning?"

"Is five too early?"

"I won't be up, but the prints will be on the table. Take my extra apartment key and let yourself in."

"Does this mean you aren't cooking breakfast?"

"Don't get smart with me, buster."

I heard his footsteps retreat. A short while later, the door slammed. I was securing the tops and bottoms of the damp negatives to the clothesline when I could have sworn someone entered and then left the apartment.

You're hearing things, Jane. Of all the people in Tipperary County, Rick Sternquist would have made sure the doors were locked when he left. That's for certain.

Still, when all the negatives had been taken care of, I grabbed the darkroom scissors, sneaked through the lab, and crept into the living room. While I looked for anything out of place, the aroma of fried food from Round the Bend tickled my nose. A white paper bag and can of Diet Coke sat on the table. I zipped over to the table like a bear to honey and found a note lying there.

Jane—Supper's on me. I'll deliver breakfast in the morning, too. Thanks for losing sleep over this. Rick

I set down the scissors, opened the bag, and pulled out a cheeseburger and fries. I bit into the sandwich and relished the flavors exploding on my tongue. I squeezed a puddle of ketchup onto a plate, dipped a french fry into it, and shoved it into my mouth. My partner knew how to get on my good side. How could breakfast possibly top this?

Chapter 39

The aroma of freshly brewed coffee entered my dreams. My alarm jangled, and still I could smell the coffee. Maybe I was still asleep and had dreamed that the alarm had rung. No, the clock was in my hand, the imprint of the knob visible on my finger. I was fully awake, or as awake as I ever was before my first cup of coffee. I sniffed again and smelled coffee again, along with the rich aroma of sausage.

I threw off the covers and went into the kitchen. Rick's envelope, which I'd laid on the table in the wee hours of the night, had been replaced by the extra apartment key. Next to the key was another note.

Jane,

Your breakfast is in on the counter, compliments of Mom, not me. Orange juice is in the fridge.

Rick

A slow cooker and a glass baking pan covered with aluminum foil sat on the counter. Behind them was my coffeemaker, its carafe brimming with the elixir of life.

I lifted the slow cooker lid and found sausage gravy. I peeled the foil off the pan and found biscuits. I resisted the temptation to shove the food in my mouth with my fingers and poured a cup of coffee to sip while I got ready for work. Once that was done, I filled a plate, poured juice and more coffee, and sat down to eat. I dug in—with a fork, not my fingers—and my mouth was full before I remembered to say grace.

Dear God, thank you for a delicious breakfast and for Cookie. I don't know how meals are handled in heaven, but if you could put Cookie Sternquist in charge of the kitchen, I'd be eternally grateful. Amen.

The breakfast dishes were almost done when Rick called. "Thank you for finishing the prints. They're just what I need for the appointment."

"I should be the one thanking you. And Cookie. Breakfast was delicious."

"Be glad I stayed at the ranch last night. Otherwise I'da brought you a box of cereal and an overripe banana." He paused. "I'm calling from a pay phone down the block from my appointment. I'll be seen as soon as schedules allow, so I've got to hurry back. Can you do a couple things while I'm tied up?"

"Sure."

"Check with Betty to see if everybody taking square dance lessons got her message and plans to be there tonight. I mean everyone, even those who don't have a phone."

"What else?"

"Clear your schedule for after school. Mom'll drop off

supper for us when she picks up Tiege. I should get there about the same time to talk about dance lessons. We can't afford any missteps tonight." He paused. "Do you understand what I'm saying?"

His code-speak made perfect sense to me. "I do."

Rick hung up. I stayed on the line. "Are you there Betty?"

"Yes indeedy, and I'ww get right on it. Shouwd I caww you during cwass with a report?"

"Please do." Excited squeals came from the playground. "The kids are here. Bye." I hung up and went to take charge of my charges. They blasted into the entryway, the prospect of a blizzard closing school for a day whipping them into an emotional frenzy.

"What about our Valentine party?" Beau quavered. "Will it be canceled if there's no school tomorrow?"

The children stilled and stared at me with worried eyes. Either I ease their concern, or they would be sprouting crow's feet before they hit double digits.

"Not canceled." I met each child's gaze in turn. "Just postponed."

Brennen looked suspicious. "What's that mean?"

"It means we'll have our party on the next school day when the kindergarteners come."

Elva closed her eyes. Her index finger moved from left to right as she counted off days on an imaginary calendar. "So the party would be on Thursday?"

"Or Friday if we miss two days of school," I said.

They continued to stare at me. Beads of perspiration began to form on the tiny slits of their foreheads bordered by stocking caps above and mufflers below. Melted snow from their boots puddled on the rug instead of on the old newspapers spread along the wall. To avoid Velma's mighty wrath, I took swift action.

"Don't just stand there," I said in a "Hi-ho, hi-ho, it's off to school we go" singsong. "The sooner we get to work, the more time we'll have to make Valentine's decorations for you to take home."

Hats, scarves, and mittens, coats and dripping boots flew in all directions. I edged into the classroom and stood at a safe distance. The students whooshed to their desks and got busy. When the phone rang mid-morning, they didn't look up.

Betty spoke in hushed tones. "Everyone wiww be at square dance wessons tonight. Bud personawwy dewivered the message to those without phones."

"Thanks for letting me know, Betty." I set the receiver in the cradle without a sound.

The students finished their lessons in record time that afternoon and left with backpacks filled with the pink and red hearts they had glued to white paper doilies. Tiege lingered in the entryway while Cookie slid a pan of chicken tetrazzini in the oven and a fruit salad in the refrigerator.

I was setting the table when Rick came in. "Do you have a search warrant?"

"I do."

"Great! What's the plan for tonight?"

"Mom is picking up Rique at his camper and taking him to their place for supper. She and Dad'll bring him straight to the dance hall. By then, the search'll be done, and I'll come to the dance hall to arrest him."

"It sounds like you've thought of *almost* everything."

His forehead wrinkled. "Wha'd I miss?"

"I won't have a dance partner."

"There's always Dick Phillips."

"Um, no." I removed the casserole from the oven, thunked it on the table, and took the salad from the fridge. "Let's eat."

We dissected Rick's plan as we ate. He really had thought of everything. Cookie's tetrazzini was delicious, and every bite distracted me. I wanted the recipe. Would there be time to ask her for it after Rique was arrested?

"Jane?" Rick's voice broke through my musings. "Did you hear what I asked you?"

"Um . . ." I set down my fork. "Would you repeat the question?"

"Did we miss anything?"

"Not that I can think of. But let's go through it again before you take off."

Finally, the time came for his part—executing the search—to begin. My part was to watch the clock so I would arrive at the dance hall late enough to avoid Oscar and early enough to greet Rique and keep tabs on him until Rick arrived.

"Be careful," I said after Rick put on his winter clothes, tested his flashlight, and tucked the search warrant into the inside pocket of his coat.

"Says the woman who has been chased by a bull and stowed away in an airplane in previous investigations."

"That was then. This is now. Tonight's going to go like clockwork."

"I hope so."

"I know so. Really Rick, what could possibly go wrong?"

CHAPTER 40

Rick left, and I set the stove timer to remind me when to leave. I puttered around in the kitchen and my classroom to distract myself until then. When the timer beeped, I put on my full winter regalia and waddled outside. The forecast predicted the snow would start after midnight. I toddled past my car and discovered it was no longer buried under a snowdrift.When had Dick Phillips shoveled it out? I squeezed into the Beetle and drove to the dance hall, arriving early.

Oscar Rumble's den of iniquity was the only vehicle in sight. I waited in the Beetle with its engine idling until the Barkleys pulled in. Then I cut the ignition and got out. As I pocketed the key, a snowflake drifted down and melted on the warm window glass. More flakes fell as I walked to the entrance with the Barkleys.

"It's starting to snow," Pam said.

"But the forecast said—"

"Never trust a weatherman," Dan chuckled. "Didn't your parents teach you that?"

Obviously not. But from the looks of the two road graders parked across the street in the vacant lot to the east of the dance hall, the Tipperary County road crew had learned that lesson and was ready for action whenever the snow began piling up. "Where's your sheriff?" Pam craned her neck and peered over my shoulder as we took off our coats.

"Finishing some work." I began removing layers and draping them over the back of a chair. "He should get here pretty soon."

"But I figured . . ." Her face fell. "Oh, never mind."

My mind went into overdrive. Had she decoded Rick's party-line message and figured out what we were up to? Had she let something slip to Rique?

"What do you mean?" I spoke sharply.

"Well, with the blizzard coming and tomorrow being Valentine's Day and you and Rick such an item, I was hoping he would propose to you tonight."

She looked as downcast as I felt relieved. "The subject hasn't come up, and I don't think it ever will. We're good friends and nothing more."

She elbowed me. "I've heard that before."

The door opened. Axel and Liv McDonald, the Yarboroughs, the Borgesons, and the Swensens entered, along with a gaggle of children.

"I thought the storm was supposed to hold off until after midnight," Galva Swensen laughed as she and Garth brushed snow off one another's shoulders. Her eyebrows lifted into the stratosphere when the door opened. When Frost and Fanny McDonald and Dick Phillips blew in, Galva's eyebrows returned to earth. She turned to me. "The sheriff and his family better get here quick, or we'll have to leave before he can pop the question."

I was explaining that we were close friends and nothing more when Winter Skye's three older sisters began to chant, "Teacher and Sheriff sitting in a tree. K-i-s-s-i-n-g."

Before long, the most mature and accomplished fifth grader in the universe, Rosalie McDonald, joined them. After that, my own students—yes, *my own students*—fell like dominoes. First Winter Skye, then Keeva, and finally Elva. The little traitors.

"First comes love, then comes marriage, then comes—"

The door flew open. Tiege burst in. He skidded to a stop and announced, "Be polite and act like you don't smell any ol' skunk. Mr. DuPeuss don't have a bathtub."

God bless your cheeky little heart, Tiege Sternquist!

The chanting died out, and heads swiveled away from me and toward the doorway, where snowflakes danced in the glow of the overhead light.

Galva turned toward the stage. "Are you going to send us home early if this keeps up, Mr. Rumble?"

Oscar slunk across the room and through the crowd near the entrance. Before he could poke his head outdoors, the Sternquists and Rique stepped inside.

Cookie went past Oscar, then gave him a second look. "Are you feeling okay, Mr. Rumble?"

He smoothed his pompadour and touched his breastbone. "Just a touch of indigestion. I musta ate something that didn't agree with me."

She moved a pile of coats from the closest chair. "Do you want to sit down?"

"Nah. I want to take a gander at this storm that's got all you ladies in a toot."

He leered at me, but went outside when Rique meandered to a halt in my vicinity. A faint skunky odor tickled my nose. As a rule, I keep away from murder suspects who splash on too much Pepé Le Pew aftershave, but not tonight. I was supposed to keep a close watch on him until Rick arrived. I pinched my nose when my eyes began to water.

Oscar came inside, pale-faced and wincing.

"Oscar," Cookie insisted, "you should sit down. You don't look good."

He waved away her concerns, sauntered across the dance floor, and climbed onto the stage.

Rique removed his coonskin cap. A fresh wave of Eau de Pepé caught in my throat. I bent over and began to cough. A blast of cold signaled the arrival of another dancer. I raised my head and watched the sheriff come toward me. Our eyes met. He gave a slight, tense nod and pulled handcuffs from his front coat pocket, shielding them so only Rique and I saw them. Rique twitched, and I doubled over coughing as a new wave of his stench came my way.

"Mr. Rumble!" Cookie cried. "What's wrong?"

The sound system squealed. Footsteps pounded toward the stage. "He fainted," a woman said.

"He's not breathing!" a man yelled.

Children began to scream.

"Get them off the stage," Rick ordered. "We need an EMT!"

I remained bent over and coughing, tears blurring my vision. I heard rather than saw several more sets of feet pound past.

"Let's move out of the way, Cookie, and let Mary and Dick through." Concern laced Bud Sternquist's voice. "Rick, you best get the ambulance ready while they work on him. It's gonna be a tough go in this weather."

"Mr. Rumble," Dick Phillips' calm voice cut through the chaos. "Can you hear me?"

"Dan!" Rick called from the stage. "Come with me!" The two men were gone in a flash.

My coughing subsided. I wiped my eyes on a sleeve and surveyed the individuals on the stage with Oscar. Mary Borgeson, Dick Phillips, Bud and Cookie Sternquist. The very people I would want around me in an emergency. Whatever was going on with Oscar, he was in good hands.

Then it hit me. Rick and Dan were getting the ambulance. I inhaled sharply and another wave of stink attacked my throat. Soon I was coughing myself silly and thinking, *If the sheriff is in the ambulance bay, who's keeping an eye on the purveyor of the god-awful polecat perfume that's doing a number on me?*

Chapter 41

Strong hands gripped my waist. My heart pounded. *He's attacking me!*

I wrenched free and made my hands into fists. I crouched, breathed deeply, and prepared to assail my attacker. It was the right reaction, except that I inhaled a whiff of DuPew and launched a new round of coughing.

Stay alert, Jane! Oxygen deprivation can make you sloppy.

Strong hands encircled my waist again, this time accompanied by a voice. "Gus fetched you a gwass of water, Miss Neweww. Can you straighten up and drink it?"

Betty Yarborough tipped my head back and pressed the glass to my lips until I took a sip. Sweet relief coated my throat, and I drank greedily.

Once revived, I straightened and remembered my manners. "Thank you," I croaked. Then I scanned the crowd and asked in a froggy, yet casual tone, "Did you see where Rique went?"

Gus sniffed. "I didn't see nothing, but from the trail of his stink, I'd say he went outside."

"He weft right after the sheriff did. That's the wast I saw of him," Betty said. "He was in an awfuw hurry."

I bet he was! I snatched up my coat on the way to the exit and ran outside. I looked right and then left. The snow and the dark revealed nothing, so I looked down. The snowy ground straight ahead, which was the most logical escape route, was unmarked. The same was true of the snow to the right and along the perimeter of the building. The snow to my left, the closest route to the ambulance bay where Rick and Dan had gone, was a trample of boot tracks. Unless Rique had sprouted wings, his boots had made some of them.

The ambulance rounded the corner and parked at the entrance. The doors of the cab opened. Dan jumped from the driver's side and headed into the building. Rick exited the passenger side, dragging Rique after him. When they passed by, I fell into step behind them.

Once we were in the dance hall, Rick shoved Rique toward me. "I've got to escort the ambulance to Tipperary. I'll radio my deputy to get over here and pick up DuPeuss. Don't let him out of your sight until then."

"Do you want me to sit on him or what?"

"Cuff him to something." Rick pulled the handcuffs from his pocket and threw them to me.

I caught them as Rick ran outside. Seconds later, Mary Borgeson and Dick Phillips wheeled the gurney bearing Oscar Rumble toward the exit. They sliced a path between Rique and me, obscuring my view of him. The shock of Oscar's motionless form and deathly pale face terrified me.

"Is he—"

"Still alive?" Cookie came from nowhere and took my arm. "Yes. Dick and Mary revived him, but it's still touch and go."

The next few seconds lasted forever. The EMTs loaded Oscar into the ambulance. Rick got into the sheriff's vehicle and positioned it in front of the ambulance. Lights flashing and siren blaring, the sheriff's truck and the ambulance turned toward Tipperary and the snow-covered highway.

"Why not a snowplow escort?" I wondered aloud.

"The nearest snowplow driver lives ten miles south of town," Cookie answered. "They can't wait for him to get here. We better pray Rick and Dan don't slide into the ditch between here and Tipperary."

"You do the praying." Betty handed Gus his coat and put on hers. "I'ww caww every rancher between here and Tipperary and teww them to get out their bwades and pwow the highway."

Scott Gibson sprang into action. "We put blades on the Forest Service pickups this afternoon. Let's get to it." Bud Sternquist and several other men grabbed their coats and flew out the door behind him.

Frost McDonald pulled on his overshoes. "Liv, can you take Fanny home? Axel and me'll open the gas station."

Silence fell after the flurry of departures. Strange, considering the number of children in the room. I glanced from one child to the next. They were all too quiet. Their faces too pale. Their eyes too wide. They had seen too much.

I gathered them together. "Mr. Rumble is the first

person I've seen loaded into an ambulance. But I have seen the EMTs take care of people before." Then I leaned closer and spoke in a confidential stage whisper. "One time, they even took care of me. They know what they're doing."

The children launched a volley of questions. Their parents roused from their collective stupor and came over. They hugged and reassured their children, shepherding them into their coats and out the door. After that, everyone else left, and I was alone in the hall.

Son of a gun!

Rique had escaped again. I loped around dance hall like a two-legged bloodhound and sniffed, hoping his scent would give him away. It didn't, though my toe kicked the handcuffs. They skittered across the floor. I ran over and picked them up.

Then I stopped running and started thinking. Considering Rique's Daniel Boone tracking ability and my little-dolt-on-the-prairie lack of the same made it unlikely I could sneak up on him and snap on the cuffs. I zipped the cuffs into my coat pocket. I would have to best him some other way. I put on all my winter regalia and waddled into the storm in search of him.

The storm came at me with animalistic ferocity. Eddies of snow swirled around my feet. Snowflakes peppered my eyes, and they shut involuntarily. I shielded my face with my hands and opened my eyelids again. Blowing snow had already obscured the footprints of those who'd left five minutes ago. So much for following Rique to wherever he was. All that remained was to avoid doing anything crazy and out think him. Or think like him.

Yes, that was it. Think like him.

He knew he was about to be arrested. He knew why. He knew he had a limited time to make his escape. He was Canadian by birth. Once there, he could disappear and live off the land. The only thing between him and his homeland was North Dakota.

How would he get there? *His truck.*

Where did he park his truck? *Outside his camper.*

Where did he keep what he needed to get away? *In his camper.*

I fished keys from my pocket and then paused. Six inches of snow blanketed the Beetle and the road. My tiny car would high center on the way to his camper. If it didn't, Rique would hear me coming, and I would lose the element of surprise. Which was, quite honestly, my only advantage at the moment.

I pushed the keys deep into my pants pocket and struck out on foot to the west edge of town where Rique's camper sat just north of Gavin Wick's house. Little dolt on the prairie was about to confront Daniel Boone. On his home court. In the snow. In the dark.

This isn't going to end well.

True enough. But it was still worth doing.

CHAPTER 42

The waddle to Rique's camper felt interminable. The wind snatched my breath away and flung snow into my eyes. Visibility deteriorated by the minute. Without the dim glow of the streetlights to keep me oriented, I would have lost my way.

My mind swirled. How could Rick and the ambulance crew make it to Tipperary in this weather? How would the deputy make it to Little Missouri? How would he find Rique and me if and when he arrived? I pushed the thoughts away, ignored the growing numbness in my fingers and toes, and slogged on. A grating noise rose above the storm as I neared the place where Rique's camper was parked.

I paused and tried to identify what I'd heard. The wind distorted the sound, batting it back and forth. I gave up and continued down the road. The wind relented when I reached the Wicks' house and turned north. The grating noise grew louder and clearer, and I recognized the sound of an engine trying and failing to catch. Light spilled from the window of Rique's camper, illuminating the cab of his truck. He sat in the cab, his profile shadowy and void of detail.

I crouched next to Gavin's igloo, watching and listening while Rique tried to start the truck again. It refused to cooperate. Just like that, it became my favorite vehicle in all of Little Missouri. Rique got out and slammed its door. He did not hold the truck in the same high regard.

Rique waded to his camper. The wind flung a string of French-Canadian swear words in my direction. They were so vile I blushed, though I don't even speak French. Or Canadian. His bad mood said this was not the time to try to apprehend him. He went inside the camper. I stayed hidden and waited to see what he did next. It was a short wait.

The camper's lights went out. I couldn't see what Rique was doing, but I could hear him. He let loose another round of swearing, and my ears burned. Before long, a beam of light bobbed and moved toward the street. Between the flashlight and his swearing, trailing Rique was going to be easy!

I eased around the igloo and stayed out of the flashlight's beam. Rique turned south and passed right in front of me. He wasn't following the chapter in the Daniel Boone handbook about creeping through snowstorms and making sure he wasn't being pursued. The visibility was too poor to allow much distance between us. Once he was a few yards ahead of me, I crept into position behind him. When he reached the corner where the Wicks' house stood, he turned east. Why was he turning toward town instead of away from it?

Tapping him on the shoulder and asking why seemed

crazy, and as I'd told Rick, I was done with crazy. Granted, tailing DuPeuss during a blizzard felt equally crazy as the wind numbed me to the bone. However, the weather conditions offered a single saving grace. Rique never once turned around to see if he was being followed. And why would he? By his way of thinking, only a tracker with the training required to survive winter storms would venture outdoors in weather like this.

I trudged along behind him, far enough away to avoid being seen, yet close enough to see him when the wind gusted and snow obscured the view ahead. Rique didn't slow down until he neared the dance hall. My breath caught when I saw my car, or to be more accurate, a vaguely car-shaped mound of snow, next to the entrance.

Rique knew I had the handcuffs. If he'd seen my car parked there earlier and connected it to the snow mound in front of him, it could put him on high alert. I scooted behind a tree, expecting him to pause and look around. Instead, he plowed on, and when he reached the building, circled left. I followed as close as I dared, slipping from one shadow to the next.

He reached the corner of the east wall and turned north to where the emergency vehicles were housed behind large garage doors. I crouched behind a row of garbage cans and peered above them. The screech of metal upon metal hurt my ears. A light came on and I saw Rique take a lap around the interior of the garage.

From my hiding place, I saw two rows of vehicles in the parking bay. On the right-hand side were two work trucks, one per side. A water tank rested on a flat trailer behind each truck. An ancient ambulance sat in the back row on the right-hand side. The space where I assumed the ambulance taking Oscar to Tipperary usually sat was vacant.

Rique stopped when he reached the vacant space. His head turned from one vehicle to the next, his back toward me. I took advantage of his position and left my hiding place, aiming for the door jamb nearest to the work trucks. When I got there, I pressed my torso against the wall and peeked inside. I saw a wrench hanging within reach on the wall and removed it. Then I unzipped the pocket that held the handcuffs, pulled them out, and waited.

Rique flung open the door on the driver's side of the ancient ambulance. It screeched in protest. He scrambled behind the steering wheel and cranked the engine. It whimpered, wheezed, and died. Rique pounded the steering wheel and swore. The old ambulance kept its composure and remained silent as a corpse. Rique climbed out and kicked a front tire, dislodging its rusty hubcap with a bang.

I raised the wrench in solidarity with the sassy old ambulance. *Take that, cow killer!*

Rique ran toward the work truck closest to the exit. He pulled at the door handle. It didn't budge. He went to the board where keys hung in rows and ran a finger along each label, slowly sounding out the words.

Now!

I put the handcuffs between my teeth and crept up behind him. He was so close I could count the moles on his neck. I lifted the wrench and inhaled. A snoutful of Eau de Pepé invaded my throat, and I coughed. The cuffs did a swan dive and landed on the concrete floor with a sickening clang.

Chapter 43

Rique whirled around. I bonked him on the head with the wrench. He crumpled to the ground. I bent over, snagged the cuffs, and ran outside. The garage lights illuminated the patch of snow directly in front of the building. I veered toward the shadows and made my way behind the garbage cans. I stuffed the handcuffs into their zipper pocket and the wrench into my parka's inner one. They were bound to come in handy at some point.

I peeked over the cans into the garage. Rique was on his feet. He swayed and used the wall for balance as he made for the exit. That coonskin hat of his had padded his thick skull admirably. I stayed where I was. Partly because the garbage smelled better than he did, and partly because he would be expecting me to run for home and lock myself in. But mostly because I wanted to see what he would do next. What he did next was to walk into the storm, turn east, and tramp through the snow toward the street. Every step increased the distance between us. That was good. But I couldn't fathom his next move. That wasn't so good.

I watched him pass through the glow of a streetlight. Thousands of snowflakes whirled around him in an ethereal dance. Once I was certain he thought I'd gone home, I crept into the shadows, staying beyond the reach of the garage lights until the last second. Then I ran full tilt into the garage, skirting the walls until I reached the light switches. I flipped them all off and plunged the parking bay into darkness. Then I crept along the west wall toward the exit.

Once outside I turned left, running a hand along the west wall of the building. The storm had grown fiercer. It batted at me like I was a piece of dandelion fluff. The wind sucked breath from my nostrils. I bent low and pressed closer to the wall. Finally, I reached the southwest corner of the building and peered around it. The beam from the light above the dance hall entrance was feeble. That suited me just fine. I rounded the corner and made for the door. I crouched low, took a penlight from my pocket, and switched it on. Cupping a hand around the beam, I aimed it at the snow in front of the entrance. It contained not one divot or boot print. No sign of Rique. Good.

I eased the door open. A sliver of light appeared. Surprised, I shut it quickly. Why hadn't the last person to leave the hall turned out the lights? Then I realized the last person had been me and decided to cut her some slack. I eased the door open and slipped inside. No melting snow or fresh boot prints marked the floor. Now I was doubly certain Rique wasn't here. Not yet. And, if I had anything to say about it, not until I was good and

ready to lure him inside and trap him there until the
deputy sheriff arrived.

The light switches were beside the entrance, and I
turned them off one by one. Using the thin beam of the
penlight, I made my way to Oscar Rumble's sound equipment on the stage. I loaded the record player spindle with
every vinyl forty-five it could hold—fourteen by my count.
Then I turned the amplifier volume to its top setting and
set the needle on the first record. With the penlight for a
guide, I hopped off the stage, went to the door, and flung
it open. The opening measures of "Somethin' 'Bout You
Baby I Like" blasted my ears and blared into the storm.
I hustled to a cluster of wooden chairs about six feet
from the entrance and squeezed in behind them. Then
I switched off the penlight, slid it inside my glove, and
waited for Rique DuPeuss to take the bait.

He took his sweet time. The needle hit the seventh
song on the stack, and my toes and fingers were tingling
back to life when he finally skidded through the door.
Between his stink, his swearing, and his stomping, I
didn't have to see him to know where he was. While
he clumped up the stairs of the stage with the delicacy
of the Budweiser Clydesdales, I eased from behind the
chairs, picked up the sturdiest one, and carried it outside.

The blizzard smashed into me as I shut the door and
wedged the chair under the knob. It wouldn't hold him
for long, and I prayed for the deputy to arrive soon. At
this juncture, my best bet was to retrace the route to the
vehicle bay where I could wait out of the wind, though
not the cold. I would be beyond Rique's reach, but close
enough to hear if he broke out of the dance hall. I inched

along the wall, squinting into the darkness. Snowflakes flew into my eyes and made them water. More flakes mixed with my tears and froze my eyelids shut. With only my hand sliding along the wall to guide me, I kept going. My fingers grew numb. Soon all feeling in them would wither. At that moment, the wall fell away. I was too scared to move. Which was worse, stumbling in the wrong direction and dying in a snowdrift or standing here until I was frozen solid?

I lurched forward into the black abyss. My knees buckled, and I fell onto something hard. I swept a hand back and forth across its surface. It was smooth with only a skiff of snow. I crawled forward on my hands and knees, feeling my way until my head bumped into something. I traced a round outline, bent forward and breathed in a rubbery odor. Was it a tire? It was. I had reached the vehicle bay!

I ripped off a glove, breathed on my fingers, and held them to an eyelid. I repeated the process until the ice melted, and my eye opened. I pulled out the penlight to search for somewhere to lie low. The back of the old ambulance proved to be the perfect place. I opened its rear doors, crawled inside, and took stock of its contents. Quickly I spread blankets on the gurney and piled the pillows on its front end. Then I crawled under the covers and lay on my back. I propped my head on the pillows and pulled up the blankets until I was all but hidden. Unless Rique came in and turned on the lights, he wouldn't find me. I couldn't see him either, but I'd left the rear doors ajar so I could hear and smell him.

I was motionless for the first time in hours—and

warmer, too. My eyelids grew heavy as the minutes ticked by. My breathing slowed.

You're falling asleep, Jane! No. I'm not.

You are. Am not.

You can't. Can . . . so . . .

Wake up! . . . Leave . . . me . . . be . . .

Through the fog of sleep, I heard an engine rumble to life. My eyes flew open. I eased up on one elbow and looked at the work trucks. Both were silent. I threw off the blankets, kicked at the rear doors, and reached out a hand until it touched the wall. I followed it to the exit and slowly poked my head around the corner. One of the road graders that had been parked in the vacant lot to the east was moving. It turned onto the road. It passed under a streetlight, which illuminated the driver's face. It was Rique DuPeuss.

No! He was not going to elude capture again. I had to stop him now, or he'd be gone for good. I raced toward the garbage cans, grabbed a lid for protection, and yanked out my wrench. I waded through the snow into the road grader's path. Channeling Don Quixote—no, make that Joan of Arc—I planted my feet and brandished my weapons. I was certain Rique would come to his senses and stop when he saw me. He wasn't totally deranged. The road grader picked up speed and kept coming. Realization dawned.

He *was* totally crazy and then some!

CHAPTER 44

I was about to throw the wrench at the grader and bail when a figure appeared from the darkness to my left. It barreled into me, and the impact sent me flying. I crashed into the garbage cans. They tipped over. Frozen trash spewed everywhere and rained down on me. The linebacker wannabe lay on my right leg. Rique was getting away, and we needed to go after him!

"Get up." I hissed.

The linebacker scrambled to his feet, hauled me to mine, and steered us to the garage. "We should get out of this storm."

"No." I yanked my arm away and pointed at the road grader. It had reached the intersection and turned west. I waved an arm in its direction. "DuPeuss is escaping!"

"In a road grader? He must be out of his mind."

At least he—whoever was hidden under his ski mask and snowmobile suit—and I agreed about that.

I grabbed his arm and pulled. He didn't budge. "We have to stop him."

"How?"

"Come on!" I pulled at him again and pointed to the other grader.

He budged.

I held onto him until we reached it. I studied the ladder-step arrangement that led to the cab, screwed up my courage, and scaled it. I yanked open the cab door and crawled into the driver's seat. Then I paused to survey a puzzling array of levers, pedals, switches, gauges, and whatchamacallits. The one thing I didn't see was a key. *Rats!*

The linebacker's head appeared. "You know how to run this thing?" he asked from his perch on the ladder thingy.

"Do you?" I shot back.

He entered the cab. "Move over."

I did.

He sat down and studied the gears. "Can't see much with this on." He took off his ski mask and stuffed it in his pocket. "That's better."

For him maybe, though not for me. I'd been hoping for the deputy sheriff. The person beside me was Dick Phillips. He studied the control panel, his gaze moving from one whatchamacallit to the next. I stared at him, open-mouthed, aghast at my own stupidity. I'd seen his snowmobile suit before. Good grief, I'd seen his ski mask too. How had I not known it was him?

"Oh, I see." He flipped the smallest lever on the panel. The engine rumbled, the cab shook, and he smiled. "It uses an ignition switch rather than a key."

Now I knew why I hadn't recognized him. This Dick Phillips used complete sentences. Furthermore, he was supposed to be in the ambulance. How had he made it to Tipperary and back already? That was impossible unless . . .

"What happened to Oscar?"

Dick ignored me and studied the array of doohickeys and whatnots spread out before us. He tested the floor pedals, tapped gauges, and grasped one lever after another.

I grew uneasy. "Have you operated a snow plow before?"

"It's a road grader."

Picky, picky, picky. "Okay then, have you operated a road grader?"

"Almost."

Since when had operating heavy machinery entered the company of horseshoes and hand grenades? Before I could ask, Dick pushed on a foot pedal and shifted a lever. Next, he eased up on left floor pedal and pushed the right one. The road grader lurched forward. I lurched backward, arms flailing and searching for a way to steady myself.

I was about to settle for Dick's ear when he grabbed my hand and pinned it under his arm. Not quite my cup of tea, but it would have to do.

Dick shouted above the engine noise, "Which way do you think he'll take out of town?"

"My guess is west. He knows his way around the Long Pines and how to live off the land. Once he gets there, no one will find him."

"You're right." Dick steered the road grader toward the street and fiddled with a lever. "I think this lowers the blade. I'll leave it be for now." He took a hard right and turned south. It was the opposite of the direction Rique had gone.

"Why aren't you following him?"

"We can't catch up with him, but we might be able to block him."

"Did you play football in high school?"

He gave me an odd look, then concentrated on negotiating the quickest route to DuPeuss and the renegade road grader.

"There he is!" I shouted when we reached Main Street. Headlights approached slowly from the north. The storm had let up, at least for the moment, but distances were difficult to judge due to the snow cover. I guessed he was approaching the school and my apartment, about two blocks from where we were now.

"Hang on!" Dick cranked the steering wheel to the right. The road grader whined in protest as it made the turn.

"Slow down!" I screamed.

"Nope. We gotta reach him before he can turn down the road that runs south of the school." He worked a lever and our speed increased.

DuPeuss must have sensed our intent because his lights began advancing at an alarming rate. They veered to the right. That was a gamble with the snow blanketing the street and blurring its edges.

Dick centered our grader between the streetlights on either side of Main Street. "If he tries to get around us, he'll go off the road."

"And take down the fence around the school," I grumbled.

Dick grinned. "Unless he tries to take us down first."

Yup. He'd played football.

The distance between Rique and us shrank. Our game of chicken grew more dangerous with each turn of the axles. We crept toward the intersection at an inexorable snail's pace. A few seconds later, the beam of our plow picked up the outline of the other grader. Soon, I could see DuPeuss sitting in the cab. Then I could see his face. The rage painted on it made me shudder.

Dick waited to touch the brake until the front of our grader entered the crucial intersection. The grader responded and crawled to a halt at an angle that blocked the road completely. The oncoming vehicle slowed, but it didn't stop. DuPeuss's decision to end his game came at the last possible second, and he came to a halt in front of the school playground.

"Let's get him"—I unzipped my pocket and pulled out the handcuffs—"before he escapes again."

Dick took the cuffs, flung open the cab door, and jumped into a snowdrift.

"Hey!" I leaned outside. DuPeuss leapt from the other vehicle and landed near the chicken-wire fence around the playground. He used it to pull himself to his feet and then began climbing over it.

Oh no, you don't!

I held my nose and aimed for Dick's snowdrift, then closed my eyes and jumped.

"My arm!" Dick bellowed.

I opened my eyes and rolled toward the fence and DuPeuss. His foot was tangled in the wire fence. I stood up and grabbed at him. He swung his free leg above me and slammed his boot onto the crown of my head.

My knees gave out, and I screamed, "Dick! Don't let him get away!" The trampled drift rose to meet me, and the white snow went black.

Chapter 45

A swift kick in my ribs jolted me into consciousness. "Ouch!" I flipped over and away from the source of my pain. I caught my breath and sat up. A figure stood above me, facing the fence where DuPeuss struggled to extricate himself from his chicken-wire prison.

"There," Dick said after a metallic click. "You aren't going anywhere until the sheriff arrives and escorts you to jail."

This guy sounded far too smug for Dick and used too many words. I crawled over and looked up. It was Dick all right. I saw that he'd cuffed DuPeuss to the fence. "I doubt that he keeps wire cutters in his pocket, but pliers are a definite possibility. We better check."

DuPeuss fought the search. When Dick pulled a pair of pliers out of the trapper's coat pocket, he swung at us with a desperate fury. His last means of escape was gone.

Dick handed them to me. "Take these inside and then call Betty. Have her get word to the sheriff about

DuPeuss. I'll stay here till Rick arrives. He shouldn't be too much longer."

"But isn't he—"

"Just go."

The weariness in his tone was unmistakable. I stifled my questions. Tall drifts impeded my progress across the playground, but visibility improved with each step as the snow and the wind died down. I slogged up the landing steps, went inside, and without removing my boots walked into the kitchen and rang Betty.

She picked up. "Are you okay, Miss Neweww?"

"Just fine, Betty. Dick Phillips wants you to tell the sheriff to collect Rique DuPeuss at the school. He's handcuffed to the playground fence."

"Stay put. I'ww caww you back before you know it." She was gone before I could raise any objections. Not that I had any. Waiting in a warm apartment while Dick stood guard in the cold felt like a reasonable division of labor to me. In a spirit of camaraderie, I filled the teakettle, set it on the stove to boil, and put several tea bags in a large thermos.

The phone rang, and I picked up. "I cawwed the deputy in Tipperary. He radioed the message to the sheriff and said Rick wiww be there in a few minutes."

"I thought the deputy was coming for DuPeuss while the sheriff escorted the ambulance to Tipperary."

"There was a change of pwans because of the bwizzard." She sounded ready to acquaint me with the details, but a siren wailed and lights flashed outside before she could.

"The sheriff's here. Gotta go." I dropped the receiver and ran for the door. Rique DuPeuss had led me on a merry chase tonight, and I intended to witness him being taken into custody.

He was putting up a fight when I reached the fence. The sheriff and Dick were too much for him. He snarled like a rabid skunk as Rick secured the handcuffs behind his back and shoved him into the sheriff's truck. Dick buckled him into the seatbelt, and Rick secured his feet with manacles.

Rick's face was grim as he slid into the driver's seat. "It's gonna be a long ride to Tipperary."

"What about your deputy? And where's Os—"

"I gotta get DuPeuss under lock and key real quick. Dick can fill you in." The sheriff shut the door, fastened his seatbelt, and left me standing in the dark, though not alone.

I turned to Dick. "Want some tea?"

This new, more talkative Dick had either lost his shyness, or he was too cold to blush. He met my gaze without turning the palest shade of red and said, "That would hit the spot."

Soon, our snow-soaked outer layers were drying in the entryway. We were sitting at my kitchen table, our hands curled around hot mugs of tea, heads bent to catch the steam rising from them. Granny square afghans covered our legs, and a plate of chocolate chip oatmeal cookies sat between us on the table. Dick reached for a second cookie, the first one having disappeared in two large bites.

I slid the plate next to me and curved an arm around it. "No more until you bring me up to date about Oscar. Is he dead?"

Dick swallowed and shook his head. "He was alive

when they loaded him in the airplane at the Wentworths' airstrip."

My throat constricted. My thoughts spiraled. The mention of the Wentworths and their runway sucked me into a vortex of bad memories.

That's all in the past, Jane! You're safe now. You're safe here.

I returned to the present and blinked. What Dick had said? Something about Oscar . . . the Wentworths and . . . "An airplane?" This made no sense. "Why an airplane?"

"The highway was so bad at first we were barely moving. Rick radioed his deputy about the road conditions. He said it wasn't even snowing in Tipperary, that the storm petered out about five miles east of where we were, and conditions were good the rest of the way to Bowman. Rick had him contact the Wentworths about using their plane to fly Oscar to their hospital. The deputy said Betty had ordered Richard Wentworth to get his ranch hands busy plowing their driveway and runway because she had a bad feeling about the ground ambulance. Nobody, not even Richard Wentworth, argues with Betty and her feelings."

I listened, amazed by the Dick's story and the words flowing from him. I didn't know what had transformed him into this loquacious man, but I liked him. However, I wouldn't be satisfied until I'd heard every last detail. "So the Wentworth ranch hands cleared the highway too?"

"No, that was Scott and Dan with the Forest Service trucks. They caught up with us just past the bridge. Once they heard what was going on, they got in front of us and cleared the highway to the Wentworth's driveway. After that, things moved fast. Richard's plane was gassed up and ready when we got there. We transferred Oscar into the plane, and they took right off."

"In this storm? Wasn't that risky?"

"He's got a lot of experience. He could fly out blindfolded if he had to. I've heard his instrument panel is topnotch, too."

"But why didn't you go with Oscar?"

"Between him and the equipment, there was only room for one EMT. Rick had to stick around and use his radio to coordinate things with the Bowman airport and hospital. So he told Mary to go with Oscar and me to come to Little Missouri to locate you and DuPeuss."

"Wow." I set the plate in front of him. "It sounds like I missed all the excitement."

Dick took two cookies and devoured one before replying. "Things looked plenty exciting when I caught up with you."

The phone rang. I hopped up. "Jane Newell, here."

"Miss Neweww, I have two messages to pass awong to you." Betty took a deep breath, a sure sign of drama to come. "First off, Mrs. Dremstein says there wiww be a two-hour wate start tomorrow."

Nice to know, but hardly dramatic. Maybe I'd misjudged her.

"And"—much longer pause—"Richard Wentworth wanded his pwane at the Bowman Airport. Oscar survived the trip. An ambuwance is transferring him to the hospitaw now."

I let out a whoop, thanked her, and hung up. When I turned back to the table, only one cookie remained. I swiped it for myself. "That was Betty."

"And?"

"The plane landed, and Oscar's on his way to the hospital."

"That's wonderful news." Dick jumped up and engulfed me in a bear hug. When he let go, he was blushing, I was speechless, our lips were deliciously close, and the cookie in my hand was a broken, melty mess. This wasn't how I'd expected my cookie to crumble, but I rather liked it.

CHAPTER 46

Again, the phone rang. We sprang apart and I hurried to answer.

"Do you know where Dick Phiwwips is?"

I had trouble finding my voice and cleared my throat. "He's here."

"Put him on the wine," Betty barked. "You sound wike you're catching cowd. Drink honey and wemon."

I held the receiver out to Dick. "It's Betty. For you."

He took it and listened for a long minute. Then he said, "Got it," handed me the phone, and hurried to the entryway where he put on his snowmobile suit.

"What's going on?"

"Nothing much."

N-n-n-n-no! He didn't get to shut me down like that.

"Well, something must be happening. Why are you leaving?"

"The road crew wants to start plowing, but the road graders aren't where they were earlier today. And the ambulance is parked where I found you waving a wrench at DuPeuss and his road grader." He pulled on his ski mask, boots, and mittens. "You wanna tell me what that was about?"

I took a page out of his book. "Nothing much."

He left. All at once, the hours I'd spent playing cat and mouse in the snow with Rique caught up with me. My muscles turned to jelly. I wanted to crawl into bed and go to sleep. I shuffled to my bedroom and pulled out my warmest, coziest pajamas. But I didn't have the energy to put them on and dropped them on the floor. Fully clothed, I crawled under the covers and fell into a deep and dreamless sleep. When my alarm rang in the morning, scenes from the night began playing inside my head. Before I could catch hold of them, the phone rang.

I picked up immediately. "Rick?"

"No, this is Betty Yarborough with the watest on Oscar. He's hanging in there."

"Thanks, Betty." I hung up.

In the next few minutes, I took four more phone calls.

Merle wanted to know where Rique DuPeuss was.

"I'm not exactly sure."

Iva Kelly wondered when the Valentine party would begin.

"Two o'clock."

Roger Holmstead, the television reporter from KOTA in Rapid City, asked for a scoop.

"No comment."

Finally, the call I'd been wanting more than any other. "Hi Jane, this is Rick."

"What took you so long?"

"Your phone's been busy all morning. I had to talk Betty into bumping me to the front of the line."

"Where's DuPeuss?"

"In the Meade County Jail in Sturgis."

"Where are you?"

"At the Wicks'. We just secured Rique's living quarters. Can I come over?"

"School starts in an hour. You'd better get here quick."

He made it in fifteen minutes. The first order of business was to box up the remaining evidence we had about DuPeuss. Then we sat down, and he briefed me on what to expect next.

"Because Rique holds Canadian citizenship, the prosecutor is being extra diligent in building his case. He asked me to bring the remaining evidence down today so he can review it before he initiates contact with Canadian officials. Once that's done, he'll begin interviewing witnesses—"

"Like who?"

"You, me, Dan Barkley, and Scott Gibson for starters. Probably some of the ranchers who lost cattle."

"When?"

"I expect he'll drive up in the next couple days. I'll let you know."

"So I have time to warn my parents?"

A car door slammed, and shrill, excited voices came from the playground. The kids were arriving.

"You do. And to celebrate Valentine's Day with your students. And to bear the wrath of Velma. She's coming in after school to clean. I hear she thinks you and Liv should have postponed your parties until Friday."

"What for?"

"Because cleaning up after a party and a snowstorm

on the same day means she'll miss her favorite television shows."

"She doesn't run the school."

"Very true, but going easy on the glitter could save your life today." He picked up the box of evidence. "Happy Valentine's Day, Jane."

I opened the door for him. "The same to you, Rick."

There was just enough time to visit the restroom before school started. Once that was done, I hurried to collect my students. Before I reached the entryway, the playground noise had escalated from excited to frenzied and was approaching hysterical. A glance out the window revealed several big kids perched on the drifts lining the sidewalk. When had Dick cleared the snow? The older students were poised to drop onto the younger kids, who were swinging their book bags like maces.

I grabbed the bell, went outside, and rang it. "Lower your weap—backpacks," I shouted as my students lined up.

"Happy Valentine's Day!" Winter Skye yelled at the top of her lungs.

The other children picked up the chant. "Happy Valentine's Day! Happy Valentine's Day!"

Ay-yi-yi-yi-yi. This was going to be quite the day.

I whispered a prayer of thanks for the two-hour late start and motioned my students inside. Two lost socks, four tangled snowsuits, five stepped-on toes, and seven reminders to line up their boots later, eleven disheveled children stormed the classroom. Most took the scenic route past their Valentine's boxes on the way to their desks.

"What time is the party?" Tiege shouted as he bounced along.

"Two o'clock."

"That's so long!" Renny groaned and flopped into his chair.

"The sooner you get to work, the faster the time will pass." I went to my desk for my three-ring binder of lesson plans. A gigantic heart-shaped box of chocolates sat on top of it. I looked for a card. There wasn't one, so I held up the box. "You tricky kids! How did you sneak this onto my desk?"

Eleven blank stares.

Elva shook her head. "It's not from us."

"Read the card." Bennan sounded uncannily like me telling him to read the directions.

I shuffled through the papers on my desk. "There isn't one."

"Maybe you have a secret *admiderer.*" Cora drew a heart in the air. So did Winter Skye, Keeva, and Grace.

"Kapow!" Jeremy struck his Batman pose.

"Is it the sheriff?" Stig asked.

Tiege spoke in my defense. "Miss Newell and him are friends and that's all!" Then he fell out of his chair.

This was going nowhere. I set down the candy box and picked up the binder. "It's time for reading class. Meet me at the table, kindergartners!"

The day limped along with me steering the discussions away from secret admirers and the children steering it back until Cookie Sternquist and Pam Barkley arrived shortly before the party began. While Cookie laid out treats and Pam set up the games, the children abandoned their assignments.

I took pity on them. "Put your papers away and get your valentine boxes."

They obeyed with astonishing speed.

Keeva eyed hers. "Can we open them?"

"Yes."

Before Beau opened his box, he came to my desk. "Want me to get yours?"

"How thoughtful of you, Beau. Yes."

For the next few minutes, all that could be heard in the classroom was the sound of envelopes being ripped opened, children saying thank you to one another, and kindergarteners asking for help reading their cards.

After several such requests, Cookie intervened. "Pam and I will take care of the kindergartners. The children want to watch you open their valentines to you."

I opened their cards one by one and thanked them profusely for the conversation hearts and squished chocolates tucked inside. When I finished, Winter Skye opened her desk and brought out a lumpy package wrapped in tissue paper and tied with yarn. She brought it to me. "Here's mine. It wouldn't go through the opening in your box."

I untied the bow and the paper fell away, exposing a little stuffed animal. Not just any stuffed animal, but a mouse. Not just any mouse, but a mouse clad in tiny pink overalls holding a lacy white heart. On it the words "There's somethin' 'bout you baby I like" had been written in red.

I stroked its fur. "It's so soft. Where did you buy it?"

"I didn't buy it. Mommy wrote the words and made the clothes. Me and Daddy made the mouse. He says I'll be as good at it as him real soon."

I dropped Winter Skye's gift and stifled the urge to run to the sink and scrub my hands with soap, carbolic acid, and bleach.

She picked up the mouse. "Don't worry. It won't break." She stroked my cheek with its tail. "Doesn't that feel good?"

Chapter 47

Forever after, I recalled only disjointed fragments of that party. Cookie plucking the mouse from Winter Skye's hand and putting it up high where "everyone could admire it." Pam playing Pin the Heart on Cupid and other silly games with the kids. The children decorating and devouring heart-shaped cookies. Me vowing to Pam and Cookie after school that, should I ever have a daughter, she would never wear pink overalls. The three of us brainstorming about what to do with Winter Skye's gift.

Pam suggested throwing it into the burn barrel. Cookie offered to bring a cat to my room over the weekend.

I pretended to be mature. "I don't want to break Winter Skye's heart. The mouse has to stay. But I'm never going to touch it again."

Pam and Cookie packed up the party detritus and collected their children from the playground. I took my cards and the mystery box of chocolates—two pounds at least—and set them on my kitchen table. I returned to the classroom for my valentine box, then took it into the kitchen. Something rattled inside it when I pitched it in the trash. I pulled out the box, took off the lid, and found three cards in it. They must have gone unnoticed after Winter Skye gave me the mouse. The cards weren't the cheap, silly variety the kids had given me. They were the full-sized, serious, Hallmark variety.

I slit open the first envelope with a butter knife. It was a lovely card from Rick Sternquist with an entirely professional note of thanks for my contributions to the case.

The next card featured Pepé Le Pew making eyes at Penelope Pussycat and was signed by none other than Rique DuPeuss. The man wasn't in his right mind. I went to the stove, intending to use a gas flame to burn it to ashes. On second thought, I took it to the lab and slipped it in an evidence bag. If necessary, it could be used as proof of his propensity to trespass on government property.

The last card was large, beautiful, and expensive. It was also unsigned. Questions began tumbling around my brain faster than balls in a bingo cage. Who had come into the building to deliver it? How had he and Rique DuPeuss gotten inside? When? Did they have keys?

"You gonna stare into space with your mouth open forever? It don't look good on you."

My heart jumped into my throat and I whirled around.

Velma Albright stood with her hands on her hips and glared at me. "Thought you'd want to know I'm here." She turned and stomped toward the classroom. "There better not be frosting in the carpet."

"Hang on!" I caught up with her and waved the cards from DuPeuss and who-knew-who at her. "Do you know anything about these?"

She stopped. Her mouth flopped open, and she stared into space. I didn't say it out loud, but it wasn't a good look for her either.

Knowing that a silent Velma was a guilty Velma, I pressed my advantage. "Do you know how they got here?"

"Hmph." She marched to the closet and grabbed the vacuum.

"Because if you don't, the other explanation is that there are other keys floating around town. I'd better call Mrs. Dremstein about rekeying the locks." I walked over to the phone.

Velma muttered something.

"What was that?"

"Don't."

"Did you deliver the note from Rick Sternquist?"

"Why would I bother"—her eyes crackled with fury—"when you let him waltz in whenever he wants? That ain't no way for the two of you to act, what with all that church goin' you do."

"Velma, I'm going to tell you something in confidence."

"You're pregnant! How many months along?"

"Zero," I snapped. "Stay here."

I ran to my apartment and took the key to the lab from its hiding place. Then I returned to the classroom, took Velma by the elbow, and steered her to what she thought was a guest bedroom. I unlocked it and told her to go inside.

Her eyes grew wide as she took in the microscope, finger-printing kit, the tables, and the outer walls of the darkroom. She looked at me, apparently at a loss for words. A stymied Velma was also a silent Velma. Good to know.

I basked in the quiet for a few seconds before taking pity on her. "This is the Tipperary County forensics lab." She remained silent while I explained its origin, Mrs. Dremstein's complicity, and my role in the investigation of Rocko's death. I didn't mention that Betty knew about the lab already. I wanted to live to celebrate my twenty-second birthday.

Velma finally found her tongue. "Do you know how Rocko died?"

"We're getting close."

"You swear there's no funny business between you and the sheriff?"

"I do."

"And I can't tell anybody what you told me?"

"Not until the investigation is wrapped up. I'll let you know when that happens."

She brightened and then frowned. "I ain't sure Dick Phillips can wait that long."

"Why should he care?"

Cold fury sparked in her eyes. She advanced in my direction. I wanted to duck under a lab table and hide.

"I never thought you was a hard woman before today, Jane Newell. Here you are, waving the card Dick give you like a rodeo flag and eating that two-pound box of chocolates he brung, and you got the gall to ask why he should care. What's wrong with you?"

Dick Phillips? The wordless wonder had struck again.

I opened the card and stuck it under her nose. "He didn't sign his card. Or leave a note with the chocolates. Go see for yourself. They're on the kitchen table."

She stormed to the kitchen, righteous indignation emanating from every pore of her body. She picked up the box and examined it with meticulous suspicion before tossing it on the table. "How come you haven't eaten one yet? You think you're too good for drugstore chocolates?"

Oh, my word! I had to talk her down from the ledge she had crawled onto before she fell off and killed our friendship.

"That's not why I didn't open them. It's because we're in the middle of an investigation, and it didn't seem wise to dip into a box of candy mysteriously set on my desk by an anonymous giver."

"Hmph." Velma crossed her arms and glowered. "So you ain't pregnant then?"

"Unless immaculate conception is a possibility, and I believe that was a one-time occurrence—"

"Enough of that church talk," she snapped. "Don't you think Dick Phillips deserves to hear what you just told me?"

For Pete's sake! The woman was impossible. Impossible and petty and a faithful friend, and I loved her with all my heart.

I counted to five and said, "You're right. He does, but like everything else, it has to wait until the official investigation is finished."

Then I picked up the box of candy, tore off the cellophane, and removed the lid. I spent a long minute studying the map that showed which chocolate lived where. Then I pointed to them one by one. "That one is caramel, that's the coconut cream, and this one is the chocolate covered cherry."

"Go ahead." I held the box out to her. "Cupid gets the first pick."

Chapter 48

Velma declared we were once again friends after her fourth chocolate. She ate one more before going off to vacuum. I locked the lab and hid the key. Being friends was one thing. Granting nosey friends access to confidential information was another.

I found myself at loose ends. It was too early for supper. My classroom needed to be readied for tomorrow, but that could wait until it had been cleaned. I'd had about as much Velma as my sanity could handle in a twenty-four-hour period. I could take a walk, but after yesterday's outdoor adventures, pulling teeth sounded more appealing. My conscience said to call my parents and tell them what I'd told Velma. I tried to ignore it, but gave up and went to the phone.

Dad picked up. "Harold Newell speaking."

"Hi, Dad. Happy Valentine's Day!"

"The same to you, Janie-Jo. You going out to celebrate?"

"No. I had plenty of excitement last night. We had

a snowstorm and the situation we talked about before came to a head in the middle of it."

"Sounds exciting." Dad paused. "You know, Janie-Jo. I don't think it's right for me to keep what you're doing from your mother any longer. It puts me in a difficult situation, and I don't like it."

"That's why I'm calling. Is Mom home?"

"We have supper reservations at The Normandy. She's changing her clothes."

"Ooh, fancy! Do you need to get going?"

"Not for a few more minutes."

Perfect. I had plenty of time to confess, but Mom would have to cut her overreaction short if she wanted to keep the dinner reservation. "Can you ask Mom to listen in?"

"Doris!" Dad hollered. "Pick up the phone in the bedroom. It's Jane."

Mom came on the line. "What's wrong?"

"Happy Valentine's Day."

"Are you pregnant?"

"Did Velma tell you that?"

"Are you?"

"No."

"Then why did you call? And don't say because it's Valentine's Day."

I closed my eyes and prayed for patience. Then I asked Betty to clear the party line. Only when she assured me that no one else was listening did I tell her what I'd told Velma—with a few minor changes, such as leaving out Dad's involvement in the investigation. It felt wrong to throw a man in a wheelchair under the bus. I did tell her about Betty's involvement.

That got a reaction. "She never breathed a word. How can I ever trust her again?"

"The sheriff swore me to secrecy." Betty sounded injured. "Did you think I wouwd disobey the waw?"

"I guess not," Mom replied. "But as for you, young lady—"

Here it comes.

"—You deliberately disobeyed me again. I've told you many times to stop all that criminal justice nonsense and become a teacher."

"Mom, I obeyed your rules while I was under your roof. But I don't live with you anymore. I'm on my own. I make my own decisions. I wish I'd been up front from the start, but Rick and are I using our fake romance to cover up our investigation."

"So you truly aren't pregnant?"

"Take a step back and think about what you just said. Do you see the irony in it? You and Velma are so thick, I couldn't risk telling you the truth for fear you'd leak it to her."

"Harold, are you going to let her talk to me like this?"

One word from Dad and their Valentine's Day date would be ruined. I spoke quickly. "Don't sic Dad on me, Mom. It won't work."

"Say goodbye, Doris. We need to go."

Mom hung up with a thunk and a Velma-esque "Hmph."

"Bye, Dad."

"She'll get over it, Janie-Jo. Talk to you later." His receiver clattered into its cradle.

"Your father's right, Miss Neweww. Your mother

wiww get over it. You may not be aware of it, but she is quite the worrier."

"I lived under her roof for twenty-one years. I'm aware."

"She wuvs you very much."

Maybe too much?

"I know, Betty. Bye now."

With the call over, I opened the refrigerator and then closed it. I didn't feel like cooking tonight, but going to Round the Bend alone on Valentine's Day was too depressing.

I opened the fridge again and contemplated the limp head of lettuce and loaf of stale bread sitting there.

The phone rang. I reached for it like a drowning woman in need of life preserver. "Hello?"

"Jane?"

"Rick?"

"Yes. Are you free for supper?"

Halleluia!

"Should I put on my fancy duds?"

"I'll be wearing a snowmobile suit."

"Killjoy."

With the thermometer sitting at one below, I put on long underwear and wool trousers. My single holiday concession was a red wool sweater. It wouldn't be visible under my down vest and parka, but who cared? I was going out on Valentine's Day with a good friend, and that was something. When Rick rapped on the door, I pushed it open with great eagerness and almost knocked him off the landing.

"Get out much?"

We walked to his truck and climbed in. Instead of

backing out, he said, "We need to talk about a couple things before we get to The Bend."

"If it's about the rumors going around town that I'm pregnant and the baby is yours, they're not true."

"I'm serious, Jane. Things are moving fast with Rique's case. The prosecutor will be in Little Missouri tomorrow to take statements. He wants you to be available all day."

"What about scho—"

"Already taken care of. Mrs. Dremstein knows, and she called Mom to be your substitute."

I reached for the door handle. "I need to get things ready."

He laid a hand on my forearm. "It can wait until after we eat. The attorney wants us to play up the romance to keep your part in all this under wraps for now. He says that reporter you know is trying to break the story."

"Roger Holmstead?"

"That's the guy."

"He called this morning, and I refused to comment."

"Interesting. Well, he knows we've been seen together more than normal and keeps asking if you're involved with this investigation. Said he might make a trip up here to find out what's going on. There's a good chance he'll be at The Bend tonight."

"Well then, let's give him a show!"

From the second we set foot in the café, we played our parts to perfection. Eye-batting and cutesy nose-wrinkling from me. Love-struck looks and goofy grins from him. Both of us casting soulful gazes at one another while we held hands across the table. I didn't see Holmstead, but our dinner theater audience drank in the spectacle. Every eye honed in on our last bit of stage business. Rick helped me into my parka. I snuggled my fingers into his coat pocket. We were absolutely adorable as we squeezed through the exit arm in arm.

Rick waited until the door closed behind us to murmur in my ear. "Don't even think about going back for a curtain call."

"Why not?" I pouted. "It would be so fun. We might get a standing ovation."

He tightened his arm around my waist on our way to the truck. A KOTA news van drove by as we crossed Main Street hip to hip. As I got into the cab, I noticed Trudy Berthold and several customers following our progress, their noses pressed against the front window. Mr. Holmstead was going to get an earful when he asked them about the sheriff and me.

"How about we go to my place and whip up wedding invitations? I'll run copies on the mimeograph machine for you to take back to The Bend and hand out."

"Has anyone ever told you that you're incorrigible?"

"Yes. I believe you did. Your mom too."

"We were right."

CHAPTER 49

The next morning, I followed the attorney's instructions to a T. Rick and I were to be at the Forest Service office at nine sharp and do nothing to raise anyone's suspicions before then. I hid in my apartment until eight fifty-five. Then I crept outside, got in the Beetle, and took the long route to the meeting. All so the children wouldn't catch sight of me driving down Main Street. As if having a substitute teacher hadn't raised their suspicions already.

My palms were sweating as I entered the building. I should have asked Rick to pick me up. No, that would have been too out of the ordinary for the attorney's taste.

"Too diddly-widdly bad!" I muttered under my breath—though it must have been louder than I thought because the man at the front desk looked taken aback.

"No, no. Not you. I wasn't talking to you. I'm just . . . um . . . nervous."

He stood and looked down his nose. "You must be Jane Newell. The sheriff said to direct you to the conference room. It's the first door on the left. Can I bring you something to drink? Decaf coffee perhaps?"

"No, thanks." I followed his instructions and paused before entering the conference room.

I can do this. It's no harder than talking to Mom was yesterday. The attorney can't be more intimidating than she. He wants to convict DuPeuss. He's on your side.

I lifted my chin, turned the knob, and entered the room with attitude. Rick, Dan Barkley, Scott Gibson, and Dick Phillips were seated on one side of the table, a man and a woman I didn't know on the other.

Rick rose and made introductions. "Mr. Gunderson, the county prosecutor, and Mrs. Knight, the court reporter. And this is Jane Newell." They stood, and we shook hands and settled into our chairs.

Mr. Gunderson folded his hands on the table. "Thank you for rearranging your schedules to be here. There have been rapid developments in this case. There will a press conference tomorrow, and we have much to get done today. My first order of business is to take your statements, with the exception of Sheriff Sternquist, who gave his yesterday. When those are done, I will apprise you of the developments mentioned previously. Mr. Barkley, you are first on the list and will remain here. Sheriff Sternquist will show the rest of you to the waiting area."

Rick led us to the staff breakroom and said we could help ourselves to the snacks and beverages on the counter. Rick and I sat next to each other. Scott grabbed a doughnut and coffee and said he'd be in his office until his turn came. Dick loaded three doughnuts and several scoops of trail mix onto a plate, poured a glass of water, and carried his haul to the far chair. He angled it away from us, sat down, and began to eat. Rick opened his briefcase, took out a file folder, and began to read.

I yawned and whispered to Rick, "Why didn't you tell me to bring something to do? Can I go home and get a few things?"

"No one is to leave the building. Me included."

"Watching you read while Dick eats isn't exactly scintillating entertainment. I'm going to go nuts!"

Rick took a book from his briefcase and passed it over. It was *Clouds of Witnesses*, the second Peter Wimsey novel.

"You're the best!" I set the book on my chair and went to make a cup of Earl Gray. The maple-frosted cake doughnut sitting with its neighbors called my name. The last time I'd had one of those was last August when my family went to Vander Meer's in Le Mars to celebrate my new job. I went to my chair and settled down for a delightful morning tea with Sir Peter.

My teacup was empty and the doughnut gone when Rick jostled my leg. "Jane!"

I jumped. "What?"

"Mr. Gunderson said your name."

I bookmarked my page with a napkin and went to give my statement. Rather than questioning me about the entire investigation, Gunderson asked about what I'd not had time to document yet, namely the events of Tuesday evening.

When he finished, he walked me to the breakroom and escorted Dick to the conference room. I made a second cup of tea, opened my book once more, and read until Rick elbowed me.

"It's time for lunch."

"I'd rather read."

"No can do." He plucked the book from my hands. "Gunderson wants to talk to us during lunch. He ordered us burgers and fries from The Bend."

"You should have said that first." I abandoned Peter Wimsey like a boyfriend who'd done me wrong.

Once we were gathered in the conference room, Mr. Gunderson apologized for the working lunch. "We hope you don't object. Mrs. Knight and I have a long drive ahead and much to attend to before the press conference."

I was too busy laying out my food to object. I smiled at him and swirled a french fry in ketchup.

"It was imperative to get your statements on record before acquainting you with recent developments in this case. I didn't want what you are about to hear to taint your testimony. I sent Dick Phillips on his way because he wasn't involved in the investigation." He wiped his mouth with a napkin and cleared his throat. "Late yesterday afternoon, Rique DuPeuss confessed to having committed the livestock killings. He also claimed responsibility for Rocko Vander Meer's death, though he says it was an accident."

My spine stiffened and I stopped eating. Rick, Scott, and Dan's expressions hardened into disgust.

"The bastard!" Dan spat.

More like crazy bastard, but I didn't quibble.

"Did he explain his reasons?" Rick asked.

Mr. Gunderson took a long pull on his coffee cup, set it down, and folded his hands. "In a long and convoluted manner, yes. It seems he applied for a ranger position with Custer National Forest over a decade ago and wasn't hired. He considered this to be a great injustice because, in his mind, he was the most qualified person for the job. As a result, he spent the next several years sharpening his trapping skills, having learned that qualified state trappers were in short supply. Five years ago, he landed an East River state trapper job. He bided his time there and did good work."

"How do you know that's true?" Scott asked.

"My paralegal is looking into it. My guess is that, yes, he performed his duties well so as to obtain a good recommendation so he would eventually be hired for the position that was his ultimate goal. That position became available two years ago. He achieved his goal when he became the state trapper for the northern tier of counties that butt up against the Custer National Forest."

Rick gestured to the west. "But most of the forest is in Montana."

"True. However, the District Ranger Station that rejected him all those years ago is here in Little Missouri, South Dakota. The state trapper duties and his personal trapping and hunting activities would give him unlimited access to Custer National Forest. That was necessary so he could exact revenge upon the Ranger Station."

"I don't get it," Scott Gibson said. "Those staffing decisions aren't made here. Even if they were, the person who rejected the application DuPeuss submitted has moved on."

"Logic doesn't seem to have figured prominently in his thinking." The corners of Gunderson's mouth jerked up awkwardly. I think he was trying to smile.

"DuPeuss spent his first year in the new position getting to know ranchers, most particularly those whose land was adjacent to the national forest, those who had government grazing allotments, and anyone, as he put it, who 'had a beef with the Forest Service.' No pun intended." Another corner-of-the-mouth attempt at a smile. He needed more practice.

"He made a list of ranchers he felt would be most likely to accuse the Ranger Station of bad faith and began killing those ranchers' cattle. He hoped the ranchers would raise a stink and force the firing of Forest Service personnel."

"Do you have anything other than his word for any of this?" Dan asked.

The attorney turned the floor over to Rick, who said, "We do. During the search of Rique's camper, we located a notebook in which he recorded each rancher's name, the date of the kill, and assigned a number to the dead animal. We now know that he also cut an ear off each animal, which he took with him and tagged with the same number."

"He's a sick man," I shuddered.

Rick shifted in his chair. "No argument about that from this quarter."

Gunderson went on. "From what DuPeuss recorded in the notebook found in his camper, he initially targeted ranchers who expressed dissatisfaction with personnel at the Ranger Station. He wanted to anger them to the point of forcing rangers to leave in disgrace. However, the dissatisfied ranchers were slow to blame people at the Forest Service for the killings. When they finally did lodge complaints, Rangers Barkley and Gibson agreed to look into the matter. That forced DuPeuss to continue his game. When he ran out of ranchers on his list, he moved on to any rancher with a grazing permit. These ranchers reserved judgment, which slowed the process further.

DuPeuss's frustration increased. It came to a head on the day Rocko died. That was when he learned of Mr. Vander Meer's true position at the Forest Service. At the conclusion of that evening's square dance lesson, DuPeuss overheard Mr. Vander Meer invite Miss Newell to the café. When she told Vander Meer she would join him there in a few minutes, DuPeuss followed him to the rear entrance of the café. DuPeuss confronted Rocko, lost his temper, and gave him a shove. He believes Rocko lost his footing on a patch of ice. The deceased fell, hit his head on a railing, and dropped to the ground. DuPeuss tried to take his pulse but didn't find one. He was certain he hadn't been seen and left."

My fingers itched. I wanted to throttle DuPeuss. Instead, I banged a fist on the table. "What a coward! Rocko might not have died if DuPeuss had gone for help."

"We will never know, will we?" Sadness laced Gunderson's words. He closed his eyes, as if honoring the dead. Then he opened them and continued. "DuPeuss said he went to his camper and realized the cow ear that had been in his coat pocket was missing. He returned to where he'd left Rocko and hid until Miss Newell left and Dick Phillips took over for the sheriff. When Phillips fell asleep, DuPeuss retrieved the ear. Then he scattered food from the café's garbage receptacle, rounded up neighborhood dogs, and set them loose to damage the crime scene."

Now Rick banged a fist. "And the next day I called on him to analyze the tracks. I bet he liked that."

"He did remark that he found your actions fortuitous in deflecting attention from him." Gunderson gazed at each of us in turn. "Despite his deception, your cooperative efforts are the reason he was apprehended. Between the case your team built and his confession, he will pay for his actions. I believe he will be found guilty and receive a steep sentence."

"But Rocko will still be dead." I blinked away tears. "That can't be made right."

Compassion flooded his eyes. "Not in this world, but most certainly in the next." A beautiful, sad, and hopeful smile played upon his lips, so natural I knew he employed it far too often.

What a poor, lovely man.

Chapter 50

The same smile graced Gunderson's face during Thursday's press conference. The live broadcast aired at nine o'clock sharp, while I was teaching the kindergarteners about the "d" sound. "Duh" as in *d*og and *d*oor and *d*oughnut. What a shame that Little Missouri wasn't big enough to support a bakery with *d*oughnuts like the maple-iced one I'd eaten yesterday. It had been almost as good as the ones at Vander Meer's in Le Mars—

The phone rang and ended my reverie. No one called this early in the school day unless it was an emergency.

"Little Missouri School," I said, my heart pounding. "Miss Newell speaking."

"Sorry to bother you." Cookie sounded breathless. "During lunch you'll want to watch KOTA's noon news report when they air the press conference. The attorney mentioned Rick and you by name. Also, can you come to supper tomorrow evening? Me and Bud are thinking you might be needing a little break."

"That sounds wonderful."

Betty joined the conversation. "Shouwd I bwock cawws from unknown parties untiw further notice?"

"Please do. Could you take down names and numbers so I can screen them?"

Because of Betty, peace ruled the morning—other than Winter Skye's meltdown when she discovered her mouse trapped under a water glass.

"It can't breathe under there!" she sobbed.

Keeva came to the rescue. "But the glass will keep the cats away."

For reasons understandable only to five-year-olds, that explanation consoled Winter Skye, and we all moved on.

As soon as my students went out for lunch recess, I turned on the television in my apartment. There was Mr. Gunderson and his sad smile thanking the Tipperary County Sheriff Rick Sternquist and his assistant Jane Newell for their diligent investigation that led to the arrest of Rique DuPeuss. The report cut to Roger Holmstead, who summarized the rest of the conference and signed off.

"Well, that's over and done with." I switched off the television, eager to concentrate on my day job.

A half hour before the end of school, Tiege catapulted out of his chair and yelled, "Holy cow! What's the KOTA news van doin' on Main Street?"

I glanced out the window and snapped the curtains shut. Then I called Betty and asked her to contact parents and instruct them to come inside and pick up their children.

"Yes, ma'am. Wouwd you give me a jingwe once the kids are gone? I've cowwected a stack of messages for you."

She wasn't exaggerating. I spent the evening replying to the most important calls—Rocko's parents, my parents, and Roger Holmstead in that order.

The Vander Meers thanked me for what I had done and asked if we could meet during my next visit to Sioux City. *Absolutely yes.*

My parents thanked me for coming clean on Valentine's Day so they were prepared for the day's media coverage. *You're welcome, I love you, and I meant to give you a heads-up that this was happening today, but I forgot.*

Roger Holmstead asked for an exclusive interview. *Out of the question.*

Then I caught up on unfinished schoolwork. A week spent chasing Daniel Boone's evil twin, celebrating Valentine's Day, turning class over to a substitute teacher, and avoiding a media spotlight meant there was much to do. Mom hadn't been exaggerating when she'd said being a first-year teacher wasn't easy.

Once my desk was clear, I ate a very late supper of cheese and crackers with an apple for dessert. Then I went to bed imagining what Cookie was making for supper tomorrow.

The children were bonkers on Friday. I chalked it up to Valentine candy sugar highs combined with pre-weekend excitement. When they ran out the door screaming and whooping after school, I was not sad to see them go.

The road to the Sternquists' was better than I'd expected. During supper, Tiege, whose wild gesticulations made the meal a contact sport, sat to my right. A relaxed and jovial Rick sat to my left. Cookie's beef and noodle casserole was delicious. For dessert, Cookie brought out a pan of warm apple dumplings.

After my first spoonful of juicy filling and flaky crust, I asked Cookie if she'd ever considered opening a bakery. "Can you make doughnuts?"

"What she's really asking is if you can make doughnuts with maple frosting," Rick said.

"No to the bakery." Cookie's reply left no room for argument. "But I can make you doughnuts now and then."

Tiege insisted we play Uno until his bedtime, which turned out to be later than mine.

When Bud saw me cracking one yawn after another, he shut down the game. "It's time for your teacher to get home, Son."

Before I left, Rick pressed *Clouds of Witnesses* into my hand and said to return it once I finished it. It was close to eleven when I rolled into to town and almost two a.m. when I quit reading because my eyes kept drifting shut. I turned off my alarm and slept until noon. I putzed away the day baking more chocolate chip oatmeal cookies and sewing a new blazer and matching trousers from a length of deep-blue wool fabric Mom had given me during Christmas vacation. Then I finished *Clouds of Witnesses* so I could return it to Rick at church.

On Sunday, I walked into the foyer and handed Sir Peter to Rick. Then I thanked Cookie for supper. Tiege invited me to sit between him and Rick during church. I said yes, and Tiege led the way to the pew, with Rick bringing up the rear. I made myself comfortable, or as comfortable as I could get, what with a perpetual motion machine at my side while sitting on an old wooden pew I suspected had been designed to keep worshippers awake rather than comfy.

The pew accomplished its intended purpose. I paid attention to the Scripture reading and the sermon except when adjusting my derriere.

"You shall know the truth and the truth shall set you free," Pastor Petersen read from the gospel of John.

His solemn, pontificating tone usually led me to tune out. Today, however, I tuned in, even as a splinter poked the soft flesh behind my knee. I shifted position.

"Stop wiggling so much," Tiege whispered.

"Shh! I want to hear this."

Pastor Petersen went on. "Early in the gospel of John, the author describes Jesus as full of grace and truth. We are his people. His Holy Spirit lives in us. And when we live according to his truth by grace, we are set free."

I thought about the conversation with Mom about my partnership with Rick. Once I had weathered her blowback, I had experienced a new freedom. No need to tell half-truths. No need to tap dance around forbidden subjects. No need to hide who I was. The truth had set me free.

After the final hymn, Rick leaned over and spoke quietly. "Dick Phillips is in the back pew. He's been staring at you for the entire service. You gotta tell him the truth about you and me before he starts bawling like a calf whose mama abandoned him in a blizzard."

I glanced in Dick's direction. Rick's description was apt, and I felt sorry for him. "You're right. Do you want to be in on this?"

"Not a chance." He lassoed his little brother with one arm and said, "Tiege, we had Miss Newell to ourselves for an hour. Let's give other folks a chance." He gestured for me to leave the pew ahead of them.

Tiege protested. I hunted for Dick. He wasn't in the foyer, so I found my coat and hurried outside. He was climbing over a drift in front of his pickup truck when I yelled from the sidewalk, "Hang on a minute, Dick! I need to talk to you."

He froze atop the drift. "What?"

I walked a few steps toward him along the sidewalk. "Could you meet me down here? I don't think I can climb up there in these shoes."

He jumped onto the sidewalk and stared at his boots.

I stood in front of him. "There's something you should know about Rick and me."

He didn't look up. "My relationship with Rick is as a friend and professional colleague. Believe me when I say it will never be anything else."

Dick raised his head. He smiled as bright as sunshine on new snow. "Well then, would you like to go to lunch with me at the café?"

Fourteen words.

My reply was far shorter. "Yes!"

CHAPTER 51

We were still in our coats when Trudy took our drink orders. She made a phone call and then went to the kitchen. Dick and I would be old news before she brought his water and my Diet Coke.

Dick studied the menu, then looked up. "I'm having the chicken-fried steak with mashed potatoes and gravy. Are you having your usual?"

"Not today. I was eating a cheeseburger and fries when the lawyer laid out DuPeuss's confession last Wednesday, and that put me off them. I'll be eating taco salad for a while."

Dick opened his mouth, then paused. "Listen." Another pause. "There's something you need to know." Long pause and a shamefaced expression that made me wonder if he'd held those cattle steady while DuPeuss killed them.

"It's about our first date."

"That was not a date. That was an exercise in humiliation." Trudy brought our drinks. When she was out of earshot, I went on. "I hope you can explain what was going on."

He downed half his water and set the glass down in slow motion. "I had a cold."

I tore the wrapper off my straw and put it in my glass. He smiled with the relief of a man who'd offloaded a great weight from his chest.

It was a good thing he had a great smile or I'da gone home right then. Instead, I gave him an ultimatum. "Either you expand on that in the next sixty seconds, or I'm leaving."

My method proved effective. Dick began talking and continued long after his deadline.

He said he'd gotten sick the day after Rocko's death. Probably due to too much time in frigid temperatures and keeping watch most of the night in the sheriff's truck. Friday afternoon, before our date, he consulted with the physician's assistant in Tipperary, who said Dick would have come down with pneumonia if he'd waited another day. The PA sent him home with a white paper bag of antibiotics, cough syrup, and a decongestant. He told Dick to take the first dose of each when he got home, and he did.

"The medicine made me drowsy. I was so tired I couldn't follow your conversation. That wasn't fair to you, so I left."

"But leaving me without explanation *was* fair?"

"Huh." Dick acted like that possibility had never occurred to him. "Guess not."

Our food arrived. I took a few bites to up my blood sugar. I also marveled at Dick's lack of dating skills. I set my fork on my plate. "Here's something you need to know. Your chances of going on a third date with me will increase in direct proportion with your ability to communicate well."

"Like how?"

"For starters, use complete sentences. Call when you're going to be late. Or because you just want to hear my voice." I picked up my fork and speared a piece of lettuce. "And most importantly, when you give me a present—say a box of chocolates—sign the damn card."

When he stopped blushing, he asked if he could take me to the final square dance lesson.

"Just the lesson or the potluck beforehand also?"

"Both."

I raised an eyebrow.

"I mean, I'd like to go to the potluck with you too."

I lowered my brow. "I'll be ready at five fifty. Call if you're going to be late."

He smiled his warm, sunny smile. I lowered my eyes and began to eat. It was far too early for him to see the power he had to melt my heart.

***

Tuesday evening, I was taking a casserole out of the oven when there was a knock at the door.

"Come on in!" I set the pan on the table, wrapped it in a thick towel, and carried it to the entryway where Dick stood. "Can you hold this while I get ready to go?"

He took the bundle and breathed deep. "It smells good in here."

"Nothing beats the aroma of ham and scalloped potatoes and apple pie." I put on my coat and gloves, then took the pies from where they sat the table. "Let's go."

A few minutes later, we entered the dance hall. Winter Skye and Keeva ran right over. Keeva gave Dick the once over. Then she frowned at me. "Don't you like the sheriff anymore?"

"We're good friends," I told her. "Like you and Jeremy are friends."

Winter Skye pointed at Dick. "Are you gonna marry him?"

"I'm not marrying anyone anytime soon." I handed each girl a pie. "Would you set these on the potluck table?"

"Well," Winter Skye went on, "me and Keeva wanna be your flower girls when you do."

"I'll keep that in mind, girls. Now go."

As Dick carried the ham and scalloped potatoes to the serving table, Keeva yelled, "Me and Winter Skye are gonna be flower girls at Miss Newell's wedding!"

Oh boy.

During the potluck, everyone except Keeva had a good laugh about her announcement. Mary Borgeson reported that Oscar was still in the hospital but improving by the day. Cookie passed around a card for everyone to sign.

"Who's going to call the dance tonight?" Pam Barkley asked.

Rick rose and gave a small bow. "Yours truly."

Scott Gibson looked at Rick in astonishment. "Since when have you been a caller?"

"Since Jane found new partner."

Axel McDonald spoke up. "But you two will keep working cases together?"

"Uh-huh." Rick's expression grew pensive. "We're hoping that won't be real often."

The adults sobered. The room went quiet until Tiege broke the silence. "Is there enough pie for seconds?"

He proved to be as good at calling as he was at being sheriff. As a refresher, he ran us through all the steps we'd learned. Then he played and called a mix of old and new tunes—from "Oh, Susanna" to "Grandma's Feather Bed", from "Will the Circle Be Unbroken" to "Don't It Make My Brown Eyes Blue" and everything in between—until we were breathless, laughing, and surprised by our own competence.

Dick was a good partner. He had the grace and rhythm of a natural athlete. He anticipated Rick's upcoming calls and directed my movements with a slight pressure of his hand upon my palm. On the rare occasions when that didn't work, when I went left instead of right, he used coordination and infinite patience to untangle my messes.

Finally, Rick announced the last dance. "We'll end with Oscar's signature tune. He lowered the needle and began to sing and call us through "There's Somethin' 'Bout You Baby I Like."

"Sing it with me," he said when the chorus began for the first time. When the final chorus began, he crooned, "Now sing it to your partner."

I caught Rick's eye. "What?" I mouthed.

He grinned at me and tipped his hat. "Sing it like you mean it."

I turned to Dick, he turned to me, and we both sang,

along with everyone else, *There's something 'bout you baby I like.*

He smiled.

My heart melted.

And just like that, we danced right into our song.

Jane Newell's Chocolate Chip Oatmeal Cookies

1 cup butter or shortening, softened
3/4 cup brown sugar
2 eggs
1 teaspoon vanilla
1 1/2 cups whole wheat flour
1/2 cup white flour
1 teaspoon baking soda
1 teaspoon salt
2 cups oatmeal
1 cup chocolate chips
1 cup chopped nuts (optional)

1. *Preheat oven to 375°.*

2.   Cream eggs, brown sugar, shortening, and vanilla.

3.   Mix in the flours, baking soda, and salt.

4.   Blend in the oatmeal first, then the chocolate chips and nuts.

5.   Chill in the oven for an hour or more.

6.   Drop the batter onto cookie sheets using a soup spoon.

7.   Bake for 10-12 minutes until crisp on the edges and soft in the middle.

ABOUT THE AUTHOR

Jolene Philo discovered Laura Ingalls Wilder and Encyclopedia Brown in elementary school and has been fascinated by the prairie and mysteries ever since. She's a voracious reader of fiction, biography, and creative non-fiction. Imagine her surprise when she became the author of several non-fiction books for the special needs and disability community. The *West River Mystery Series* combines her love of mysteries and northwest South Dakota's short grass prairie, where she and her husband Hiram lived for seven years when they were first married. Jolene and Hiram live in central Iowa with their daughter, son-in-law, and their two children. Jolene instills book love into her grandchildren by reading to them as often as she can. You can keep up with her reading and writing adventures at her website, www. jolenephilo.com.

PLEASE WRITE A REVIEW

Dear Reader,

At Midwestern Books we have worked hard to make this excellent book available for you. We truly hope you have enjoyed it. It is our mission to tell stories from a Midwestern perspective that honors its culture. Thank you for including us in your reading selections.

Please, would you consider going to the Amazon website and write a review for this book. Reviews are crucial for helping others to know about this book and encouraging Amazon to promote it. We very much need help from readers like you to get the word out about our books and the enjoyable stories they share. Thank you for helping us.

Midwestern Books

OTHER TITLES FROM MIDWESTERN BOOKS

See Jane Run! Book 1 of the West River Mysteries. Amidst the scenic wonder of a quirky corner of western South Dakota, Jane Newell starts her career in a country school. She soon discovers that someone close to her is a killer, and she is determined to find out who it is.

See Jane Sing! Book 2 of the West River Mysteries. Just back from Thanksgiving break, Jane Newell stumbles over the body of a teenage boy while hunting for a Christmas tree. Jane ignores Sheriff Sternquist's warning not to investigate when she discovers a tangle of clues.

Stay Out of that Room! Two sheltered teen aged girls spend a summer on lake Minnetonka with their wackadoodle great aunt when a secret room lures them to break her rules, while hunky neighbor boys heighten the stakes.

Cosmic Background Radiation. Grieving his brother, Josh confronts rural life to save his family. Strange dreams take him back 2,700 years to a parallel life with his brother alive and a girl he just met as part of the household.